Francesca Hairston had come tonight because she knew *he* would be here, and there *he* was.

Nelson Santiago was stretched out on the sofa lining the opposite wall. Four glasses rested on the coffee table in front of him. The first three were shot glasses, facedown. The fourth glass was a tumbler of what looked like scotch, in which all the ice had melted.

Great! The man to whom she'd chosen to entrust her life was a lush.

But she couldn't let that deter her. She crossed the room to stand beside the sofa, leaned down and shook his shoulder. "Mr. Santiago, Nelson. I need to talk to you."

She straightened, waiting for a reaction from him. He shifted a little and then one of his arms came to life. It rose, grazing the back of her leg as it traveled upward. "Nelson," she said in a sharp voice.

He opened his eyes then and looked up at her with sleepy curiosity. "What can I do for you, sweetheart?"

"For starters, would you mind taking your hand off my butt?"

DEIRDRE SAVOY

is a native New Yorker who spent her summers on the shores of Martha's Vineyard, soaking up the sun and scribbling in one of her many notebooks. It was there that she first started writing romance as a teenager. Since then, Deirdre has published ten books, all of which have garnered critical acclaim and honors. She lives in the Bronx, New York, with her husband of ten-plus years and their two children. In her spare time she enjoys reading, dancing, calligraphy and "wicked" crossword puzzles.

DEIRDRE SAVOY

An
Innocent
MAN

KIMANI
ROMANCE

KIMANI PRESS™

ISBN-13: 978-1-58314-776-4
ISBN-10:   1-58314-776-4

AN INNOCENT MAN

www.kimanipress.com

Printed in U.S.A.

Dear Reader,

I hope you enjoyed Nelson and Francesca's story. I really enjoyed working on it and traveling to a new place—Atlanta. As most of my stories are set either in New York City, my hometown, or Martha's Vineyard, my family's vacation getaway, it was nice to "visit" somewhere new, if only fictionally.

I'd love for you to let me know what you think of the story. You can reach me at aboutdeesbooks@aol.com or by snail mail at P.O. Box 233, Bronx, NY 10469.

All the best,

Deirdre Savoy

For my daughter, who proves the Mother's Curse
is a powerful thing indeed. I pass it on.
May she have a daughter just like her—
and the strength to withstand the experience.

ACKNOWLEDGMENTS

As always, I would like to thank my family for their
support. They spread the word about my books, give me
a good smack when I need it, and in general keep me
sane. Thanks especially to my younger sister Shari-Ann,
whose brain I pick regularly for medical information
(some of which actually has to do with books).

Thanks to my agent Manie Barron and my
editor Evette Porter, for having faith in me and my work.

Special thanks to Tee C. Royal and Dee Stewart of
RAWSistaz for bringing the Atlanta area alive for me and
for all their support over the years.

Prologue

The only truth in her nightmare was the fear. Panic, fierce and never ending, raged in her chest like a wild animal that could not be controlled. Bile, thick, caustic, foul-tasting, clogged her throat, cut off her breathing. The dagger, its ornate handle, gleaming, fell once, twice, three times. At once, she was both inside her own body, suffering blow after blow, and outside her body, watching, relishing, glorying in the devastation of her own making. Tears spilled from her eyes as her life's blood spilled from her body.

She forced her body upright as she willed herself to consciousness. It wasn't real. None of it was real. Gasping for breath, she glanced around the small room that had been hers since childhood and knew the dream had, once again, released her. Instead of relief, a peculiar emptiness overtook her. A void of emotional desolation that was almost more terrifying than the dream. She didn't know what to do about the dream or her life or the dread each inspired in her. She only knew she couldn't go on like this. She'd crack up if she did, if she hadn't already, if the dream weren't an omen that her mind had already slipped.

If only she had more time. In two short weeks, it would begin—the things she feared most of all because she still couldn't be sure if her truth was *the* truth. That's what paralyzed her and made her easy prey for nocturnal horrors. She *had* to know and she had to act now, before she made a mistake that was irrevocable.

She knew only one man who could help her. She'd seen him only once close up, almost a year ago, at her brother's engagement party. She didn't know what it was about him that reached out to her. At barely six feet, he wasn't even that tall. He wasn't that handsome, either, with a face carved in granite planes and a thin scar that ran the length of his left cheek. He wore his wavy, jet-black hair long and pulled back from his face into a short ponytail at his nape. Even in a sport coat and dress slacks, she noticed the broadness of his chest, the heavy musculature of his body.

The entire package lent him a savage look, the look of a primitive masquerading as a civilized man. The man was a troglodyte, who spoke in terse monosyllables if he deigned to answer at all. He'd turned her down flat a year ago. She didn't intend to let him refuse her a second time.

Chapter 1

Francesca Hairston glanced around the festively decorated room with a feeling of discontentment. Her brother Matthew had married into a large and loving family. Every weekend heralded someone's birthday or anniversary, the christening of some child or the birth of another. Although Frankie had a standing invitation to all such events, she mostly eschewed these gatherings, as she could barely keep straight in her mind anyone's name, age, marital status or relationship to anyone else.

Tonight she'd come with several cards, one of which would hopefully fit the evening's occasion, tucked in her purse, as well as a fifty-dollar bill that would smooth any feathers in the event one didn't. She'd come tonight because she knew *he* would be here, though so far *he* was nowhere to be seen.

And she would have known it if he were here, conscious and accounted for. Nelson Santiago, now her cousin-in-law by marriage, was a man of commanding presence. That is, when he showed up.

Frankie made her way from the crowded family room, to the hallway that led to the room that served as a library. She needed a moment to regroup and recover from her disappointment at not finding him here. She didn't begrudge the family its happiness, but she didn't belong among them, not in her present mood. She needed a moment to decide whether to leave or to tough it out and hope he'd still show up.

The door creaked slightly as it opened. Otherwise the room was silent save for a low, persistent buzzing she couldn't place. She closed the door behind her and flicked on the light. She saw him then and frowned. Nelson Santiago was stretched out on the sofa lining the opposite wall. If he'd been wearing a jacket when he arrived he must have removed it. The sleeves of his white shirt were rolled up to the elbows. One hand rested on his stomach. The other arm hung straight down over the edge of the sofa. Four glasses rested on the coffee table in front of him. The first three were shot glasses, facedown, as if someone had drained their contents and upended them as proof. The fourth glass was a tumbler of what looked like Scotch in which all the ice had melted.

She crossed her arms and canted her hips to one side. Great! The man to whom she'd chosen to entrust her life was probably a lush who couldn't hold his liquor.

But she couldn't let that deter her. She moved farther

into the room, letting the door close softly behind her. She'd had half a mind to let it slam. That would probably wake him, but she didn't want to make any noise that would draw others' attention. While she had Nelson Santiago alone, she wanted to keep it that way. What she needed to ask him demanded privacy, at least a little bit of it.

She crossed the room to stand beside the sofa. For a moment she simply stared down at him. Asleep or passed out or whatever he was, she wondered what his reaction would be to being awakened by her and her renewed request for his help. She couldn't dwell on that too much—certainly not enough for her to change her mind. She leaned down and shook his shoulder. "Mr. Santiago, Nelson. I need to talk to you."

She straightened, waiting for a reaction from him. He shifted a little and the arm hanging over the sofa came to life. It rose, grazing the back of her leg as it traveled upward. She froze, her body chilled by his unexpected touch. Gathering her wits, she leaned down and shook his shoulder again. "Nelson," she said in a sharp voice.

He opened his eyes then and looked up at her with sleepy curiosity. "What can I do for you, sweetheart?"

Disgusted, Frankie rolled her eyes. "For starters, would you mind taking your hand off my butt?"

His fingers flexed as if to confirm what they rested on. Then his hand descended the same lazy way it had gone up. "Now what?"

If he'd gotten any satisfaction from groping her body, it didn't show on his face. If anything, he seemed to still be half asleep. Now that his restraining grip was off her, she took a step back. "I need to talk to you."

He squeezed his temples with his thumb and middle finger, probably what he'd been trying to do when she got in the way. When he focused on her again, his gaze was more lucid, but not much more. He blinked again and, without warning, swung himself up to a sitting position. She had to back up quickly to avoid getting in his way. He sat forward, pressing the heels of his hands to his eyes.

"Rough night?" Frankie ventured, more than a little sarcasm in her voice.

He didn't say anything to that, only cast her a short, sharp look. "You're Matt's sister, right?"

"Guilty as charged." She suspected there was disapproval in that brief look he cast her and in the tone of his voice. That she couldn't fathom, considering that apart from her attire, she was exactly the same. The last time she'd seen him, she'd had on the one good dress in her closet here in New York, the one pair of heels she possessed, and she'd worn her shoulder-length hair free, not tucked up under a cap as she did now. Maybe he looked at the jeans, boots and T-shirt and viewed her with the same disdain her mother did—as a woman too lacking in femininity to recognize that she was a girl. Even if he did, so what? She didn't care what he thought of her except in relation to his willingness to help her.

She sat in the chair perpendicular to the sofa, licked her dry lips and screwed up her courage. "What would it take to change your mind about what I asked you before?"

"Investigating some old rummy down in Atlanta?"

Frankie shook her head. That's what he'd gleaned from the information she'd given him? No wonder he wanted no part of her. "An old rummy named Harlan Jacobs accused of raping and killing several young women on the Excelsior College campus where I used to teach."

She watched his face for any sign of reaction to her correction, but there wasn't any. "So what do you say?"

"No."

She blinked, surprised by his terse answer, though she probably shouldn't have been. It was the same answer she'd gotten last time. But then she'd simply been convinced the wrong man was in custody. Now was different, and if he were the slightest bit astute, he should have picked up on her desperation. "Why not? Isn't that what you do?"

"Yeah, but most of my clients offer me something you haven't."

"What's that?"

"An explanation, some reason other than idle curiosity for wanting me to get involved."

She bit her lip. She couldn't argue with him there. She'd told him what she wanted but not why she'd wanted it. She'd hoped to keep her motives to herself. She'd kept silent when he'd asked her, figuring he'd ferret everything out of her before he was satisfied. And she wasn't prepared to tell him everything. She might not ever be. She sighed. At least now she had some reasonable explanation she could give him.

"I've been called by the district attorney to testify at Jacobs's trial, which starts in two weeks. I saw him running from the scene of one of the crimes." That last part of it wasn't exactly the truth, but it would do for now.

"Then what's the problem?"

"I'm not sure the man I saw running away was Jacobs. That man, whoever he was, wore a mask. You know, one of those plastic thingies that distort the features. It could have been any white male of average height for all I know. Campus police picked up Jacobs for whatever reason and they expect me to help them put him away."

"Again, what's the problem?"

"How would you feel about putting away a man you weren't sure was guilty?"

He tilted his head to one side, apparently considering what she said. Hoping to sway his decision in her favor, she added, "I can pay you whatever you ask."

His jaw tightened. "I don't need your money, lady."

Was there anything worse in the world than a man with his macho showing? "Don't get Cro-Magnon on me. I only meant that I didn't expect a family freebie. I know this is your living."

"No."

Frankie's head dropped down to her chest in frustration. The first question she'd asked him was what would it take for him to change his mind, and she was beginning to wonder if there was nothing. That didn't mean she'd give up, but maybe it was time to come up with another strategy, whatever that might be. She lifted her head and her gaze snagged on a framed photograph hanging on the wall—Nelson's grandmother surrounded by several of her grandchildren, including him.

She sighed dramatically. "I wonder how your grand-mother would feel knowing I came to you for help and you turned me down?"

But before he could respond, the door pushed open and said grandmother came in.

"Nels—" Both her words and her advance into the room stopped abruptly. "Francesca, I didn't know you were here."

Frankie gritted her teeth at the use of her given name and the effusiveness in the older woman's voice. Frankie stood to receive the older woman's hug.

"It's been a long time," Luz said.

Frankie recognized the chastisement in the other woman's voice. Everyone in this crazy family thought everyone appreciated family and family gatherings; its matriarch being the chief proponent. Maybe she should invite them to a few more Hairston family gatherings. That would cure them. Still, Frankie liked the older woman and didn't want to displease her. "I'm making up for it now."

Stepping back, Luz settled an assessing gaze on her, then shifted her gaze to Nelson. "Or maybe it's my grandson that interests you today?"

Frankie offered her a tight smile. Seeing Nelson was what brought her here today, but not the way Luz appeared to mean. Frankie couldn't blame her for jumping to that conclusion, since the last family event she'd attended ended with Nelson taking her home. Even her brother, who should have known her better, had jumped to the same conclusion. She hoped this evening ended on a more successful note than that one had.

To Luz she said, "Actually, I got a craving for some home cooking that wasn't cooked by my mother's cook."

"Then come." Luz linked her arm with hers. "We've got plenty of food out back."

No match for the older woman even if she had objected, Frankie allowed herself to be led from the room. She doubted Luz was as interested in feeding her as in finding out what she and Nelson had been up to all by their lonesomes. Too bad Frankie had no intention of telling her. But Frankie did cast one last glance over her shoulder at Nelson. He was basically where she'd left him, except he'd sat back against the sofa and draped an arm along the back of it. His deep black eyes were on her and his face bore the expression of a man who'd just won a battle. Let him think what he wanted. He really didn't know her if he thought she was done with him already.

She let a smile wander over her lips. Ding ding. Round number two was on.

After the two women left the room, Nelson picked his glass up from the table and walked the distance to the open doorway. He leaned his back against the jamb in a way that gave him an adequate view of Francesca Hairston and his grandmother making their way toward the back door. Despite his intentions, his gaze wandered to her hips and the gentle sway of her backside as she walked. At least that was the same. The only other time he'd seen her she'd been dressed in some sleeveless number with her hair wild around her shoulders. If he were the type of man to get his head turned by a pretty face and slamming figure he might have tried to get more out of her than that cockamamie story about investigating some old guy rotting in jail. There was something else different about her today, too, beyond the outfit that probably cost more than he made in a month. Her family came from wealth, and she didn't seem to have a problem throwing it around.

Well, whatever. It didn't really matter. Though she'd told him more, as sure as he knew his own name he knew she hadn't told him everything—not enough for him to want to waste his time and expertise pursuing it. In his experience folks who didn't want to explain why they needed his services were up to no good. And while he'd pegged her as a basically harmless woman, he had no intention of getting involved in her melodrama. She was like a lot of people he'd seen who got cold feet the minute they were called on to back up their stories in court.

But there had to be some reason why the police had picked up this Jacobs and some reason why the D.A. liked him for the crimes. Unless she knew something she wasn't telling him—like some sort of personal relationship with the man, which she neglected to mention—her best bet was to let twelve jurors decide if the cops and lawyers had done their jobs.

Nelson sighed. Then there were his own personal reasons for not wanting to be involved in this case. Reasons he had no plans to share with her. That left him with the task of convincing her to take no for an answer.

He found her later out on his grandmother's porch standing at the railing. Though the day had been warm, the night was cool. Someone had leant her a sweater that dwarfed her small, slender frame and leant her the look of a young girl. He came up beside her, resting his elbows on the railing, mimicking her posture.

Without looking at him, she said, "Finally come to your senses and decided to help me?"

"No. Finally decided to quit asking?"

To his surprise she smiled at him. "Never."

Good God, what was he going to do with this woman? He knew she hadn't gone to his grandmother or he'd have heard about it already. If he'd given her an answer before, he'd have told her his grandmother hadn't approved of anything he'd done since he was sixteen years old. But he'd given his family enough disappointments not to want to bring another one down on his head. Still, he couldn't fathom this woman's tenaciousness, why it mattered so much to her that he acquiesce. "Why me?"

She turned to face him and crossed her arms. "There's the fact that I know you. You used to be a cop, in Special Victims, no less. You know about these things, and I'm not foolish enough to think I can do this by myself. And most of all, I trust you."

"Why is that?"

"Did you not notice all those people inside who would kick your ass if you let anything happen to me?"

She had him there. "Why should something happen to you?"

She shook her head as if in disbelief that he hadn't figured it out himself already. He had, he just wanted to hear her say it. "I'm the only witness who can identify a man suspected in a string of heavy-duty crimes. If I'm right and Jacobs is innocent, someone out there will want to shut me up."

"Not if you mind your own business."

"I'd consider that if it weren't for the little matter of the subpoena. I have to show up whether I want to or not." She sighed and turned away from him, looking straight out toward the yard. "Just so you know, I'm going to do this whether I get your help or not."

He figured that for an idle threat. She wouldn't be so persistent about getting his help if going off on her own was in her plans. Then again, she might try to hire another of his P.I. brethren, which was preferable, he supposed, but that didn't guarantee that whoever she picked up might not try to take advantage of her in one way or another, and barring that, there was no guarantee that someone else would be as vigilant as he would.

Damn. Despite his objections to getting involved, he didn't want to see anything happen to her. He felt himself giving in, even as he fought against it. "This is a fool's mission, Frankie."

Her head lowered and she was silent for a long moment. "Then call me a fool. Just help me."

The earnestness in her voice undid him. With a sigh of capitulation, he said, "Here's what I'm offering. You tell me everything you know about the case. I'll check it out for you and let you know if the right guy is in custody."

He thought he'd made a generous offer, as generous as he intended to get. But she shook her head. "I have to be there."

He should have known she'd refuse.

She offered him a tight smile.

There was no hope. "Lucky for you I like gutsy broads." He nodded toward the house. "Let's get out of here. Then you're going to tell me everything I want to know and do exactly as I tell you. Is that understood?"

"Yes, *Mien fuhrer.*"

"I mean it, Frankie. If you want me to put my butt on the line for you, I don't want you doing anything that might put either of us in more danger."

She raised her hand as if being sworn in. "I promise to behave. And if you knew me, you'd know what a big deal that is."

He didn't doubt it. He led her back through the house, making his goodbyes as he went. His last goodbye was to his grandmother, who walked them to the front door. She told them good-night with a familiar matchmaker's gleam in her eyes.

As he and Frankie walked to the car, he asked her, "Why didn't you tell my grandmother I turned you down?"

She gave him a lopsided grin. "I didn't want to pressure you." She winked at him and slid into the passenger seat of his car.

Chapter 2

Frankie let them into the apartment that had once belonged to her brother before he married and moved upstate with his wife and kids. Actually, it still belonged to him, since he'd refused to sell it to her. She tossed her keys on the low table by the door. "What's your poison? Coffee? Soft drink? A little wine?"

Nelson followed her in, closing the door behind her. "Nothing, thanks."

Frankie shrugged. "It's your funeral. Make yourself at home. I'm going to get something." She headed to the kitchen, retrieved a bottle of Corona from the fridge, popped the top and headed back toward the living room. She'd kept most of her brother's furniture, including the facing black leather sofa and love seat. Nelson had already taken a place on her sofa, so she opted for a spot on the love seat. Or rather she set her beer on the table in front of the love seat. Before sitting, she pulled off the oversize shirt she had on and tossed it onto the cushion. She itched to take off at least one of the bras she had on, but that would have to wait until later.

She flopped onto the love seat. She picked up her beer and took a sip from it. "So, what do you want to know?"

"Start at the beginning."

She nodded and lifted her foot onto the edge of the sofa to remove her boot. "The first murder happened eighteen months ago. One of the students went missing from her dorm room. The killer strangled her first, I guess to subdue her, raped her, then slit her throat. At first the police thought it was an isolated incident. They had the girl's boyfriend in custody for a while. Twenty-eight days later, the same thing happened to another girl. By the time they picked up Jacobs, four more girls were dead."

"The same MO each time?"

"Yup, strangulation followed by rape followed by a knife across the throat."

"What were the victims like?"

"Different ages, races, heights. The only thing they had in common was that all the women were athletes."

"Why'd they focus on Jacobs?"

"He was one of the janitors that worked in the sports center. He had a 1983 conviction for sexually assaulting his niece. He had no alibis for any of the murders."

"Sounds like they had reason to at least pick him up."

"Pick him up, yes. Keep him? I don't know. I know Jacobs—he's an odd bird. But the man was fifty-seven years old, and only five seven with a bad back. And these girls were all athletes. I couldn't imagine him subduing any of these girls, even if he strangled them first. One of the first girls murdered was on my soccer team. She was five eleven and do you have any idea what kind of strength you build up playing soccer?"

Having removed both her boots, she grabbed her beer and pulled her legs up so that her feet rested on the sofa. She took a long pull from the bottle, letting her emotions settle as the cool liquid heated her insides. She didn't want to get worked up, figuring he'd bolt at the first sign of a hysterical woman regardless of the fact that he'd already agreed to help her. She probably could have told him that part of her desire to make sure the right man went to jail was to make sure her player's killer was brought to justice. But it had seemed easier to ground her motivation as far away from herself as possible.

"What was her name?"

"Kerry Washington. She was only nineteen years old."

"I'm sorry."

She looked away, surprised at his perceptiveness. "Thank you." She took a last sip of her beer and set the bottle on the table. "As you put it before, what now?"

"We head to Atlanta."

She nodded. "When? Tomorrow?"

"Tomorrow night. And by the way, we'll be driving."

"Why?"

"These days firearms and flying don't mix."

Frankie's eyebrows rose. She hadn't considered that. She hadn't considered much more than securing his help. "Are you armed now?"

"That depends on what you mean by armed."

She was too tired and a little too buzzed from the beer to contemplate that effectively. "What time should I be ready?"

"Six o'clock."

She could do that—pack a few things, suffer through lunch with her mother long enough to let her know she was going out of town for a few days. She'd try to get a few hours' sleep if the nightmares didn't come and be ready to go. "All right."

He took a card out of his back pocket and placed it on the table. "If you need to reach me before then, my numbers are on there." He stood. "Lock up behind me and try to get as much sleep as you can before then."

She nodded and stood. "Just in case I didn't manage to say this before, thank you."

He cast her a look that said she had to be kidding. She'd as much as blackmailed him into helping her, so what did he want with her gratitude, anyway. Despite her methods, she was grateful to him. And he was intent on getting out of there. She followed him to the door.

"Is there anything in particular I should bring with me?"

"Just be ready on time."

"That I can do."

He pulled the door open and stepped into the hall. He turned to her and for a long moment their gazes met. There was something about those dark, dark eyes that got to her on a feminine level. No matter, he seemed on the verge of wanting to tell her something—probably to talk her out of this fool's mission as he called it. But he broke their mini staring contest first. He glanced down the hallway toward where the elevator waited. "Don't forget to lock up."

It figured that his last words to her were an order of sorts. "Will do, sir." She offered him a salute, then closed the door. For a moment, she rested her back against the frame. Phase one of her mission was accomplished. By this time tomorrow, they'd be on their way to Atlanta. She'd find out what she needed to know. Maybe then she could sleep. Maybe then she could put her life back together without fear. Maybe.

"Lock the damn door."

She jumped at the sound of Nelson's voice coming through the door. Shaking her head at her own reaction to his barked order, she turned the three locks and put the chain on. Though he'd scared her half to death, at least he was watchful. If what she suspected were true, he'd need to be.

Hearing the sound of the locks turning, Nelson moved off toward the elevator at the end of the hall. As he rode down to the lobby, he contemplated what she'd told him. Despite all she'd said, there was so much more he needed to know—names, dates, places and, more than that, what motive someone might have had for wanting these particular girls dead. He didn't think it was a coincidence that they were all athletes or that the victims were random. The killer, whoever he was, had gotten into at least one of the girls' rooms, so he may have known his victims beforehand and probably killed them because they knew him, too. To his mind, that made Jacobs a more likely subject, not less. Maybe each of these girls had offended him in some way and what he did to them was his brand of punishment.

Whatever. As soon as he got home, he pulled out his laptop to search the Web. A string of crimes like Frankie described would have made headlines, even in a sleepy Southern college town that would more likely seek to bury its tragedies than admit something so sordid was going on. By the time he was finished, he'd found out the names of each victim, dates for the crimes, pictures of each girl and a background on Jacobs.

What he didn't find was any mention of Frankie being a witness to any of the attacks or mention of any witnesses at all. That intrigued him since the district attorney planned to use her as a witness in the trial. He packed his suitcase, including the material he'd printed out. Once they got to Atlanta, he'd lay it all out in some format he could make sense of.

But when he got into bed, sleep didn't come. Usually, he didn't suffer from bouts of insomnia, but usually his mind wasn't caught up in thoughts of Francesca Hairston, either.

Surprisingly, it was the woman herself, not her case, that preoccupied him. One particular moment, actually, when she'd done a mini-striptease for him in her living room. He doubted she'd been trying to entice him, but when she'd pulled the big shirt over her head, the shirt underneath had ridden up, exposing a flat washboard stomach and a belly ring. Considering that pierced belly buttons didn't usually do a thing for him, his own reaction surprised him. She'd asked him if he knew what kind of muscles you built up playing soccer, which made him wonder if she were that toned all over. That wouldn't be a bad thing at all.

Mentally, he shook his head. It had been a long time since he'd paid any attention to a woman's physical attributes. Not to say he didn't look or appreciate, but it had been a long time since watching any woman sparked any heat in his body or any prurient thoughts in his mind. So why'd he have to pick some five-foot, hardheaded spitfire to fantasize about?

He flopped onto his stomach. What he really needed to concentrate on were his girls. Frankie had lucked out in that he'd cleared his schedule for a few days intending to spend that time with his daughters. Twelve-year-old Dara would understand his change in plans; sixteen-year-old Bonnie wouldn't. Either way, he'd see them both tomorrow to explain.

At noon the next day, Frankie pulled into the drive in front of her parents' Scarsdale home. She both loved and hated that house, which to Frankie's mind was more of a museum than a place to live. But all that space came with plenty of hidey-holes in which to avoid her mother and, when circumstances demanded it, her mother's tiresome guests.

Her mother's ancient butler answered the door with a warm smile for her. To everyone else, he was Anderson, but she greeted him as she always did. "Hey, Andy, what's shaking?"

"These old bones, miss."

"Is my mother here?"

"She's having luncheon on the patio. Should I let her know you're here?"

Frankie had figured as much, which was why she hadn't bothered to call ahead. "I'll tell her myself, thanks."

Anderson moved off while Frankie headed deeper into the house toward the side doors that led out onto the patio. Once she reached the doors, she stood watching her mother a moment. Though she loved her mother, she wasn't looking forward to the confrontation to come—and with her mother it was always a confrontation. It was impossible for Frankie to be true to herself and still be anything her mother wanted in a daughter. That was the crux of the problem. At first, Frankie had been hurt and angered by her mother's continuing disapproval of her; now it just saddened her. Oh, well, she couldn't stand there all day. She may as well do what she came to do and go.

Frankie pushed through the double doors and stepped out on to the tiled path leading out to the patio. When she reached the table where her mother sat, she pulled out the chair opposite and sat.

Margaret Hairston didn't look up from the task of serving herself another portion of lobster salad before she spoke. "I wondered how long it would take you to wander out here. You know it's not polite to watch people."

Frankie sighed. "Of course I know that." She could have added that she was girding her loins for this very conversation, but didn't.

"Why don't you have Anderson bring you a plate? There's plenty of food."

Aside from the fact that she was capable of getting her own plate, she declined. "No thank you. I'm not hungry."

"You're slouching."

So she was. She straightened in her seat for the sole purpose of moving the discussion along without interruption. "Don't you want to know why I'm here?"

"I thought it had dawned on you that you could visit some other time than when you wanted something." For the first time, Margaret Hairston focused her full and disapproving gaze on her. "Really, Francesca. Your sense of fashion has always been a bit bizarre, but in the past year it has become atrocious. Did you borrow that shirt from the Jolly Green Giant or are you hiding the fact you've gotten fat?" A horrified expression crossed her face. "You're not pregnant, are you?"

"No, mother. I'm not. Believe it or not, that I would tell you." Or try to.

Margaret huffed. "I should hope so. Maybe you'd better get around to telling me what you want."

"I don't want anything. I came to tell you that I'm going out of town for a while, back to Atlanta. I've got some unfinished business there that I need to tie up."

"Will Nelson Santiago be going with you?"

Frankie tilted her head to one side, considering her mother. How had her mother known anything about Nelson?

"Don't look so surprised, dear. His grandmother called me this morning to tell me the two of you left his cousin's engagement party together last night."

Frankie leaned back in her chair. She should have known the family grapevine would have activated the moment they slipped out together. But why would they care? "The man is married, or hadn't you noticed?"

"He's divorced. Has been for five years."

"Then why does he wear a wedding band?" She'd noticed it the night before as they stood by the railing.

"Probably to ward off unwanted attention. You may not have noticed this, but he's not exactly hard on the eyes."

She had noticed that, but it surprised her that her mother had noticed any man who didn't look like he was born wearing a tuxedo. Nelson Santiago definitely didn't fit that mold. Divorced or no, the fact that he hadn't bothered to take off his ring made him married enough for her. "Sorry to disappoint you, Mother, but there's nothing going on between Nelson and me."

Margaret put down her fork and a pinched look came over her face. "You could at least try, Frankie. That's all I'm asking. You'll be thirty by the end of the year."

So that's what this was about, the damn inheritance that would be hers if she married before her next birthday. "I don't care about that money, Mother."

Margaret flashed her a knowing smile. "That's what your brother used to say, but he capitulated in the end."

Frankie ground her teeth together. That's because in the nick of time Matthew met Nina and the two of them fell in love. Barring that, he would have let the inheritance go, as she planned to. It irked Frankie more than a little that her mother believed that either of her children was so shallow as to marry anyone just to gain a little money.

Frankie pushed back her chair and stood in one motion. "I tell you what, mother, why don't I head to the nearest soup kitchen and pick up a guy there? I mean, if I'm going to share the wealth, why not with someone who really needs it? No? You want a son-in-law presentable enough for family dinner. Let's see, you think half of five million dollars is enough of a bribe to get some man to marry me, or should I throw in some of my trust fund, as well?"

"You are being ridiculous. That's not what I meant at all."

"Yes, it is, Mother. That's exactly what you meant. I really am sorry to be such a disappointment to you, but why can't you trust me to do what makes me happy?"

"Are you happy, Frankie?"

Frankie bit her lip. The only answer she could give was no, but that had nothing to do with either men or money. More important, she wanted to know why when they argued her mother always had to get the last word. "I'll let you know when I'm back in New York," Frankie said finally, whirled around and hurried back to the house.

"Why are we here?" sixteen-year-old Bonnie asked as Nelson pulled up in front of his grandmother's house in Queens.

He'd picked up the girls around noon, taken them to see some snorefest girlie movie they begged him to see. They'd stopped at a fast-food restaurant, and after they'd eaten the girls had practically bankrupted him in the adjoining arcade. He'd purposely avoided telling them about his need to leave so as not to ruin the rest of the day, but judging from the belligerent look that came over Bonnie's face, maybe he should have taken his punishment sooner than later.

"Your mother will be picking you up here later. I have to go out of town for a few days."

Bonnie's mouth fell open and she glanced over her shoulder at her sister in the backseat. "Didn't I tell you? I knew he couldn't go through with it." She flopped back against the seat, her arms folded.

In an effort to mollify his daughter, he said, "You know that I wouldn't put off spending time with you guys if it wasn't important."

"Yeah, whatever, Dad. You go chase the bad guys. Dara and I can take care of ourselves."

Nelson ground his teeth together. How did he ever end up with such a drama queen for a daughter? He turned off the ignition and pocketed the key. "Let's go."

He got out of the car, leaving the girls to do whatever they liked. A moment later, he felt Dara come up beside him and lace her fingers with his. "Bring me back a present, okay?"

Dara had her mother's features, but his hair. She wore hers long, held back by a headband. He ruffled her bangs. "What kind of present?"

Playfully she swatted his hand away. "I'm too old for that."

Maybe, but it hadn't been long ago that she wasn't. "Well?"

"Where are you going?"

"Near Atlanta."

She crinkled her nose. "What do they have there?"

"I'll have to let you know."

They reached the door, but before he had a chance to knock, his grandmother opened the door, her focus on Dara not him.

"Mi vida, ven aca. Dame un beso."

"Abuela," Dara said at the same time, throwing her arms around her grandmother.

Still holding on to Dara, Luz asked, "Where's the other one?"

Nelson nodded back toward the car where Bonnie still sat, her arms folded.

"Leave her be," Luz said. "Come in. I made you something to eat."

How not surprising was that? With his grandmother, every occasion was an occasion for food. When they got to the kitchen, the table was already laden with several dishes. Both he and Dara sat and began to fill plates.

"¿Quiere tostones?" Luz asked him, and before giving him a chance to answer, she plunked a few of the slices of green bananas on his plate.

He glanced up at her over his shoulder. "I don't like tostones. Nathan likes tostones," he said, referring to his cousin.

Luz shrugged. "I'm an old lady, how am I supposed to keep everybody's likes and dislikes straight?"

Nelson shook his head. Serving folks food they didn't like was one of his grandmother's ways of letting folks know they'd displeased her. He put his fork down. "Okay, what did I do now?"

"What's going on with you and Matthew's sister?"

"Nothing. She has a problem I'm helping her with." His gaze slid to Dara, whom he knew was listening to every word. "Hence your unexpected chance to visit with your grandchildren."

"Oh."

She sounded so let down he wanted to laugh. "What do you want from me, *Abuela?*"

"Another grandchild might be nice, before I'm too old to hold it."

He looked at Dara again. "Has your sister been taking lessons from Grandmama Drama over here?" He hooked his thumb toward his grandmother.

"I don't know," Dara said, "but could we have a boy this time? Sisters are a pain in the butt."

He glanced over his shoulder at his grandmother with a look that said, See what you started?

Luckily, Bonnie chose that moment to make an appearance, which put the other conversation on hold. She stood at the end of the edge of the kitchen, her arms still folded, her head down. "Sorry, Dad."

Nelson took his napkin from his lap and tossed it on the table. He went to Bonnie and hugged her. "You through with your fit already?"

She nodded and one of her hands wound around his back. "I just miss you, Dad."

Not wanting to be left out, Dara came up beside him. "I miss you, too."

He ended up with an arm around each of his daughters. "I miss you guys, too." And though he knew his girls were just trying to guilt him for leaving them, he was really going to be pissed if this thing with Frankie turned out to be nothing.

Chapter 3

When Nelson pulled up in front of Frankie's apartment building, he was still in a foul mood. Although his daughters' attempts to make him feel guilty were transparent, they were nonetheless effective. He didn't often disappoint his girls. He made sure of that. But he wondered if something else, rather than his absence, was really on Bonnie's mind. He'd asked her before he left, but she hadn't really given him an answer.

Now he had Francesca Hairston to deal with. He saw her as he neared the apartment. She was standing with her back against the building, a small military-style duffel at her feet. Wearing an oversize jersey and a baseball cap pulled low on her forehead, she gave the impression of some waif abandoned on a doorstep. In this neighborhood, he was surprised she hadn't gotten a ticket for loitering.

He didn't understand her—at least her dress code, anyway. A picture of her as she was a year ago flashed in his mind. She'd struck him as a very sensual woman. And the impression wasn't his alone. A younger cousin of his had tried to catch her attention, but hadn't gotten anywhere. Nelson didn't know why he was bothering to contemplate this now. For all he knew, she merely wanted to be comfortable for the long ride. Either way, it wasn't his problem.

He cut the engine and got out of the car. By the time he reached her, she'd moved away from the building and picked up her bag. He took the bag from her and slung it over his shoulder. Dara had a stuffed bear that weighed more. "Is this it?"

"Why? Were you expecting a line of Louis Vuitton luggage and a personal assistant?"

When she said it like that, his assumption did sound ridiculous. "Something like that."

"I'm afraid you've got me confused with my mother. Besides, we'll be staying in my house in Atlanta."

Which is presumably why she didn't need to bring much. They walked toward the curb. "Nice wheels," she said when she saw the fire-engine-red Ferrari. "Where'd you get them?"

"My garage."

She cast him a skeptical look. "This is your car?"

He opened the trunk and tossed her bag inside. "Why is that so hard to believe?"

Shaking her head, she shrugged and got into the car. "A little conspicuous, no?"

Nelson sighed. When he'd decided to take the

Ferrari, his only concern had been enjoying the car's smooth ride on the long trip. Trying to impress Francesca Hairston hadn't figured into it. But to find her so singularly unimpressed? He should have figured that. During his stint on the computer last night, he'd done a little research on the Hairstons as well. Unlike his wife's family, which was merely rich, her family had real wealth, old money earned the old-fashioned way—on the backs of poor folks.

He closed the trunk and got in beside her. While he fastened his seat belt, he surveyed her profile. Without makeup of any kind, she really would look like somebody's too-pretty kid brother if it weren't for the long braid hanging out of the back of her cap. "Ready?"

She put on a pair of sunglasses. "As I'll ever be."

If that's the best he was going to get, so be it. He gunned the engine and pulled out into traffic. Though heavy, the flow was nothing like it would have been even an hour earlier. That was part of the reason he'd wanted to wait until now to leave. The other part of it was that he'd never mastered the art of making conversation out of nothing. With a little luck, Frankie would sleep most of the way.

Apparently, Frankie hadn't mastered that skill, either. She stared out the window, not that there was much to see inside the Lincoln Tunnel. For some reason he couldn't fathom, he wondered what she was thinking. He sensed a shift in her, a withdrawal into herself. Considering this trip was her idea, he didn't understand the distance he sensed in her.

Again, it was none of his business. He just hoped she

hadn't changed her mind, or if she had, she'd let him know before he saw half of the Eastern Seaboard.

To test the water, he asked, "So how do you want to play this when we get there?"

She turned toward him, an impish grin on her face. "That son-of-a-bitch district attorney who subpoenaed me is actually a friend of mine."

"How good of a friend?"

"Does that matter?"

"Probably not."

"Then why'd you ask?"

"Just wondering if you honestly thought any D.A. would turn over evidence to a witness that might change her mind about testifying in his case?"

"When you put it that way…"

"Then again, maybe you can blackmail him, too." She cast him a look that said she hadn't blackmailed anyone. She could take that stance if she wanted to.

After a moment she looked away. "What do you suggest instead?"

Another benefit of his research last night was discovering that a friend of his from the force was now the head of campus security at the college. That would make it easier, considering that both police squads from the city and surrounding county had formed a task force to hunt down whoever was killing the girls. As low man on the totem pole, he'd know if the cops made a mistake and probably be disgruntled enough to want to share. "I have a lead or two."

That seemed to surprise her. "Already?"

"That's why they pay me the big bucks."

"Speaking of which, how many bucks am I going to owe you when this is over?"

Like with any other case, that would depend on how long it took, as well as other factors. But if she thought he'd charge her one cent, she was mistaken. "Let's worry about that when this is over."

"Does that mean you haven't figured out how much you think you can gouge me for?"

If it weren't for the smile on her face, he would have assumed she was serious. "No."

Surprisingly, she didn't say anything to that. Silence stretched between them, and after a moment she went back to staring out the window. Nelson exhaled. This was going to be a long ride.

Frankie startled awake, once again in the grip of her dream. Breathing heavily, she looked around. She was in the car, the one Nelson claimed was his. She closed her eyes and concentrated on breathing. They were stopped at a gas station and, while Nelson was gone she wanted to get her emotions under control.

Damn. Until the subpoena arrived, the nightmares that started after her attack had nearly faded into distant memories. But in the last few days, they'd come back with a vengeance, assaulting her every time she fell asleep. She'd promised herself she wouldn't slumber during the ride, but the late hour and the hum of the car's engine had made her succumb.

After a moment she sat up enough to get a good look out the window. Nelson was just coming out of the con-venience store attached to the gas station. Wearing black jeans, a black short-sleeved shirt that bared muscular forearms and reflective sunglasses, he had this dark-and-dangerous thing going on that was totally at odds with the car. No way did she believe it was his, despite what he said—not because she doubted he could afford such a car, but left to his own, she doubted he'd buy it. She'd take him more for a tricked-out Harley or that big black monster of an SUV he drove.

He opened the passenger side door and got in. "Look who's back among the living."

If she could help it, she'd stay that way. "What time is it?"

"About three o'clock. If you want something to drink or have any other needs, now is the time."

Despite the long drive, she wasn't particularly thirsty, but her bladder felt about to burst. "I'll be right back."

The station bathroom was surprisingly clean. She relieved herself, washed her hands, then studied herself in the mirror above the sink. "You look like hell," she told her reflection. Dark circles shaded her eyes, either a testament to her recent lack of sleep or the late hour, she wasn't sure which. She would have splashed some cold water on her face if there were anything resembling a paper towel in the place with which to dry off. Not that her appearance mattered at this point, or would. The cold water might have helped keep her awake.

She went back to the car and got in. "Ready?"

Was he going to ask her that every time she got in the car? This time she skipped the flip answer and just nodded. Once they'd pulled out of the gas station, she asked him, "By the way, where are we?"

"Just outside Charlotte."

They were in South Carolina already? He must have waited until she fell asleep to drive like a maniac.

"We should be at your place by six. I figured we'd get a couple of hours' sleep before we get started."

That sounded like a plan. No one they needed to talk to would be available when they got there. She drew her knees up and wrapped her arms around them. Already she felt the pull of her own sleepiness. She needed something besides her own will to keep her awake.

She glanced over at Nelson. His gaze was focused straight ahead on the road. The set of his jaw suggested he was annoyed, or at the very least, slightly pissed off. She should probably leave him alone, but she couldn't risk falling asleep again. In these close quarters he couldn't miss it if she started flailing around, lost to her nightmares.

She tried looking out the window, but at this hour and with no moon and an unlighted highway, she couldn't see much. She searched her mind for something to say, but she doubted Nelson was the type of man to appreciate small talk, not that she could think of any at the moment, either.

"Tell me about this town we're going to."

She shrugged. "Like something out of *Mayberry R.F.D.* About eight thousand people including the college kids. Too damn much foliage, greasy food, spandex. As exciting as a clump of dirt by New York standards. No real crime, until last year. Until then, the biggest problem was how to allow development in the town without losing that down-home feel."

"How'd a city girl like you end up there?"

"It wasn't New York."

"No doubt. But I meant how did you get the job?"

"Actually, a friend of mine who turned it down told me about it. She was looking for a big-time job at a college with a major sports program, not a hole-in-the-wall school where most of the athletic budget comes out of my pocket."

"Do you just coach, or teach, too?"

"I don't do either anymore, but I also taught self-defense to campus women and in the community center in town."

"Really?" She thought that might catch his attention and it did. He turned his head to survey her for a moment. "You'll have to show me some of your moves."

He said that with more skepticism than admiration, which made her want to show him her smack-in-the-head technique. "Anytime."

He cast her a wicked smile and looked away, making her wonder what he was thinking. Lord knew a man who didn't even apologize for having his hand on your ass couldn't be trusted. Besides, for all she knew, he'd checked her out, too, while he was scaring up whatever leads he claimed he had. Either way, she'd said all she intended to about herself. It was time to turn the tables.

She slanted a glance up at him. "So, what's your story? Why'd you go from being a cop to being a P.I.?"

"I was looking for a safer line of work."

Something about the way he said that suggested he hadn't quite been successful. "How's that going for you?"

"What do you think?"

Considering that he was here with her now, she guessed she had her answer, though honestly she didn't know how much danger awaited them. If Jacobs was guilty, then absolutely none whatsoever as he'd been in the county jail since his arrest. But if someone else were responsible for those girls' deaths, all bets were off. She had no idea who else it could be or what they were capable of doing.

She didn't want to focus on that now. Instead she let her feet drop to the floor. She turned slightly in her seat to face him more fully. "Do you mind if I ask you a personal question?"

He slid a glance her way. "Depends on what it is."

"Whose car is this, really?"

He made a sound that in some universe might pass for laughter. "It's my cousin Nathan's."

She could believe that. Nathan was one of the few in-laws she actually remembered, not only because his sister married her brother, but because he'd made quite a name and quite a fortune for himself as a singer. Now him, she could believe the car belonged to.

"Feel better now?"

In a way she did. That meant her instincts weren't off about everything. "Actually, yes."

He shook his head as if in incomprehension. "Any more questions?"

Her gaze went to his hand, to where she knew his ring was even though she couldn't see it. She was curious about why he wore it, but perhaps that was even more than she wanted to know about him. Besides, his comment wasn't designed to find out if there was something she wanted to know. It was meant to alert her that he knew what she'd done—shifted the focus of their conversation off her and onto him. So, he wasn't a stupid man. That was good to know.

She offered him her sweetest smile. "Not at the moment."

"Go back to sleep, Frankie."

There was humor in his voice as well as command. She probably should go back to sleep, but she knew she wouldn't. Instead she watched as the sun began to dawn over the horizon.

The sun had risen fully by the time they pulled up in front of Frankie's house. As soon as Nelson cut the engine she stepped out of the car. All the houses on this block were two-story white clapboard, set back from the street. Their sashes and railings were accented with different pastel colors, in her case a pale lavender. In her absence, the lawn had been kept neat by her neighbor Rachel's son. Even if she hadn't paid the kid, his mama probably would have made him do it, anyway. People in this area took pride in their homes and their neighborhood. None of them would have tolerated a neighborhood eyesore, even if that meant fixing it themselves.

"Nice place."

She hadn't noticed Nelson come up beside her. "Thanks." At one time this house had been her sanctuary. Her place away from New York, from her mother's criticisms and her past mistakes. Living here had been the only time in her life she'd felt like a real grown-up, a woman capable of standing on her own without

anyone else looking over her shoulder. Then some
madman had ruined it for her, ruined everything. And
as much as she wanted to go inside that house, she
dreaded it, too. *He* was there. She'd thought time had
dulled her memories, but now that the nightmares had
come back, she knew that wasn't true.

"I'll get the bags," Nelson said.

He moved off, but she wondered how much of her
mood he'd picked up on. He'd proved to be at least
slightly observant on the trip. If she didn't want to tip
her hand she ought to be more careful. She fished her
keys out of her pocket and pasted a smile on her face.
The first time would be the worst, then it would get
better. She could get through this. She had to.

A white tiled path led up to the house. She traversed
it alone, figuring it was better to have whatever reaction
she might have alone. She hadn't been in this house
since that night. The closest she'd been was to her
neighbor's house, where whatever Rachel Gibbs could
manage to pack up for her awaited.

The first thing she noticed that was different was that
the porch steps didn't creak under the weight of her
ascent. The entire time she'd lived here, she'd promised
herself to get them fixed but never had. In her absence,
someone else had taken care of it. When she got to the
door she took a deep breath before inserting her key and
turning the lock. The door swung open onto a small foyer.
Beyond that was the living room. She stepped inside, past
the foyer, to stand at the edge of the living room.

She surveyed the area. Everything was as it should be.
Even though none of these things in this room were hers,

that mattered to her. The former owner had died with no relatives to claim her possessions. Frankie hadn't seen any point in throwing out perfectly good furniture she rarely used, anyway. The only testament to *his* being here was the absence of the throw rug that had been on the floor and the replacement of the lamp that had broken with another. The room looked oddly…normal. That was the only way she could think of it.

She hadn't realized she'd been holding her breath until that moment, because she let it out as relief flooded her. In an odd way, she wanted to laugh. Part of the reason she'd strong-armed Nelson into coming with her was that she'd known she had to come here but had been afraid to stay in the house alone. Now she felt silly for making such a big deal in her mind about coming back here.

"Why didn't you wait for me?"

Frankie gasped and whirled around. Even though he'd been on her mind, she'd forgotten the real Nelson was only a couple of feet behind her. That flesh-and-blood Nelson had given her a bigger fright than the room had. She whirled back around, away from him, so he couldn't see the strength of her reaction.

She must not have turned in time, because she sensed him come up behind her, not close enough to touch her, but almost. "Are you all right?"

She dragged in one more gulp of air, hoping to sound normal. "You startled me. That's all." She pasted that same smile on her lips and turned to face him. "Maybe we can both use those couple of hours of sleep you talked about."

By the skeptical expression on his face, she knew he

didn't believe her. She couldn't worry about that right now. She needed to get somewhere to collect herself. She walked past him to where he'd left the bags. She slung hers over her shoulder. "The bedrooms are upstairs."

Without waiting for a response from him, she headed toward the staircase to the right. She didn't have to look to know he followed her. She felt the heaviness of his weight on the stairs behind her. If he had anything to say about the scene in the living room, he had the good sense to keep it to himself. What more could a girl in her situation want?

The upstairs bathroom was at the top of the landing. Her bedroom was to the left with the guest bedroom on the other side. She veered to the right, flipped on the light and stepped into the room. The bed was made. That was a bonus. The sheets had to be clean, not left that way when she left, since she never bothered to put sheets on the bed unless she knew someone was staying over.

She turned to face him. "I hope you like the accommodations, since it's all I've got."

He dropped his bag by the door. "It'll do."

He was still watching her with that hawk's gaze. Impressive, but if he thought he was going to get anything out of her with just a look, he was mistaken. "I'm across the hall. If you need anything, help yourself. You've already seen the bathroom." She realized she was babbling and closed her mouth.

"Just to be on the safe side, I don't want you letting anyone into the house, or going anywhere without me for the time being. Our best bet is to play it low-key until we know the lay of the land here. If someone other than

Jacobs is responsible, we don't want him getting wind of what we're doing before we find out anything."

"All right." For a not-so-tall guy, he seemed to take up the entire doorway to the room. She managed to squeeze past him and step into the hall. "See you in a couple of hours," she said over her shoulder as she headed toward her room. Once inside, she shut the door. That way, if her nightmare claimed her, the only one to know about it would be her.

Once Frankie left, he went back downstairs to check out the rest of the house. Downstairs was the living room, a small kitchen and a larger dining room, as well as a small parlor at the front of the house. He checked the refrigerator and found it stocked with a variety of fresh items. He'd known Frankie had called to have the electricity and phone turned on. But if there was food, that meant someone had been in the house before them. A neighbor had probably done the shopping, but he wondered what the likelihood of someone in a small town keeping their mouth shut about her coming back was. Any number of people could know she was here already. Damn.

Back in his room, Nelson toed off his boots and lay down on top of the covers. He told himself to wake up at nine o'clock, which was usually all it took to set his internal alarm clock, and shut his eyes. Despite having been awake all night, sleep didn't immediately come. His mind kept replaying the expression on Frankie's face when he'd come in the door. He'd vaulted up the path behind her, ready to lay into her for not waiting for him. She'd invited him to this party as part investigator, part bodyguard, yet she'd gone into the house alone. What had stopped him from letting her have it was the look of pure terror on her face.

He'd sensed that something was wrong the moment he'd walked in the house to find her standing, just standing, rooted to one spot. Any normal person coming home came in, put down their keys, looked around to make sure everything was in its place. But she just stood there.

Something was going on with her that she hadn't confided in him, some reason why this case mattered to her as much as it did. He had his suspicions, which for the time being he would keep to himself. But she was going to tell him. He'd see to that or he'd go home. Family or not, he wasn't going to risk his neck for a woman that wouldn't be straight with him.

Either way, he was already looking forward to this case being over. This was the second time in three days he'd tried to fall asleep with thoughts of Francesca Hairston keeping him awake.

Chapter 4

Nelson woke at the appointed hour. As he looked around the unfamiliar room, it took him a second to realize where he was—Francesca's house in Branson, Georgia. The walls were covered with some god-awful wallpaper depicting peach-tree branches and ripe fruit. A ceiling fan churned air that was already warm enough to make him perspire. The bed had been comfortable enough. Even now, while sleep still pulled at him, he had to force himself to get up. Hopefully tonight, if nothing untoward happened, he'd do a better job of getting some z's.

He went to his bag, grabbed some toiletries and fresh clothes and headed toward the bathroom. Frankie's door was still closed. He'd wake her once he'd showered, if she hadn't gotten up on her own steam by then. He groaned in pleasure as the warm spray of the shower hit his skin. After the long drive, every muscle in him ached. A little warm water went a long way in relieving the tension.

He toweled off and dressed in a his usual black T-shirt and black jeans, an ensemble that could be dressed up or down as the situation called for. Since she wanted to see the district attorney first, he'd throw on a light-weight jacket. As he left the bathroom, he noticed Frankie's door was still closed. After straightening his room, he went to hers and knocked on the door.

"Frankie, time to get up." Getting no answer, he knocked again, harder. Still getting no response, he turned the knob and opened the door a crack. "Frankie?"

He still got no answer, but then Frankie wasn't there to give him one. Her bed had obviously been slept in, because the sheet was turned down where she would have lain. But clothes and other items were scattered all over the bed. He stepped into the room, walked up and picked up an electric-blue bra from the top of the pile. It seemed as alien in Frankie's bedroom as an actual martian might be. At least, the Frankie he'd seen in the last couple of days—the woman who dressed as if oversize clothes were all they had left at Nieman's—he couldn't imagine putting this on. Not that he couldn't imagine her in it. That presented an image problem of a different kind altogether.

He blocked that thought from his mind, tossed the bra back on the bed where he found it and moved farther into the room. There was a door on the other side of the room, which he assumed to be a bathroom. He knocked, but again, no answer. He yanked open the door. Wrong again. This door led to a small terrace off the bedroom. He pulled the door shut, noticing the door was slightly off its hinges, making him have to finesse it back in place.

So where the hell was Frankie? On the odd chance she hadn't made all this mess herself, he pulled out his gun and headed for the stairs. Moving as swiftly and quietly as he could, he descended the steps. When he got far enough down, he crouched to survey the living room. No sign of Frankie there, either. Nothing out of place or out of the ordinary. He was thankful for that, at least. He descended the rest of the way down the stairs and headed toward the kitchen.

He heard her before he saw her, or rather he heard someone rattling with the broiler to the stove. His view of who it was was blocked by the island that stood in the middle of the room. Undoubtedly, no one had broken in to cook a steak, but he wasn't taking any chances. He moved farther into the room to the right, his gun still poised. He saw her at the same time she decided to lift her head out of the oven. Well, not exactly the same time. She afforded him one brief moment to view her backside, molded to perfection in a pair of skintight jeans, tilted in the air. Damn.

He was about to put his gun back where it belonged, when he noticed a motion to his left, the direction of the dining room. He turned to see an older woman coming through the doorway. The moment she saw him, the platter she held in her hands slipped from her fingers to crash to the floor. "Sweet Mary and Joseph," the woman said, putting up her hands as if being taken hostage.

Abruptly Frankie got to her feet, her back still to him. "What the—"

Her voice trailed off as she spun around. The same pallor came over her face that he'd seen earlier that morning when he'd startled her. Almost immediately her features shifted to a look of supreme annoyance. "Do you have to go waving that thing around?"

He'd already tucked his weapon back where it belonged, but undoubtedly she'd seen it. His answer would have been "yes" if she'd bothered to wait for him to answer. Instead she went to the older woman, draping her arm around the woman's shoulders and leading her to one of the two chairs at the small kitchen table.

The woman plopped into a seat, fanning herself. "My word, I've never had a thing like that happen to me before. Like to give a body a heart attack." She glared at him pointedly.

"Rachel, this is my cousin Nelson that I was telling you about. Nelson, this is Rachel Gibbs, my neighbor across the street."

"Hey," Rachel said.

"Hey," Nelson echoed. "Sorry about that."

"Nelson used to be a cop in New York City. He thinks everyone is dangerous."

"I can see that." Rachel sat forward, adjusting the salt-and-pepper bun at the back of her neck. "Someone ought to clean up that mess before it stains the floor."

"Relax," Frankie said, putting a hand on her shoulder. "Nelson will get it." She speared him with a look that defied him to say or do otherwise.

He ground his teeth together. Was this woman crazy

or was she deliberately defying him? He responded with a similarly pointed look. "I need to talk to you. Now."

She shot him a disgruntled look, but she excused herself from her friend and sauntered past him on the way to the living room. He followed her, stopping at the entrance to the other room when she turned to face him. "Exactly what is going on here this morning?"

"What do you mean?"

He gritted his teeth, wondering if she were being purposefully obtuse. But since she'd asked, he'd start at the beginning. "What happened to your room?"

"Nothing. I couldn't sleep so I started going through some of the things I left here. I admit I left things a little messy, but Rachel came over."

"Speaking of Rachel, what is she doing here? I thought I asked you not to let anyone in here."

"I didn't let her in. She has a key. She wanted to surprise us with breakfast, since when she came in to check the place out she noticed the stove wasn't working."

She tucked a strand of hair behind her ear. He hadn't noticed before that she wasn't wearing one of her hats, but had her hair plaited in a single braid that hung down her back. Neither did she have on one of her big shirts, but a form-fitting top that barely covered her navel. "What was I supposed to do, Nelson? Say no? She's been very good to me. I couldn't do that."

"She's the one who stocked the refrigerator?" He asked that more to verify his own suspicions than as a condemnation of her actions.

She sighed. "If it had occurred to me that you wanted our coming here to be some big secret, I would have gotten us a hotel room under assumed names, but don't you think we'd have been a bit more conspicuous going food shopping in the local Piggly Wiggly?"

She had him there, since that expedition would also be a waste of time better used in other ways. "Exactly when did I become your cousin?"

"You are my cousin—technically, anyway. If you'll remember that's what got you into this mess in the first place."

No kidding. If it weren't for their familial relationship he'd be home right now being tormented by his own daughters' taste in entertainment.

"Are we done now?"

For the time being. "Yes."

"Good. Your breakfast is in the dining room." She cast him a brilliant, if fake, smile. "And the broom and the dustpan are in the tall cabinet by the sink." She pivoted to head in the direction of the stairs.

"Where are you going?"

She turned around but continued her journey across the floor walking backward. "To finish getting dressed, if that's all right with you."

Considering that probably meant she'd add a hat and one of those big shirts, he definitely did mind, but he didn't really think she cared. "I want to leave in fifteen minutes."

She winked at him. "I'll see what I can do."

The district attorney's office was in the Gwinnett County courthouse, about a thirty-minute ride. The building looked like the same one used in *Inherit the Wind*—white stone with lots of columns and the Ten

Commandments hanging over the door. Robert Parker's office was on the second floor toward the back of the building.

When they knocked on the door, a baritone male voice called, "Come in."

Clearly, the man had been expecting someone else, because he was standing, his arm extended as if to shake someone else's. The expression on his face changed from one of business polite to one of surprise and interest. "Francesca, is that you? What are you doing here?"

"You subpoenaed me."

"That's not for another two weeks."

Parker must have noticed Nelson then, because a look of curiosity, and maybe challenge, came over his face. "Who's this?"

"My cousin, Nelson Santiago."

The challenge faded from the man's eyes as he extended his hand. "Pleased to meet you."

"Likewise." Nelson surveyed the man as he shook his hand. He looked to be about thirty-five, with dark brown eyes, black hair cut close to his scalp, but not shaved, and a copper complexion a few shades darker than his own. In his dark blue, three-piece suit, Parker struck him as a man of ambition, though Nelson couldn't imagine what in this town there was to be ambitious about.

Frankie had told him that this man was a friend of hers, but he could see already that he was more than that, or at least he thought he was. That had to be the mismatch of the century—Mr. Buttoned Down with Little Miss Grunge. He supposed stranger things had happened.

Parker stepped back, gesturing toward the interior of

the office. "Well, come in. Sit down. What can I do for you folks?"

While Parker returned to the seat behind his desk and Frankie took one of the visitor's chairs, Nelson took a spot to the side, leaning his back against the wall. He'd rather observe and let Frankie see what she could get out of him.

While Frankie ignored him, Parker cast him a quizzical look, as if he wondered at his purpose for both being there and remaining aloof. The man could wonder if he wanted to. Nelson wasn't telling him anything.

Parker turned back to Frankie. "What's going on with you? I almost didn't recognize you in that get-up."

"It's my new look."

Parker chuckled. "Is it too late to send it back?"

"Very funny, but I didn't come here to talk about my wardrobe. I came here to talk about the trial. Why did you subpoena me? Couldn't you just ask me to testify?"

"If I had, would you have?"

"That's beside the point."

"No it isn't." Parker cast Nelson a look that said he wished he'd disappear by whatever means necessary. "I figured the only way to get you back here was to make it legal. You left without telling me."

"Was there really anything left to say?"

Parker clenched his jaw. "I guess not." He picked up a pen and tapped it on the blotter. "Is that all you wanted to ask me?"

"Do you really need my testimony in the first place?"

Parker blinked and dropped his pen on the blotter. He sat forward. "Yes, I do need you to testify. You saw

Jacobs wearing the same coveralls from which fibers were found at every single crime scene. He was picked up two blocks from your house. Damn straight I need you to testify."

"I saw *a* man. Half the handymen in the county have coveralls like those."

Parker cast him an annoyed look before leaning even more forward. The first part of what he said, Nelson didn't catch, but the second part he did. "I don't understand your reluctance to help put this man away."

Frankie sighed. "I better go." She got up and looked at Nelson to follow.

Parker stood. "Fine, Frankie, do what you want. You always do. But I do expect you to testify when and where and how I want you to. You'll be hearing from me, and this time you'd better return my phone call."

"Fine."

For the first time since they'd come in the office, she looked at him with a mixture of anger, defiance and something else he couldn't fathom. She stalked out of the office without saying another word.

Parker glared at him. "Why don't you see if you can do something with her." He gestured in the direction Frankie had gone.

Yeah, like he'd have any better luck. He was tempted to ask Parker what he'd whispered to her, but decided against it. Whatever was going on, he'd rather hear it from Frankie.

Frankie leaned her back against the passenger door of Nelson's car, folded her arms and waited for him to catch up with her. That had gone just peachy. Not only had she not gotten any cooperation from her friendly, local district attorney, she knew Nelson had to figure out that there was more to her relationship with Robert than mere friendship. Considering that Nelson probably would have noticed that at some point, she didn't know why it bothered her that he knew. It certainly didn't change anything.

At least she was certain Nelson hadn't heard what Robert said to her about Jacobs. She was reasonably certain he would have had some reaction to that, if only to give her one of those glares he was becoming famous for.

At any rate, that was water under the bridge. He'd said he had a lead or two and she hoped one of them would take them someplace.

After a minute Nelson joined her. Once he unlocked the doors, she slid into her seat, fastened her seat belt. She didn't really want to talk about what just happened, but she figured the best way to head off a lengthy conversation was to put it to bed early. "So you were right. That was a complete waste of time."

He gunned the engine and pulled out of the lot. "Want to talk about it?"

From the surprisingly sympathetic tone in his voice, she knew he meant her relationship with Robert, not her failed attempt to get out of testifying. "Not particularly." To emphasize her point, she leaned her elbow on the door frame, rested her cheek on her hand and stared out at the landscape on her side of the car.

"How long were you two seeing each other?"

She turned her head to glare at him. "Correct me if

I'm wrong, but didn't I just say that I didn't want to talk about it?"

"Yeah. Indulge me for a minute, though. How long were you seeing him?"

"That's none of your business." Not that she could figure out why he cared. "You want to delve into someone's personal life? Let's pick yours. Why do you still wear your ring when according to all sources you're divorced?" The question was out of her mouth before she remembered she didn't want to know that much about him. Now that it was out, she didn't expect him to answer her, anyway.

He surprised her. "She divorced me. If I ever decide she was right, I'll take it off."

Frankie blinked, not knowing what to say to that. By the earnestness in his voice and the grim set of his jaw, she knew he'd told her the truth, at least the truth as he knew it. She said the only two words it made sense to say. "I'm sorry."

"Answer the question."

Bristling from the command in his voice, she said, "What was that again?"

He said nothing, but he took his eyes off the road long enough to cast a look her way. He had his sunglasses on again, so she couldn't see his eyes, but she didn't need to see them to know what kind of look he'd given her.

She gave a sigh of frustration and capitulation. "Fine. About six months."

"Was it his fault you broke up?"

"No."

"Your fault?"

In a way it was, but she'd had no control over that, so as far as she was concerned it didn't count. Since she didn't want to explain all that, she said, "Look, it was nobody's fault. It just ended. It wasn't like it was some big deal. We weren't madly in love or anything. It was something to do. You must have noticed there isn't much of that to go around in this town."

"If it wasn't anybody's fault, you might consider cutting the guy a little slack."

Now he was trying to tell her how to run her love life? This guy was too much. "Well, thank you, Dr. Phil, for that brilliant piece of insight. Why do you care, anyway?"

"Because if there comes a time when we actually do need something from him, it would help if you didn't antagonize him."

"Oh." In the back of her mind she'd thought he'd asked out of some personal interest in her. Not a sexual interest, obviously, since among other things he was still caught up in his ex-wife, but concern for her well-being. She didn't know why she should be so disappointed finding out that his interest was linked only to how her relationship with Robert might affect their investigation, but she was. "Point taken."

She sighed again, returning her gaze to the view outside her window. She must be more exhausted than she thought if she found herself caring what this man or any man or anyone thought of her. The only person in her life who she thought knew her, liked her and accepted her for herself was her brother. Her father loved her, but made no attempt to understand her. Her mother had been trying to remake her into the image of her older sister, who had died before Frankie was born. Claire, as described to Frankie, had been one of those girlie girls you could dress up and never worry she'd get dirty or muss her hair. The perfect little lady—everything that Frankie was not.

She had plenty of female friends who tolerated her, but thought she was weird. The debutantes she'd grown up with wondered how anyone with her background would want something as déclassé as a degree in sports education. Her friends from college, most of whom came from families that were financially comfortable, wondered why anyone whose allowance paid for every conceivable want would even bother to work.

As for men, she rarely allowed them to get close enough that what they thought made any difference to her. Robert had been the sole exception to that, in that they had known each other socially before they ever made it to bed.

Nelson's hand grazed her thigh. "How are you doing over there?"

She crossed her leg and his hand fell away. "Just a little tired, I guess. If you don't mind, I'm going to try taking that nap again when we get home."

He cast her another of his skeptical looks. She met his gaze levelly. She didn't care what he thought, as long as he left her alone.

Chapter 5

Once he'd left Frankie at the door to her room, presumably to take a nap, Nelson got the papers he'd printed out from the Internet from his bag and went down to the small parlor at the front of the house. This was as good a place as any to lay out the information. No one coming into the house would have to see what he'd done, not that he was hoping for many visitors. They'd only prove to be a distraction neither he nor Frankie needed. Only one potential visitor mattered. Nelson pulled out his cell phone and dialed the number he'd already gotten from information.

Donald Meyer, former NYPD lieutenant, wasn't in when Nelson called his office, but the person answering the call had promised to give him the message. Using Scotch tape and a few pushpins, he posted the picture of each of the girls and whatever pertinent facts he'd gained about their murder in the order they had occurred. First was Diana Hill on February 1, then Kerry Washington, Frankie's player, a month later, followed by Taneisha Webb, Gladys Chin and Brianna Lopez.

Thirty days separated the first two killings, but all the others occurred within much shorter and seemingly random intervals. Like Frankie said, the girls were of varying heights, played a variety of sports, had differing areas of study at the college. Kerry and Taneisha were black, Evelyn and Diana Hill were white, and Gladys Chin was Asian.

As far as Nelson could tell, there were no similarities between the girls except their athleticism, and that each girl's body had been found in the same deserted stretch of road within twenty-four hours of them going missing. That was probably another reason they'd looked at Jacobs. As a janitor, no one would have thought twice about seeing him move in and out of the buildings, not that anyone reported seeing him. But the girls even hailed from different states in different parts of the country.

Nelson stepped back from his handiwork and surveyed the wall. He wished he had a photo of each of the crime scenes and a look at the murder book for each victim. How the bodies were left, whether they were posed or sexualized in any way, might offer some clue into the killer's psyche. The murder book, the logs of every report and piece of information the detectives collected, might show some hidden pattern to the killings, such as what, if anything, the killer took as a souvenir. He doubted Meyer could get him the latter, but the former would be easier to come by.

The last picture Nelson hung up was a shot of Jacobs himself being led into the courthouse. Skinny, balding and looking every day of his fifty-seven years and then some, he could see why Frankie would question Jacobs ability to have committed the murders. The most damning evidence against him was his criminal record, and that the killer reportedly wore coveralls similar to the ones Jacobs wore every day.

"Santiago?" he heard Frankie call.

"In here." He noticed that after she'd gotten his acquiescence to help her, she'd either called him by his full name or surname alone, never his first name—at least not when they were alone. He wondered what to make of that but came up empty.

She appeared in the doorway a moment later wearing a voluminous white robe that buttoned down the front, and her hair was back in that single braid. Considering how hot it was and how ineffective the ceiling fan in this room was at cooling anything, he couldn't comprehend her choice of outfit. "What? No schmatte this time?"

Fingering her hair, she walked farther into the room. "It's pretty silly to wear a hat in the house." She turned to survey the items on her wall. "If you wanted to redecorate my house you should have said something. I admit the wallpaper in here is ghastly."

She stepped closer to the wall, surveying each of the items he'd tacked there. "These are all of the girls."

It was a statement, not a question, but he said, "Yes," anyway. "When did you see Jacobs?"

She stepped back. "The night Brianna Lopez was murdered."

"There's no mention of that in any of the newspaper articles I've seen. How did that hap—"

The sound of his phone ringing cut him off. He unclipped his phone from his belt and looked at the display. It read the same number he'd just dialed for Donald Meyer. Nelson connected the call. "Hey, Don."

"Hey man, did I hear it right that you're in this neck of the woods? What? New York got too exciting for you so you had to try it out in the sticks?"

"Not exactly." He glanced at Frankie, who suddenly seemed terribly interested in one of the photos on the walls. He knew she was listening to every word he said, so he wondered why she bothered to pretend she wasn't. "I'm down here working on a case."

"Those murdered girls."

He sounded so certain it made Nelson curious. "How did you know?"

"We ain't got no other crime down here, except the occasional boy getting friskier than the average girl allows. What can I do to help?"

"Any information you've got would be useful."

"Where can I meet you?"

"You know where Francesca Hairston lives?"

"I can find it. How does an hour and a half sound?"

That was fine with Nelson. He and Don said their goodbyes and he disconnected the call. Meanwhile, he could sense Frankie's impatience to know what was going on. He didn't keep her guessing. "That was Don Meyer, the head of campus security. He used to be NYPD before a heart attack forced him to retire."

That should answer both her questions as to whom he was talking to and how he knew anybody out here.

"One of those leads you told me about?"

"Yes."

A look of appreciation came into her eyes. "Not bad. That man wouldn't give me the time of day when I asked him what he knew."

"That's what I'm here for."

"Ain't you just?" She tightened the sash on her belt. "I guess I'd better go put some clothes on. Why don't you see if you can get the pilot lit on the stove and maybe we can have some dinner tonight."

She pivoted and left, leaving him to wonder why she needed to bother with clothes. No outfit she could come up with could possibly conceal more than that robe did, unless she planned to put on a burka and veil. Besides that, he'd hoped to have at least a few moments with Don without Frankie being present. There were some questions that he wanted to ask that Frankie didn't necessarily need to hear the answers to. Although she presented a tough-cookie exterior, he didn't know how much of what he'd find out she could handle. He'd have to come up with some excuse to get her out of the room.

He got the stove lit without too much trouble. He found two steaks marinating in an aromatic liquid in the refrigerator—their dinner, he presumed. He took the container out of the fridge and placed it on the counter. He looked around the kitchen and found other ingredients for a meal and got them started on different burners on top of the stove.

By the phone mounted on the wall, he found a list of numbers. He pulled out his cell phone and dialed the one he wanted. He was just disconnecting the call when Frankie came into the kitchen. She wore a long white blouse that narrowed at her waist and flared slightly at her hips over a pair of black pants. On her feet were black ballet-type slippers. Her hair was pulled back into a ponytail high on her head. She actually had on some makeup, a subtle application of mascara, lip gloss and blush.

She stopped by the counter where he was slicing onions and mushrooms to sauté. She popped a slice of mushroom into her mouth. "My, you've been busy. How are you with windows and floors?"

"Passable." Maybe he should keep his mouth shut, but he couldn't help adding, "You clean up pretty nice yourself."

She lifted one shoulder in a shrug that seemed to dismiss his compliment. "And again, no shmatte." She snagged another piece of mushroom and bit into it. "I didn't see any point in continuing to terrify the populace with Frankie au naturel."

She must be joking, since with or without makeup she was a pretty woman. Even so, that wasn't the interpretation of *au naturel* that consumed his brain or other places farther down on his body. Despite her attempts to camouflage her figure, his mind had filled in all those parts of her kept hidden, and he had a vivid imagination, too vivid for his own good.

She popped one last slice of mushroom into her mouth. "I guess I'll make myself useful setting the table."

She gathered silverware and linens from a couple of drawers and left. He stared after her, doubting she cared much if the table were set or bare. She'd wanted to get away from him. He saw that in the way she hurriedly gathered the tableware. She'd seemed perfectly comfortable with him until he mentioned her appearance. Damn. He knew something was up with her and he was trying to guess what it was. Despite what he told himself about not needing to understand her, he planned to find out.

Frankie wiped her mouth, then arranged her napkin in her lap. The steak Nelson had cooked was divine, the rice nicely done, the salad crisp. He'd even made gravy and the ubiquitous biscuits people in the South loved. She knew he was watching her, though so far into the meal she'd avoided eye contact and any conversation other than "Pass the salt, please."

Honestly, she didn't know what to say to him. She'd seen the way he'd looked at her in the kitchen, though she'd pretended she hadn't noticed. She just got out of there as soon as she thought of an excuse to. She knew the look of desire in a man's eyes, and for a split instant she'd seen it in his. That look was as familiar as it was, for a variety of reasons, unwelcome.

If it were up to her, she'd have stayed in her robe. She'd felt comfortable and protected. But she didn't want everyone she knew to question how she looked as Rachel had done that morning and Robert a couple of hours later. She needed to restore some measure of outward normalcy, though she felt anything but normal.

"So how is it?"

She met his gaze. For an instant she couldn't fathom what on earth he was talking about.

He gestured with a movement of his fork toward her plate. "How is it?"

"I should have hired you as a chef instead of an investigator. Everything is wonderful. Thank you."

He winked at her. "I'll have to tell Bonnie there's someone in the world who enjoys my cooking."

"Who's that? Your wife?"

"My daughter. She thinks carbs are the dietary equivalent of anthrax."

Not in her wildest dreams did she picture him as a father. "How old is she?"

"Sixteen going on thirty-five. Her sister, Dara, is twelve."

She heard the pride in his voice and saw its reflection in his eyes. "No sons?"

"No."

"Guess you wouldn't have had much luck telling them they needed a haircut, anyway." Still, he didn't strike her as being old enough to have a twelve-year-old child, let alone a teenager. "You must have gotten married right out of the womb."

"Close. Right after college, but we'd known each other since high school."

"I didn't think people did that anymore."

"What?"

"Marry their high school sweethearts."

He grinned. "I'm a throwback."

"Nelson the Barbarian? It has a certain cachet, I guess." She looked down at her plate. Despite the flavorfulness of the food, she hadn't really eaten much, just pushed it around on her plate. "Do you boss them around like you do me?"

"Who? The girls? Even if I did, it wouldn't make much difference. They listen about as well as you do."

"Smart girls."

The doorbell rang, silencing any answering comment he would have made.

"I'll get it." She was out of the room before he got out of his seat. Her radar might be off about him, but she knew him well enough to assume he'd try to leave her out of whatever conversation he had with Don Meyer. She'd hired Nelson to protect her, but not from the full truth of what happened. That she couldn't stand for.

But before she could get her hand around the knob, he stood in front of her blocking her way. She drew back in surprise, crossing her arms in front of her.

"You should know better than that by now, Frankie."

"For goodness' sake. I can see the man through the door." She gestured toward one of the glass panels on either side of the door. "Do you think someone trying to hurt me would bother to ring the bell?"

The bell sounded again, followed by Don Meyer's baritone voice. "You people planning on letting me in?"

Frankie shot Nelson a pointed look. He moved aside slowly so that she could open the door. Don Meyer was in his late fifties, but the heart attack had added another five years to his appearance. Male-pattern baldness robbed him of but a few light brown hairs on the crown of his head, which he meticulously slicked down to look like more. He carried a beat-up old briefcase in one hand, which she assumed contained whatever information he'd managed to scrounge up.

Frankie stepped back, opening the door wider for him to pass. "Good evening, Chief Meyer," Frankie said.

"Hey, Ms. Hairston." He turned in Nelson's direction, extending his hand. "Good to see a familiar face."

"Same here."

Chief Meyer stepped inside. Both men waited for her to close the door before proceeding.

Meyer said, "Knowing you, you've got plenty to go on without my help, but let me see what you've got."

Nelson led the way to the parlor. He stopped in the doorway. To Meyer he said, "Take a look."

Meyer walked past Nelson to enter the room. When she stepped up to do the same, the grim expression on Nelson's face told her he'd bar her from the room if he thought he could get away with it. Not in this lifetime. She met his glare and walked past.

She came up beside Chief Meyer. He looked over his shoulder at her, then returned to gazing at the material Nelson had put up on the wall. "Looks like you've pretty much got it covered," Meyer said.

"Do you have anything else to add?" she asked him. But before the words were completely out of her mouth she heard the sound of her front door opening. "Yoo hoo, anybody home?"

That was Rachel's voice. Frankie focused a narrow-eyed glare on Nelson. He looked as innocent as a little baby lamb, so she knew he was guilty of inviting Rachel over here to distract her. He knew that she wouldn't send Rachel home or reveal to her the true purpose of the chief's visit, which meant she'd have to occupy Rachel in another part of the house. He'd probably told Rachel to use her key, too, that way she couldn't have met the older woman at the door and told her that now wasn't a good time to visit. Damn.

"You have company," Nelson said, she supposed in an effort to get her moving.

She intensified her glare. "Don't think I'm not calling the locksmith tomorrow morning."

She met Rachel in the living room and invited her into the kitchen for coffee. Once they were both seated at the table, each with a healthy slice of the coconut cake Rachel had brought over, Frankie said, "He told you to come over here, didn't he?"

Rachel set down her mug. "It was more of a suggestion, really. He told me the chief was coming over. The two of them were old friends and you'd probably be bored to tears listening to them. And since I didn't have nothing to do but watch my toenails grow, I thought, why not? We have a lot of catching up to do ourselves."

"Really?" Frankie had thought they'd done that this morning. Nothing much was new with either of them, or at least that's the opinion Frankie gave Rachel. "What's on your mind?"

Rachel took a deep pull from her cup before answering. "Is that boy really your cousin?"

Frankie blinked. She hadn't expected that, and she wasn't answering until she was sure where the conversation was heading. "Why do you ask?"

"Y'all don't look nothing alike."

"He's my cousin by marriage."

Rachel nodded. "That explains it." Rachel leaned across to pat her thigh. "Then there's still hope yet."

Though she knew she was going to hate the answer, Frankie asked, "Hope for what?"

Rachel sipped from her cup. "Well, everybody around here knows that you cut things off with Bobby after, well, you know. I was hoping you'd found some nice young man up in New York to make things better."

Frankie swallowed down the last sip in her coffee cup, fighting the urge to gag. She could think of a lot of words to describe Nelson Santiago, but "nice" wasn't one of them. And contrary to Rachel's wishes, Frankie had spent the last year avoiding men rather than seeking them out.

"He's spoken for," Frankie said when she could talk, since to her mind he was in every way that counted.

"Too bad." Rachel leaned forward as if to whisper a secret. "That boy looks like he could put a hurting on a woman and she wouldn't wake up complaining the next morning."

Now, that she didn't have any trouble imagining. Heat rose in her body, pooling between her legs. There was something about that man that appealed to her on a primitive level that had nothing to do with reason.

"I tell you," Rachel continued. "If I were thirty years younger, I'd be tempted to forget I said 'I do' and help him forget he said it, too. Heck, I might do it if I was just twenty."

"Rachel," Frankie said in mock surprise. The way Rachel talked about her long-dead husband, Frankie knew she'd do no such thing. Still, she couldn't help teasing. "What would your husband have said if he'd heard you making light of your marriage vows?"

"I don't know what he would have said about it then, but he's dead now, so he don't have nothing to say about it." Rachel laughed. "I only said I'd be tempted, and since I ain't forty years younger, you can get that look off your face."

"I was only pretending to be shocked."

"I'm not talking about that look and you know it." Rachel stood. "At any rate, it's time I got these old bones in bed. I'm going out the back door so as not to tip those boys off. You say bye for me to Nelson and the chief."

"I will." Frankie walked Rachel to the door. "You have a good night."

"You, too." Frankie let Rachel out, then leaned her back against the door. Now it was time to find out what those boys were up to.

"That's one sick puppy."

Nelson nodded his head in agreement, saying nothing. His eyes were still on the crime-scene photos Don had brought over without Nelson having to ask. Each girl had been strangled, raped and had her throat slit. The fact that each girl had also been stabbed six times in the abdomen postmortem had been kept out of the papers as a means of identifying the killer. Only the doer would know exactly what had been done.

Apparently the killer had left the women however they were when he was through with them—throats slit and bruised, clothing torn or missing, legs and arms splayed at odd angles, but surprisingly little blood, suggesting the girls had been killed elsewhere and dumped there. Little larval activity had started, confirming that the girls had been killed and dumped within a short period of time, less than a day. "Rigor?"

"In some of the girls but not others. Not enough time for it to set in."

Nelson gathered the pictures together and returned them to their folder. He doubted they'd have much more time before Frankie's curiosity drove her into the room. He didn't mind discussing those pictures in the abstract, but after seeing them, he was glad he'd hidden them from her. It was one thing to look at pictures of strangers; it was another when it was someone you knew.

Don shifted in his seat. "After they found the first girl, the good ol' boys from Gwinnett swore her boyfriend was the one who did it. The Brandt family owns half the town here and what they don't own they control. Junior's been cutting up since he was a kid, but daddy always got him out of it. I imagine the boys around here were happy to pick him up on some charges they thought might stick."

"What kind of cutting up?"

"Just a for instance, he got picked up a couple of years ago, wandering around the back roads, drunk out of his mind and stark naked. He said he was looking for his keys. I remember it was a couple weeks after Halloween. The only clothing they had to fit him was a Batman costume from the lost and found. Or that's what they told him."

From the smile on Don's face, Nelson assumed that wasn't the case. He wondered how Brandt had looked in his mug shot complete with cape and cowl. "Why'd they let him go?"

"He was in police custody when the second body showed up. The M.E. said the murder had occurred during the time he was in custody. They had to let him go."

"And after?"

"Between my guys, the cops, the boys from the sheriff's office, the student patrols, you'd have thought no one could breathe funny without someone catching them do it. But four more girls were attacked before we got Jacobs in custody. Then it stopped. The man must have been part ghost, since no one ever saw him anywhere near any of the girls."

"You're sure it's Jacobs?"

"I'm not sure of anything, except the murders stopped when they picked him up."

Nelson considered that, an alternate thought occurring to him. "And they never came up with any connection between the girls?"

"None."

"Did the killer take anything? A souvenir?"

"Not that anybody shared with me."

He had only one more question—what the hell Frankie had to do with any of this. But before he got it out of his mouth, there was a knock at the door. Nelson rose to answer it, blocking Frankie's entrance through the door with his body.

"I thought you boys might like some coffee and some of the cake Rachel brought."

She carried a tray laden with a white carafe, two coffee mugs and two slices of cake on dessert plates. He took the tray from her, but didn't move from his spot guarding the door. "Thanks."

From behind him, Don said, "I've got to be going, anyway."

Nelson set the tray on the table inside the parlor. "I'll walk you out." He waited for Don to pass before following. It only took a moment to let Don out the door and say good-night. He knew where Frankie would be, though. She'd raced into the room the second he and Don were out of the way. That's why he'd made sure to set her tray on top of the folder of pictures Don had given him.

After he closed the front door behind Don, he went back to the parlor. Just as he'd supposed, Frankie was in the room with her back to him, but she'd found the pictures despite his attempt to hide them. He knew because they were scattered all over the table and at her feet. Damn.

He leaned his back against the door frame and called her name softly. Her only response was to let the pictures in her hands fall to the table. "Frankie," he repeated.

She did turn then, with her arms wrapped around herself. In her eyes he saw the revulsion and pain she must have felt looking at the pictures of the girls. But there was something more in her expression that he didn't understand. He took a step toward her. "Say something."

For a moment her lip trembled, as if she were on the verge of speaking. Instead she bolted past him, out the parlor door.

Chapter 6

"Frankie," he called after her, but she didn't stop. If he wanted to, he could have caught up with her, but since he thought he knew where she was headed, he let her be. He went into the parlor instead, gathered up the pictures she'd scattered and put them back in their folder. He took the folder upstairs and tucked it between the mattress and box spring of his bed. In the unlikely event she wanted to look at them again, she wouldn't know where to find them.

On the way up the stairs he noticed the closed bathroom door. He went back to it and knocked. "Are you all right in there?"

Getting no answer, he eased the door open. She was sitting on the floor, her back against the claw-foot tub, her knees drawn up. She'd wrapped her arms around her knees and rested her forehead on her arms. "Frankie?"

She lifted her head but didn't look at him. "I thought I was going to…"

She more cut herself off than trailed off. He didn't have to be a genius to fill in the rest for her. He'd known seeing those pictures would upset her. Being right didn't give him any consolation. "Are you okay now?"

She did look at him then. "How do you do it? How can you look at something like that without having it affect you?"

"I can't."

"Those poor girls. What he did to them. It's one thing to think about it intellectually…" She trailed off, sniffling. "They must have been so scared. They fought back, didn't they? Even though he tried to debilitate them, they fought back."

He saw in her eyes that she needed to believe that. He was glad he didn't have to disappoint her. Each girl showed wounds that suggested she'd tried to fend off her attacker. "Yes."

Looking away, she nodded. "Thank you."

He didn't know what to say to that. It didn't matter, though, since he doubted she would have heard anything he did say. She laid her cheek on her knees, her shoulders shaking. The sound of her muffled sobs reached him. His heart went out to her, making him wish he had some way to comfort her. If she were any other woman, he wouldn't hesitate to hold her until she quieted. But she'd closed in on herself. Even her head faced away from him. Clearly, she didn't want his interference, but he couldn't leave her that way.

He sat on the floor facing her so that his legs were

on either side of her and pulled her to him. She flinched, but she didn't fight him. He rubbed her back, whispering Spanish words of comfort learned at his grandmother's knee.

He wasn't sure if anything he said even registered with her, but after a moment she sat back, swiping at her eyes. Still, her gaze didn't meet his. "I'm sorry."

She had nothing to be sorry for, or to be embarrassed about, or whatever she was feeling. He understood how she felt, or at least he thought he did. Even so, he doubted sympathy from him was what she was looking for. He decided to try another tack. "Not a problem. You forget I have two daughters. I'm used to this sort of thing by now."

She glared at him then. "If that's supposed to be some sort of commentary on female emotionalism—"

He cut her off. "It's a testament to teenage hormones. My oldest still thinks feminine temper tantrums are the best way to wrap a man around her finger, and I haven't been doing the best job of convincing her she's wrong." As he spoke, he pulled his handkerchief from his back pocket and offered it to her. "Truce?"

She took the handkerchief from him. "I didn't know men still carried handkerchiefs."

"I told you I was a throwback."

She dabbed at her eyes, but she missed a spot of moisture on her cheek. He brushed it away with his thumb. She started, and as if she suddenly realized the intimacy of their positions, she pulled as far back from him as she could. "It's getting late." She pushed to her feet. "Good night, Nelson."

He would have grabbed her leg, but he figured she'd freak out, like almost every other time he'd touched her. He had the feeling she wouldn't have allowed him anywhere near her tonight if she hadn't been lost in her own misery. He decided to stop her with words instead.

"Jacobs was here, wasn't he? That's why the police were looking for him in this neighborhood when they picked him up."

For an instant, she froze in place, saying nothing. He sensed the ambivalence in her and also the moment of capitulation when she decided to level with him in the droop of her shoulders. But she didn't bother to turn and face him.

"Yes, he was here, whoever he was. The night Brianna Lopez was killed. I came home late and he was in here, in my living room. He attacked me the moment I came in. But he misjudged, I guess because I'm so much shorter than his other victims. The rope caught me on the chin, not around the throat. I put my elbow in his solar plexus and tried to get the hell out of here."

She didn't elaborate, but he knew there was more. He wished she'd turn so that he could see her face, gauge her feelings about what she was telling him. Her voice sounded flat, as if she was numb or didn't care. That couldn't be the truth. Maybe she'd gone on emotional shutdown after her crying jag. He didn't know her well enough to tell. All he could do was prompt her to tell him what she knew. "What happened then?"

"I don't know. That's all I remember. The next thing I remember is waking up in a hospital bed."

"What makes you think Jacobs had nothing to do with this?"

"I didn't see his face, but this guy was muscular and strong, much too strong to have been Jacobs. Is there much more to this interrogation, or can I get some sleep?"

No, the interrogation wasn't over. He had plenty of other questions on his mind, including the most pressing one. But those could wait until later, when he had some hope of getting a face-to-face answer. "Go to sleep, *munequita.* We'll talk tomorrow."

Finally, she turned to face him, her arms folded. "What did you call me?"

"Literally it means *little doll.*"

"That better not be a short joke." She pivoted and left the room.

No, it definitely wasn't a short joke. It was an endearment that had slipped from his tongue effortlessly. Since he wasn't a man given to frilly language even with his girls, he'd surprised himself, too. He didn't know what it was about this woman that got to him, that fired both his libido and his protective instincts.

Though she appreciated the latter, she definitely wasn't interested in the former. Not that he had any plans to act on any attraction he felt. He was a grown-up with more than average self-control. But her reaction to his touch made him wonder what had really happened that night. There was still more to this story that she seemed determined to dole out to him in dribs and drabs.

He didn't know what else she kept from him, but at this point he knew three things: there was some connection between the victims that no one had yet figured out; Frankie was hiding something from him; and if he ever got his hands on whoever hurt her, that man was dead meat.

* * *

Frankie leaned her back against the door to her room surveying the mess she'd made that morning. Most of the mess, anyway. She'd cleaned up part of it when she came upstairs to change her clothes. She could understand why Nelson had looked at this and thought someone besides her might have been responsible.

But it wasn't her messy room that disturbed her, but her messy emotions. Not only had she cried in front of Nelson, she'd told him three-quarters of what she'd promised herself to keep to herself. But all Nelson Santiago had to do was ask and she spilled her guts. To her credit, those pictures had been an incredible shock. It was one thing to know in the abstract what happened to those girls and quite another to see it in glossy four-color.

She'd been to each of the girls' funerals, all except Brianna's. Due to the wonders of makeup and mortuary science, no one would have guessed the horrors of their last moments alive. She wished she didn't know, but now that she did, it made her more determined to make sure the right man went away for their murders.

Frankie pushed off the door. She'd better clear off some of this mess, enough so that she could lie down and go to sleep. But even after she'd lain down, sleep didn't come. Every time she closed her eyes, she saw his face. She didn't know why she'd let him touch her in the first place. She hadn't been so lost in her own misery that she hadn't noticed. Truthfully, it had felt good to be held by someone who didn't want anything from her except to see to her well-being. But when he'd wiped the tear from her cheek—that was too intimate a gesture for her to allow.

Still, she wouldn't have imagined such a rough man could have such a tender touch. It wasn't the only contradiction about him that intrigued her. She would have thought a man like him would have preferred some high-action police assignment, not chasing down sex fiends and child molesters. He'd told her he left the NYPD in search of a safer line of work, but she didn't buy that, either. Clearly, from the way he'd redecorated her walls and the gusto with which he'd attacked this case, he'd enjoyed his work. So why had he left?

She shifted onto her side, trying to get comfortable. One more question plagued her, one she knew she should leave alone or at least confine to her own solitary contemplation—what the hell had he done to his wife to make her leave him?

The next morning, Nelson was sitting at the kitchen table finishing off his second cup of coffee when Frankie came into the room. She had on a pair of jeans, a close-fitting black T-shirt and her feet were bare. Her hair was twisted up into some sort of loose bun at the back of her head. She cast a smiling look at him. "What? No breakfast this morning? I hope you weren't waiting for me to cook."

He turned his head to follow her entry into the room. She went to the refrigerator, took out a carton of orange juice, then went to the cabinet to retrieve a glass. Was it his imagination or was this the same woman who last night cried inconsolably in his arms? From her demeanor, you wouldn't think she had a single care. "I wasn't hungry."

She filled the glass about halfway then downed its contents. "Does that make you opposed to a little French toast?"

"Not particularly."

She filled the glass again and returned the juice to the refrigerator. "Knock yourself out." She lifted her glass in salute to him. "This is all I'm having this morning." She pivoted, obviously intent on leaving the room.

Before she got to the doorway, he moved to block her path. "Where are you going?"

She backed up a step. "I thought I'd listen to the news in the living room. Why?"

She didn't fool him. Her smile was too bright and her gaze didn't meet his. He stroked back a lock of hair that made it out of her hairdo. "How are you really, Frankie?"

She tucked the strand behind her ear. "I'm fine."

"Are you?"

She cast him a hard, narrow-eyed look. "What do you want from me, Santiago? You expecting me to go all weepy Mary again? Forget it. That wouldn't have even happened without those pictures. Or is this your way of saying I told you so about me not listening to you?"

"This is my way of saying I'm concerned about you."

"I'm not paying you to be concerned."

"You're not paying me for anything, so whatever I do is my business."

She pressed the heel of her hand to her forehead and shook her head. "Please don't do this to me, Nelson."

He didn't see that he was doing anything to her. Without a doubt, she had more invested in this investigation than finding out who killed her student, or even her own attack. He couldn't imagine what that might be, but it was something. He was sure of that.

He cupped her chin in his palm and stroked his thumb across her cheek. "What is it about this case that has you so tied up in knots?"

For once, when he touched her, she didn't pull away. Her lips parted and her throat worked, but before she got a word out, the doorbell rang.

She stepped back and crossed her arms. The plastic smile was back in place. "Am I allowed to answer that?"

Nelson ground his teeth together in frustration. "I'll get it." He stalked to the door and pulled it open. Several young women pushed past him, casting looks at him over their shoulders as they went. The last of the girls to come through, a statuesque redhead in a lavender sundress, sauntered through the door, giving him a bold feminine once-over.

She extended her hand toward him. "I'm Julia. And you are?" she prompted.

Nelson almost laughed at the guileless Southern belle routine. The last woman who'd tried that nonsense on him had been from Brooklyn. "Almost old enough to be your father. Frankie's inside."

The smile fell away from her face and she marched past him. Shaking his head, he closed the door and followed. By the time he joined them, the women had gone to the living room. Frankie was sitting on the sofa with the girls gathered around her.

As she approached, she looked up at him. "Girls, this is my cousin Nelson. Nelson, meet the Excelsior College soccer team. Most of them, anyway."

The girls issued a collective "Hi Cousin Nelson."

Frankie put her hand on her chest and bowed her head. "Ah, I have trained you well."

The girls dissolved into giggles, leaving him to wonder what that was about. But he also knew any chance of getting any more information out of her at the moment had flown. That was okay. As long as the girls were here she'd be perfectly safe, and he thought he knew someone who'd prove more accommodating.

He smiled in a way that encompassed all of them. "I've got to go out for a minute. Can I trust you ladies to watch out for Frankie until I get back?"

The girls offered him a chorus of "Of course." Julia was the only one to bat her eyelashes and add, "As long as you promise not to take too long."

Oh, brother. He winked at Frankie. "I'll be back before you know it."

She cast him a look that said she would get him later. That was fine with him. By then, he hoped he'd know all he needed to know.

After Nelson left, Frankie focused on the girls. She had no idea where Nelson had sneaked off to and at the moment didn't want to know. She didn't think she could handle any more evidence as graphic as what she'd seen last night. She'd be content to hear about it later.

"What are you guys doing here?" Frankie asked no one in particular.

"You didn't think you could sneak back into town and we wouldn't find out about it, did you?" That came from Linda Spence, the most gregarious girl of the bunch. "You should have told us you were here."

"I wasn't sneaking in anywhere. I just got here yesterday." Most of the girls looked at her in a way that said one day was one day too long. She smiled, appreciating the girls' loyalty, their concern and their bravery. Not only had these young women kept a vigil by her hospital bedside, while all the murders were going on they had resisted their parents' attempts to pull them from the school.

"What's up with you guys?"

For the next half hour, they filled her in on the new coach, new players, and the return to normalcy on the campus—which also lead to speculation about the upcoming trial.

"Do you think they'll convict him?" Linda asked.

Frankie could have said that she was the wrong person to ask, since she wasn't convinced he needed to be convicted. But the quiet way in which Linda asked, coupled with the fact that she didn't meet Frankie's gaze when she asked, made Frankie suspicious. "Why?"

Linda shrugged. "He just didn't seem the type."

Julia rolled her eyes. "And Ted Bundy looked like a troll, too."

"You know what I mean," Linda countered. "You'd think you'd sense some sort of danger being around someone capable of that."

Again, Linda didn't meet anyone's gaze when she spoke. Seizing on an idea, Frankie stood. "I don't know where my manners are. Linda, you want to help me in the kitchen for a minute?"

Linda nodded and followed her. As they stood in the

kitchen making a tray of iced tea and the remainder of the cake Rachel had brought over, Frankie asked, "You're not so sure Jacobs did it, are you?"

Linda shrugged. "I don't know. He was always nice to me. And…"

"What? If you think you know something, I wish you'd tell me."

Linda sighed. For the first time Linda met her gaze. "I don't know anything for sure, but some of the girls were into a few things they should have left alone."

"What can I do for you, Mr. Santiago, or should I call you Nelson?"

Nelson slipped into the visitor seat across the desk from the district attorney. He didn't bother to answer. He didn't care what this man called him. He hadn't liked him the first time he met him and his assessment of the man hadn't improved. "Tell me about the night Jacobs was at Frankie's house."

Parker straightened his vest. "Shouldn't you ask her about that?"

Evasive little bastard. Even if Frankie had lied to him about not remembering anything, he doubted the man in front of him refused to comment out of any loyalty to her. If that were true, the esteemed district attorney might at least look him in the eye when he said that instead of fiddling with the papers on his desk.

Nelson shrugged. "I'm already here talking to you."

Parker pursed his lips. "What do you want to know?"

"Tell me about the attack. What did he do to her?"

"The same as the other girls. He tried to strangle her.

Apparently that didn't work and he attempted to subdue her by other means. The bastard put her in the hospital with a concussion and…and…internal injuries. Is that what you wanted to hear?"

No, that wasn't what he wanted to hear, but close to what he'd expected. "Was she raped?"

He shook his head. "I don't know. The rape kit was inconclusive. We had, um, been together that night. Her neighbor across the street heard the commotion and came running over with a baseball bat. He ran off before Rachel got a look at him. In all likelihood Frankie owes her life to that woman."

And no wonder Frankie hadn't been able to turn her away. "What makes you think what happened to Frankie has anything to do with the rapes on campus?"

"Why wouldn't it?"

This guy couldn't be that obtuse. "For one thing, all the other attacks were on students. Was there any forensic evidence to tie the same actor to this scene?"

"Only fibers from his clothes. But we found Jacobs two blocks away warming a bench in Eagle Park. He looked beat-up. He said some kid tried to mug him, but his description of the kid was too vague to be credible."

Parker said that with a certain amount of pride in his voice, an emotion Nelson understood. At least Frankie seemed to give as good as she got. "Can you get me in to see him?"

"Who? Jacobs?" Parker shook his head.

"Look, we both know how stubborn Frankie is. She's not going to testify unless she's certain that she should."

"I know you don't like me. That's fine. I don't really

give a damn. But don't insinuate I don't care about what she's feeling or what her wishes are. That night, she left my apartment after I asked her to marry me. It wasn't the first time, but her answer was always the same—no."

Of all the things Parker told him, that was the only thing that surprised him. She'd told him that her relationship with Parker was for entertainment purposes only. Maybe for her it was, but not for him. "Seems to me that after a while a guy would give up trying."

"I might have if it weren't for one thing. Until that night Frankie was pregnant with my child."

Chapter 7

After leaving Parker, Nelson drove back to Frankie's house. Anger simmered in him, directed at what or at whom he wasn't exactly sure. He knew part of it was the fact that Frankie had lied to him about her relationship with Parker. Why she'd done that he hadn't a clue. From the beginning, he'd asked her to be straight with him. Why did she find that so impossible to do? Or did she prefer him to get sandbagged every time someone opened their mouth about her? What was that supposed to accomplish?

He sighed as he pulled to a stop at a red light. He knew he was being too hard on her. Considering everything that had happened to her that night, everything she'd lost, he could understand why she wouldn't want to talk about it with him, a virtual stranger. Maybe he was just mad at the situation. He hadn't wanted to get involved in this for reasons that had nothing to do with blowing the time he had to spend with his daughters. He didn't need this shit. Damn.

By the time he reached Frankie's house, his mood hadn't improved and he didn't much care. He'd taken Frankie's key when he left. He used it to open the front door. Frankie was still sitting where he'd left her. Bottles of wine and soda as well as a variety of snacks crowded onto the small coffee table. As he came to stand at the perimeter of the room, conversation lulled. Frankie, as well as her players, looked up at him expectantly.

"Looks like it's time to go," one of the girls said. They gathered their things and within a couple of minutes they were out the door, closing it behind them.

After they'd gone, he turned his attention to Frankie. She was sitting so that her head rested against the back of the sofa. Her feet were propped on the edge of the coffee table. Her relaxed posture annoyed him, as did what she said next.

She lifted her wineglass to him in salute. "Way to clear a room, Santiago. What are you going to do for your next trick?"

He sighed. "Don't, Frankie. Just don't."

"Okay, what did I do now?"

"What's important is what you're going to do now. You're going to tell me exactly what's going on. Otherwise I'm out of here."

"What's going on is that I'm trying to figure out who attacked five girls on this campus. What do you think?"

"Honestly, I don't know. All I know is that I'm tired

of getting zapped with what you haven't told me every time I turn around."

"Who were you talking to?"

"Your former boyfriend. You know, that relationship that wasn't any big deal or anything."

She took a swig from her glass. "Okay, so the man proposed once or twice or a hundred times. What about it?"

"Is there some reason other than pure contentiousness that you didn't tell me this?"

She sighed, a gesture of capitulation. "Forgive me for trying to keep a few private things private." She refilled her glass and sat back. "Have a seat. I'll tell you what you want to know."

He did as she asked, taking a seat in the chair perpendicular to the sofa. "Why did you lie to me about your relationship with Parker?"

"I didn't want to take the chance that it would get back to my family that I had been pregnant without telling anybody. I don't think they would understand that."

He could understand that. All it would take was him opening his mouth to his grandmother or maybe his cousin for such a tale to make its way through both families. "Why didn't you tell them?"

She sipped from her glass. "I tried to. I called my mother, but she started haranguing me about something else. I figured I'd speak to her some other time when she was more amenable. Before I had a chance, the conversation became unnecessary."

Her voice sounded flat, emotionless, as if she were discussing the weather or some other subject unimportant to her. He could think of only one reason for that. "You didn't want the baby?"

She hadn't been looking at him before, but her head turned toward him in a sharp move and anger flashed in her eyes. "Do you honestly think I'd contemplate bringing a child I didn't want into the world? I know what that's like—not to be wanted, or at least not for who and what you are."

Coming from her, that sentiment surprised him. That emotion must have shown on his face, because she continued.

"You don't think I know what that feels like? Let me tell you a little story about the Hairston family. Once upon a time my family had two children, my brother, Matthew, and my sister, Claire. Nice family, until Claire dies at nine years old. A year later, I was born and my mother has been trying to remake me into the daughter she lost ever since."

She leaned forward to refill her glass. "And in case you're wondering, no, Robert doesn't count, either." She sipped from her glass. "You want to know the first time he proposed? It was two days after my parents came down here for a visit. Apparently, he hadn't realized until then that I was one of the New York Hairstons and that an alliance with me could do something for his career. Incidentally, my parents hadn't even come down here to see me. They got invited down here by the Dean of Schmoozing or whatever, who hoped to shake some money out of my family tree."

"You been at this pity party long?"

She snorted in a self-deprecating way. "You think?"

She ran her hand over her hair, mussing it. "Look, I wasn't trying to act like some spoiled rich girl. I didn't entertain the idea that he'd give up his job and move where I wanted to be. I would have been willing to stay here in Boringsville so Robert could see his child if he proved to be a good father. If not, I would have used my family's considerable influence to make sure he never saw the kid again."

Looking down, she swirled the contents in her glass. "Maybe it's just a little selfish, but I didn't want to marry someone simply because they were willing to step up to the plate. For once in my life I wanted someone to want me for me, not what I had or what I could offer them. Oh, hell."

She brought her glass to her lips and downed half its contents. "I probably would have said yes, eventually. I do believe kids need two parents. I wasn't in love with him, but if I could get my hole-in-the-wall team to the national championships, I could have made that work. I just couldn't let it go down easy, you know? I had to be difficult."

In her voice, he heard a combination of guilt and self-condemnation. He'd heard similar sentiments spoken in similar voices—too many to count. "You can't blame yourself for what happened that night."

"Why not? If I hadn't walked out when he asked me again, I wouldn't have been here. If I'd been thinking clearly, I might have paid more attention. I did everything I counsel women not to do to keep themselves safe, starting with not keeping a decent lock on my door."

"It wasn't your fault, Frankie. It never is."

"That's it, Santiago. Spout the party line. So maybe it wasn't my fault. Is that supposed to make me feel any better?"

No, he didn't think any platitudes would offer her any solace. He wished he could, however. He sensed the pain in her, even though her voice had gone back to that dry-eyed monotone after her brief show of anger. Last night she'd wept for girls she'd barely known, but not a tear for herself. Either way, he'd heard enough, except in one area.

"How is it none of this was in the newspapers?"

"Robert kept it out, in deference to me. His cousin is the owner of the local paper and all the media was taking their cue from them." She sat forward and put her feet on the floor. "Are we done?"

"Why?"

"If we are, I've got to start getting ready for tonight."

"Where do you think you're going?"

"I think I'm going to Tara, a club outside town. One of the girls told me she knew of at least one girl who made her tuition working there." She flashed him one of her famous grins. "Don't worry, you get to come, too."

At least he didn't have to fight her in that regard. "Why don't you tell me where it is and I'll check it out."

She shook her head. "I'd have to turn in my gutsy-broad card if I did that."

So she would. Damn. Since he doubted anything he could say would change her mind, he didn't bother. "Tell me what she told you," he said.

She winked at him. "Later. First I've got to find something to wear."

* * *

Hours later, Nelson waited for Frankie at the base of the stairs. She'd spent the entire afternoon closeted in her room, refusing to come down even for food. Honestly, after her revelations this afternoon, he was worried about her. It seemed to him that whatever troubles she carried, she preferred to bear them alone. Being the same way himself, he could understand that. He could also understand the feeling of not being wanted for who and what she was. He'd been there. But as sure as he knew his own name, he knew there was more to this. Something didn't add up to him. But for the moment he was tired of pulling information from her bit by bit. Besides, he had the feeling it would be all he could do to survive tonight's adventure.

Later, seeing Frankie walking down the stairs toward him, that impression deepened. His gaze traveled upward from a pair of black high-heeled sandals over shapely legs covered in fishnet stockings to a teeny-tiny postage stamp of a skirt and a low-cut spangled top that dipped deep between her breasts and left her belly bare. Her hair, wild and unbound, floated around her shoulders. She wore enough makeup on her face to keep Tammy Faye Bakker happy for a week. But rather than giving her a hard edge, it lent her the look of a little girl playing in her mother's cosmetics. He wondered if that image was the one she was shooting for.

She stopped a few steps up, one hand on the banister, the other on her left hip. "Hey, big boy," she said in a manner reminiscent of Mae West.

Finally, he figured out what had been different about

her—her breasts. Right now they threatened to spill out the top of her top, but every other time he'd seen her lately he would have sworn she wasn't that well endowed. He folded his arms, and met her gaze. "What exactly are you supposed to be?"

She didn't pretend to mistake what he meant. "I believe the closest approximation would be poor black trash." She grinned. "Sorry, but my nun's habit is in the cleaners."

She didn't need to look like a nun, but she was out of her mind if she thought he'd take her anywhere looking like that. "No."

Her eyes narrowed. "No what?"

"No, you are not going out like that."

"I hate to disappoint you, Dad, but you're not *my* Dad. Though if you were, that look on your face would probably have me headed for the sackcloth and ashes about now." She descended the rest of the stairs to walk past him. "You coming?" she tossed over her shoulder.

Nelson gritted his teeth. She had a point. If they were going to the sort of place he thought they were, she couldn't show up looking like Goldilocks. Then again, there were some fetishists that would like that, too. He turned to follow her. Only then did he notice the sway of her hips and the fact that her top was held together by a thin string that crisscrossed her back. Whatever else the night proved to be, for him it was going to be torture.

"Tell me what you know about this place."

Frankie slid a glance at Nelson. For the last few minutes, as they started off toward the outskirts of town, they'd ridden in silence. That suited her fine, since despite the devil-may-care attitude she'd exhibited for Nelson's sake, she needed to get her emotions in order.

Actually, she'd been fine until she'd walked down the stairs to find Nelson staring up at her. There was no mistaking the look in his eyes and no denying the answering quickening in her body once she'd seen it. That surprised her. Until that moment, she'd thought that night had killed her ability to feel sexual attraction, except on an esoteric level. She thought back over all the times he'd touched her and she'd felt nothing but coldness inside. Oddly, that felt normal. Maybe it was the damn hootchie mama outfit she had on that made the difference. Or maybe they'd spent long enough in close-enough proximity that she'd started to thaw. It had to be just her luck that the first man to arouse her in a year happened to be wearing another woman's ring.

Frankie licked her lips, which seemed dry despite the layers of lipstick and gloss she'd applied. "Linda told me that both Kerry and Gladys had worked at this place— Kerry because she needed the money and Gladys just liked the attention. Or at least Linda knew of these two."

"Why didn't she say something during the investigation?"

"Would you want to be the one to bring to grieving parents' attention the fact that their child had been taking off her clothes or worse for money?"

"I guess not."

"Besides, Linda only knew about these two girls. She figured the information would only be important if all of the girls were involved."

"But she told you."

Frankie shrugged. "I have one of those faces."

He shook his head. "It seems to me those girls wanted you for who and what you are."

In the darkened interior of the car it was impossible to see the expression on his face, but there was an earnest quality in his voice that reached her. She hadn't considered it before, but he was right. Her girls had appreciated her the way she was. "Let's put a moratorium on discussing my life for the moment." She shifted in her seat to lean her head back against the headrest and close her eyes. "Tell me about your wife. You told me you met in high school?"

"She was a sophomore at Science. I was a junior at neighboring DeWitt Clinton High School. It was still all boys then. I saw her in the stands at one of my football games."

"You played football? Aren't you a little, well, short for that?"

He chuckled. "It was high school. I didn't have much shot of going pro, even before I blew one of my knees."

"How did that happen?"

"About half a team fell on me. Until then, I didn't know knees bent that way."

"Ouch."

"Precisely."

She swallowed. "So it was love at first sight?"

"For one of us and you're looking at him."

"She made you work for it, huh?"

"More that her family didn't approve. Hers had money, mine didn't. The only saving grace was that her grandmother liked me."

"Granny put in a good word for you?"

"Something like that."

"Is there any chance of you two getting back together?"

"Me and Grandma?"

"That's not what I meant."

"No, there's no chance. Anything else?"

She frowned, hearing the same words she'd spoken earlier. She supposed he resented being grilled on his past as much as she did on hers. If so, she wondered why he hadn't shut her down at the first question.

She shifted in her seat to better see him. "Why did you tell me all that?"

"I wanted to prove to you that self-disclosure doesn't have to be painful. Besides, I was only picking at your personal life for information that might help the case. You were just being nosy."

"Not nosy, curious."

"Why?"

She shrugged and looked away. Since she didn't have an answer, she decided to change the subject. "I'm surprised you haven't given me a lecture on proper comportment once we get there."

"Comportment. I'm not even sure what that is."

By the humor in his voice she knew he was teasing her. "One of the many subjects I flunked in charm school."

"Do I really need to tell you to be on your guard and not to wander off by yourself?"

"No."

"Then I guess we have comportment covered. What exactly do you plan to accomplish tonight?"

She knew what he was doing, offering her one last

out before they got there. They hadn't discussed it, but he had to know she didn't have any sort of plan. At most, she hoped to speak to one of the girls and find out if any of them knew Kerry or Gladys. "I just want to see what kind of place this is."

They rounded a corner in the road and the house came into view. The two-story white structure did remind her of some antebellum plantation house, complete with a columned entrance. The house was surrounded by a grove of dogwood trees and a variety of shrubbery. If it weren't for the pulsing beat of music that reached her ears as they drove into the clearing, the red lights illuminating the entrance and the presence of two behemoth bouncers standing by the door that served a parking lot, she would have sworn she belonged in another era.

Nelson cut the engine. "You're still sure you want to do this?"

Frankie sighed. No, she wasn't sure she wanted to do this, but it needed to be done. She nodded toward the entrance. "Let's go."

They met around the front of the car and walked together toward the front door. She tensed a moment as Nelson's arm wrapped around her waist. She hoped he didn't notice her reaction, but that was not to be.

He leaned down to whisper in her ear. "Relax, sweetheart."

At least he'd misinterpreted her response. "I'm fine. Really."

They made it upstairs to the front door with the bouncers giving them only a cursory glance. Once inside, they stopped, giving the interior a once-over. The stage was at the center of the floor. On it a young woman alternated obscene gyrations with swinging around the pole stationed at the center of the stage. A bar ringed the stage, where several men sat watching the woman avidly. Several wooden tables were stationed around the room, serviced by topless and nearly bottomless waitresses. A series of banquettes lined the walls, occupied by men and women, the latter of which were probably paid for. The air was clouded with a layer of smoke that, to some extent, owed nothing to tobacco.

Nelson broke the silence. "Scarlett O'Hara must be turning over in her fictional grave."

Frankie turned to look at him, since there was only humor, not censure, in his voice. "Is this what you expected?"

"Pretty much. I was hoping it went a little lighter on the tacky." His fingers on her waist flexed. "We can go now, if you want to."

She shook her head. He'd assumed correctly that her major interest in coming here was to find out what sort of business her students had gotten sucked into. But she also wanted to find out as much as she could about anyone who might have come into contact with them. "What do you think the odds are of getting a decent banana daiquiri in this place?"

He chuckled and laced her fingers with his. "Come on."

Chapter 8

Nelson led Frankie over to one of the banquettes another couple vacated. He sat so that he could keep an eye on the room and pulled her down next to him. She turned toward him and crossed her legs. She tucked a strand of hair behind her ear. "What now?"

For all her talk of athletic prowess and feminine failings there wasn't a thing unfeminine about her. He draped his arm along the back of the banquette to rest his hand on her back. "We have a couple of drinks, see how restless the natives get. See if we see anyone you know or anyone acting suspiciously."

"That's it?"

That's all he'd allow her to do. Once he'd learned where they were headed he'd called Don Meyer to see what he knew about the place. Apparently, the show on the stage was simply a teaser for the more lucrative business of prostitution. The club operated without benefit of a liquor license and under the protection of someone who made sure raids were kept to a minimum. Who that benefactor was, Don didn't know. But when Don had sent his people over to ask questions once it had been found out that Kerry Washington worked here, the local cops had told him to leave it alone. Which meant someone powerful enough to influence the local cops had an interest in keeping the place open.

"That's it."

She said nothing, but he could tell from the set of her mouth that she was unhappy with his answer. He could understand her frustration. She wanted to find out something, anything that would explain the girls' deaths.

She cast a look around, shaking her head. "You wouldn't think a place like this would exist in such a dead town."

She looked at him for confirmation, but he had to disagree with her. This was exactly the sort of place you could expect, where any sort of perversion could be found under one roof. "Big cities have no lockdown on vice. The only difference is the numbers."

She shrugged. "I suppose. But I always figured Kerry as a little naive. I can't imagine her working here in any capacity."

And if she'd ever been here during operating hours it would have been impossible not to know what she was getting herself into.

One of the waitresses with teased blond hair and an

eyebrow piercing approached their table. "Can I get y'all something to drink?"

He looked to Frankie for her choice of beverage, only to find her staring back at him with a knowing look in her eyes.

"White wine, please," she said.

After he ordered the wine for her and a Scotch for himself, the waitress left them. He turned back to Frankie, who regarded him with the same look. "What?"

"Don't try to play little Mr. Innocent with me. I saw you looking."

"I never said I didn't look. I'm as red-blooded as the next American male. But I'm only into natural endowments."

She blinked and shook her head. "How could you possibly tell in this lighting whether or not they were fake?"

"The shape, the way they move."

"So you've made a study of this, have you?"

"Not a study, no."

"I will never understand you men. You obsess about something you know is false?"

"Not me." Unconsciously, his gaze drifted lower to settle on her cleavage. He didn't know what made him say this, except maybe the buzz he got simply breathing the air in the room. "By the way, why do you spend so much time trying to hide yours?"

Her mouth dropped open, but she quickly recovered herself. "I'm not trying to hide anything. Do you know what it's like running around on the field with your boobs flapping around in your face? It's painful to say the least."

"That wasn't part of your abandoned cover-up campaign?"

"No, that's just a part of playing sports I've gotten used to over the years."

"Glad to hear that."

"Why?"

Before he got a chance to answer, not that he had an answer that would suit her, the waitress came back with their drinks. She set down their glasses, he paid her and she left.

He handed Frankie her glass, watching as she took a delicate sip of the wine. "How is it?" he asked.

"If it tasted any more like nail polish, I might actually gag."

He sampled his own drink. To call it watered down would have been an understatement. He leaned back against the banquette. He brushed her hair behind her shoulder, letting his fingers linger on her soft, bare skin. Remembering how she flinched when he'd touched her before, it surprised him that she didn't pull away or readjust herself to get out of his grasp. Part of him wanted to push her to see how far he'd get before she shut him down. He let his fingers graze her collarbone. "Where were we?"

She bit her lip, scrutinizing him. "Is this place getting to you or something?"

His knuckles grazed her cheek. "Not this place."

She rolled her eyes. "Please tell me you are not trying to flirt with me, Santiago."

"Would it be a problem if I were?"

"For one thing, don't think just because you brought

me to this charming place and bought me this swell drink you're getting laid tonight. I'm not that cheap a date. In the second place, you're not my type."

"What type is that?"

She winked at him. "The type that's actually thinking about me when they're in my bed." She set her glass on the table. "I'm going to the ladies' room and then I'd like to go home. This place gives me the creeps."

He sat back and leaned his elbows on the banquette as he watched her make her way across the room. Despite the height of her heels, she possessed a smooth, confident stride that turned more heads than his in her direction. He hoped none of those fools tried to put their hands on her, because in his present mood he wouldn't mind a good fight.

He realized he was using his thumb to spin the ring on his finger and stopped. When she asked him why she wore it, he'd given her his stock answer, or at least what he told himself why he wore it. Five years ago, he'd thought he and Sandy had been happy or at least comfortable with their marriage. In the intervening years, he'd come to realize he simply hadn't been paying attention. But once illumination came in the form of walking into an empty house, he'd tried to make it up to her, to make some sort of reconciliation. But for Sandy that was it, no second chances allowed.

To her credit, he'd never had any complaints about how she raised the girls. She'd never tried to turn them against him. On the contrary, she relied on him for everything save the girls' financial needs. Not that he didn't pay child support, but with her family's money, she didn't need it.

For a year, he'd worn that ring, hoping for another chance, even though the papers were signed and the property divided. As he saw it, she owed him that chance. They'd been together most of their lives. That had to count for something. That's what he'd thought, until Bonnie, angry with both of them for not being together, had let it slip that there was a new man in Mommy's bed. Sandy didn't bother to deny he'd been in the picture for some time.

He should have taken the ring off then. He'd thought about it. But something stubborn and vindictive in him had allowed him to leave it on, a tangible reminder to her every time she saw him that the breakup of their marriage had been her doing, not his, at least not the way she'd led him to believe it was. He was willing to take the blame for not being there for her; for the death of their marriage he was not.

He drained the remains from his glass, still watching Frankie over the rim. He knew that she, like most people, saw that ring and assumed he harbored some lingering devotion or affection. She might be wrong about that, but she was right about something else: he wanted her. He could guarantee her that if he were ever lucky enough to share her bed, he wouldn't be thinking about anything except those muscular legs wrapped around him.

Despite that, he knew he'd leave her alone, most of all because she'd been through so much. Honestly, the attraction he felt for her wasn't purely physical. He admired her resilience, her determination and her loyalty to her students. But the last thing he needed would be for her to feel like he'd used her and to have

that get back to his family. They were disappointed in
him enough.

Frankie paused, casting a glance back in his direction. *Damn.* From the expression on her face he figured
she was up to something. He waited until she disappeared down the hallway that led to the rest rooms, put
his glass on the table and followed her.

Frankie walked to the ladies' room door and pushed
it open. There were two stalls and two sinks with a large
rectangular mirror above them. It wasn't the worst
bathroom she'd ever seen, though whoever had decorated it had a serious love affair with pink. Unfortunately, it was empty. Damn.

At least when she'd turned back to check on Nelson
a couple of moments ago he was still in his seat. That
should afford her at least a couple of minutes before he
came looking for her. Regardless of what she told him,
she didn't plan to leave here empty-handed. Since all
she wanted to do was have a talk with one of the girls,
she couldn't imagine she was putting herself in much
danger. Now if someone would just show up.

The sound of a toilet flushing startled her. A second
later, a woman came out of the far stall and went to the
sink. Frankie realized immediately why she hadn't
noticed the woman's presence. She was dressed from
head to toe in the same bubble gum pink of the
bathroom. Or rather, what few items she wore were
pink: high-heeled mules, stockings, miniskirt and a top
that scooped low on her abundant chest. Frankie didn't
need Nelson's input to figure out this woman had

implants. On their own, breasts didn't grow that big. At least she hoped they didn't.

The woman glanced at her over her shoulder and issued the ubiquitous greeting. "Hey."

"Hey." Frankie went to the mirror and retrieved her lipstick from the tiny pocket in her skirt. As she put it on, she snuck a look at the woman beside her. The girl was young, probably in her mid twenties, but already her face bore signs of dissipation. "You were just on stage, weren't you?"

"Yeah. That was me. The bastards that run this place give us a dressing room but no private john."

In other words, if she had a choice, she wouldn't be standing there talking to her.

"Have you worked here long?"

The woman cast her an assessing look, probably trying to figure out what she wanted. "Long enough."

Since it was obvious she'd been pegged as a citizen, not a stripper, Frankie abandoned her plan to ask questions under the pretext of looking for work. "Did you know a girl named Kerry Washington? She used to work here about a year ago."

"Who wants to know?"

Instead she pulled her school ID from her pocket and laid it on the sink.

The women broke out in a grin. "I'd half pegged you for a reporter, but a schoolteacher?"

"Did you know her?"

She handed the ID back. "I knew Kerry. Sweet kid. She used to tend bar some nights, no heavy lifting, if you know what I mean. She was trying to make her tuition,

I think. It's a shame what happened to her. They've got that old guy in jail about to go on trial."

"Did he come in here?"

"Pervert liked 'em young, as I remember. You know, the whole Suzie Schoolgirl thing. He liked Kerry. When she went missing I remember thinking he was probably responsible. Then all the other girls started turning up dead."

"Did any of the other girls work here?"

"Just one. Some stuck-up Chinese bitch. She didn't last long."

From the way she said that, Frankie figured the other girls had made sure of that. Having exhausted all the questions she could come up with, she tucked her lipstick and her ID in her pocket. "Thanks, um?"

The woman smiled and tilted her head to one side in a self-deprecating gesture. "I go by Pink here."

Frankie smiled back. "Can't imagine why."

"Yeah, well. We all have to have our *thang*."

"So true." Frankie turned to leave.

"You know, if you ever wanted to moonlight, you could get a lot of mileage out of that schoolmarm thing. You sure enough got the goods."

Frankie winked at her. "Something to think about." So, too, was the man she assumed was waiting outside the room for her. There would be no convincing him that this had been a simple bathroom break, not that she wanted to convince him of that. But he'd probably be annoyed at her at the least, which meant she had to deal with that.

She saw him the minute she opened the bathroom door. He was leaning against the opposite wall with his arms and ankles crossed. The expression on his face gave away nothing.

She took a step toward him. "Been waiting long?"

He pushed off the wall and took her hand. "If you're through playing Harriet the Spy, let's go."

"Fine. Don't you want to know what I found out?"

"Outside."

Once they made it down the front steps, Nelson let go of her hand. "Tell me."

Frankie huffed out an exasperated breath. "Kerry did work here, as well as Gladys. And Jacobs was a regular. To quote my new friend, Pink, he liked 'em young."

"That's it?"

"That's what we came here to find out, isn't it?" That's what *she'd* come here to find out.

He took her arm. "Let's go."

She followed him to the car, mainly because his grip was too strong for her to simply pull away. When they reached the passenger side of the car, he opened the door for her to get in. She slid into her seat a moment before he slammed the door shut.

He rounded the back of the car and got in beside her. "Put your seat belt on."

She ground her teeth together, but did as he asked. He gunned the engine and peeled out of the spot, throwing her back against the seat cushions. It didn't take a genius to figure out he was angry with her.

"Did I hurt you?"

"What?"

He glanced at her then down at her arm. "Did I hurt you?"

Until that moment she hadn't realized she'd been rubbing the spot on her arm where he'd held her. She dropped her hand to her lap. "Of course not. But would you mind explaining what exactly has you so bent out of shape?"

He shot her a hard glance. "I don't particularly enjoy being lied to. You said you were going to use the bathroom."

"How do you know I didn't?"

"Your hand was dry and room temperature. I assume that if you'd actually gone into the bathroom to use it, you would have washed your hands."

For a moment she stared at him. Never would it have occurred to her that he took her hand for any ulterior motive. "What is the big deal? I told you before we left the house that I hoped to talk to one of the girls to see if they knew Kerry."

"For one thing, I thought you had enough sense only to do that with me present."

"An opportunity presented itself and I took it."

"Bullshit. I saw the look in your eyes when you looked back at me. Damn it, Frankie. I don't know what you think you're playing at. You're not Nancy Drew and this isn't *Pretty Woman*. That hooker-with-a-heart-of-gold myth is nonsense. Most of these women are down on their luck because they're on something and have to support their habit. They're dangerous, Frankie, not poor misguided souls in need of a hand up."

Since her experience with working girls of any kind was severely limited, she wasn't in a position to argue with him. She searched her mind for something to say to mollify him. Coming up with nothing, she kept her mouth shut.

In a quiet voice he asked, "Did you give her your name?"

"I showed her my school ID. I figured she'd talk more readily if she knew I wasn't a reporter or a cop."

He muttered something she was sure he hadn't intended her to catch. "Well, then here's another thing to worry about. On the off chance that someone at the club was involved in the murders, and if they picked up on you talking to your new friend, in all likelihood they now know exactly where to find you."

Nelson glanced over at Frankie. She'd been silent the last few minutes, staring out the window. He knew he'd come down hard on her, maybe too hard. But he needed to impress on her the danger she might have put herself in. He'd worried from the beginning how far she would go to find out who killed these girls. He didn't want to find out only after someone hurt her.

He brushed his fingertips along her thigh. "Are you all right?"

"Stop for a minute, would you?"

"Sure." He pulled over to the side of the road and cut the engine. By the time he turned to look at her, she was already halfway out of the car. By the time he got his door open, she'd walked forward, caught in the beam of the headlights. She seemed to be walking along aimlessly, but he doubted she had no purpose in coming here.

When he caught up with her, she was looking upward.

"You don't see the stars like this in New York," she said. "That's one of the few things I like about this town."

She sounded pensive, not upset, so he relaxed. "If you wanted a moonlight walk with me, we could have found a better spot than this."

She glanced over her shoulder at him. "Don't start with me, Santiago." She took a step away from him. "This is where he dumped them, you know. This stretch over here in the middle of nowhere. He left them here like so much trash at the side of the road."

Nelson gritted his teeth. If he'd known that's why she wanted to stop he would have kept on driving. He wrapped his arms around her from behind and pulled her to him. Luckily, she didn't bother to fight him. "If this is because of what I said…"

She shook her head. "You were right. I am just feeling so frustrated."

He kissed her temple. "I know, sweetheart."

"The worst part is, it was just money. She could have asked me. I would have paid her damn tuition if I'd known she needed it. Then she might not have been somewhere that he could have noticed her in that way."

"You're not blaming yourself for this, too?"

She shook her head. "No. Just wishing things had turned out differently."

He turned her in his arms so that she faced him. Her arms were still crossed in front of her, keeping him at a distance. Nonetheless, he brushed his fingertips across her cheek. "Torturing yourself with what could have been is a good way to make yourself miserable."

She shrugged. "Oops, too late."

He didn't know what to say to that, what words of comfort or encouragement to offer. Instead he pulled her to him, running his hands over her back in a soothing motion. For a moment, she melted against him, her softer body melding to his harder one. For a moment, he was content to bury his nose against her fragrant hair and hold her. Then she was pushing away from him with her hands on his chest.

Immediately, he released her. "What's the matter, baby?"

She bit her lip. "Remember when I said I wanted a man who was thinking about me?"

He nodded.

"I'd think you'd want the same thing for yourself." She pulled away from him, went back to the car and got in.

Chapter 9

"Daddy, when are you coming home?"

Every time he'd spoken to Bonnie in the last couple of days, he heard the same question. Today he heard if from Dara, too. "Why the sudden interest in your old man?"

"Bonnie is driving everyone crazy. She's so mean."

Nelson held his humor, not wanting to alienate his daughter. But coming from Dara, "mean" could signify anything from something truly horrible to being thwarted in her attempt to raid her sister's closet. "What did Bonnie do now?"

"Nothing, really. She's just moping, and every time I try to talk to her she snaps at me."

"Why don't you try leaving her alone for a while?"

"All right," Dara said in a voice that said he'd taken

all the fun out of her existence. "So when are you coming home?"

"Soon." He didn't bother to tell Dara that at the moment he didn't know significantly more than he did before he left. In some ways, he had more questions now than before, particularly where Frankie was concerned. She'd been silent and pensive the first part of the trip. But once they got back in the car, there was a faraway layer to her demeanor that got to him.

Who had she been thinking about when he held her? He doubted it was the esteemed district attorney. He believed her when she told him that she'd stayed with Parker for the sake of her unborn child. But who, then, if it *was* a who? Maybe the whole situation weighed on her so that she could enjoy nothing, not even a man's embrace. That might be true, but he didn't think so.

He'd let her go when she wanted to be released, but what he'd really wanted to do was shake her until she'd told him everything. How many secrets could one tiny woman keep?

"Are you listening, Dad?"

"Of course, sweetheart," he said, though he'd zoned out from whatever Dara was saying. "I've got to go, sweetie. Do me a favor and let your mom know I'll be here a few more days."

"Okay, but then I'm going to need two presents."

"That's extortion."

"Yup."

"Fine. I'll talk to you later." He disconnected the call just as Frankie came into the kitchen. He'd known she was awake since the house phone had rung twenty minutes ago and she'd answered it. Still, he didn't put it past her to have listened to his end of the conversation, but then he hadn't said anything much that would interest her.

"Good morning." She breezed past him wearing the same voluminous robe, headed toward the coffeemaker.

"Morning." He closed the newspaper he'd been reading before it was late enough to call his daughters. "Hungry?"

"Famished, but we have a breakfast meeting. Guess who that was on the phone before." As she spoke she added cream and sugar to her coffee.

"The pope? He wants his dress back?"

"Very funny. No, that was Jacobs's attorney. He wants to meet with us. Apparently someone's been spreading rumors that we're trying to get his client freed."

"Who would that be?"

"He didn't say. But he did hint that he has some evidence that no one as yet has listened to him about. He didn't elaborate, but I figured it couldn't hurt to listen."

No, it couldn't, but it would take more than the word of the man's attorney to convince Nelson the man wasn't guilty. He didn't put much faith in lawyers, either prosecutors or those who petitioned for the defense. "What time do we need to meet him?"

"We should probably leave now. We're meeting a couple of towns over to avoid any speculation."

"Whose idea was that?"

"Mine."

There went one strike against the lawyer already. "Give me five minutes." He took his cup to the sink and rinsed it, then went upstairs and retrieved his jacket, figuring he ought to look presentable. When he got back downstairs, Frankie was waiting for him by the door. "Ready?" he asked.

She nodded. "What evidence do you think he has?"

Nelson didn't care to speculate. He just hoped the lawyer wasn't wasting their time. Especially since he sensed the anticipation in Frankie. She didn't need to get her hopes up for nothing. "Only one way to find out."

He opened the door and they stepped out into the warm Georgia sunshine. Across the street a man was mowing the grass in front of her friend Rachel's house. "Who's that?" he asked.

"That's Rachel's son, Myron. Why?"

He shrugged. For the moment, at least, he'd keep it to himself that he saw that same man watching her in the club last night.

Walter Fletcher was a round, balding man not much taller than Frankie was herself. Her first thought when she saw him was that this must be what Weebles looked like when they came to life.

Fletcher stood as she and Nelson approached his table in the restaurant. "Ms. Hairston, I'm so glad you could meet me."

Frankie shook the hand the man extended toward her. "This is my cousin, Nelson Santiago."

The man shook Nelson's hand. "Should we sit?"

Frankie sat in the chair Nelson held out for her, the one next to the window. He sat beside her with Fletcher sitting across from them. "What have you got for us, Mr. Fletcher?" Nelson said.

"Well…" Fletcher's eyes widened and he sputtered. Frankie bit her lip to hide her humor. Obviously the man was used to Southern charm, not New York bluntness. She might have become flustered, too, if Nelson questioned her in the same demanding tone.

But before Fletcher actually got anything out, the waitress appeared. "Maybe we should order first," Fletcher said with obvious relief in his voice.

Frankie ordered waffles with country sausage. Fletcher ordered eggs, toast, grits and an extra serving of bacon. Nelson just ordered coffee, which he drank black. After a few minutes, Nelson set down his cup. "Okay, Mr. Fletcher, what's on your mind?"

Fletcher put his fork down and cast an agitated look at her. Fletcher hadn't mentioned Nelson in their conversation. He'd asked to meet with her. That to her mind meant he didn't know Nelson was involved, that whoever had told Fletcher about her figured Nelson really was her cousin and therefore no threat, or Fletcher had hoped to separate her from Nelson for this discussion. She wasn't sure which scenario made more sense. It depended on who'd sprung a leak. Either way, she'd decided she wasn't going to say a word and let Nelson do his thing. After his lecture last night, she didn't need another one.

"First," Fletcher said, "Harlan wanted me to convey to you, Ms. Hairston, that he is very sorry about what happened to you, but that he is not the man responsible. He—"

Nelson cut him off. "Let's start with this new evidence you have."

For once Fletcher showed some backbone. "I'm getting to that. Second, I believe they're railroading my brother into a conviction because of his record."

Frankie glanced at Nelson to gauge his reaction to that bit of information. He was staring straight at Fletcher like the Great Stone Face, giving away nothing. Despite her resolution to remain quiet, she asked, "Jacobs is your brother?"

"Half brother, really. We have different fathers but we were raised in the same house together. Harlan did not rape my daughter."

Nelson did look at her then, with an expression that said "This ought to be interesting." To Fletcher, he said, "Go on."

"For a number of years my wife and I served as foster parents. Mostly it was short-term arrangements. We'd get the kids while Mom settled whatever issues child welfare had. But we had this one girl that stayed with us for a few years. She was a handful, having suffered every type of abuse before we got her, but my wife was devoted to her. The real trouble didn't start until we adopted her when she was thirteen. All of a sudden she was this wild child neither one of us could control."

Fletcher sipped from his cup. "My brother and I had been estranged for a long time. To get back at my wife and me, my daughter sought him out and seduced him. At the time, she was fifteen going on forty-five. He didn't know who she was or how old she was. When she finally told him the truth, she expected him to side with her and say what lousy parents we were, but he called us to come get her. That's when she decided to press charges against him. It was a game to her, but it cost him twelve years of his life."

Fletcher sat back. "I'm not saying my brother is blameless, but he's certainly not the predator he's been made out to be."

Frankie didn't know what to say to that, so she said nothing. One thought that niggled in the back of her mind was why Jacobs had picked girls over the age of consent as his victims if jailbait was really his thing. Pink told her he liked them young, maybe just not that young.

"What do you expect us to do for you, Mr. Fletcher?" Nelson asked.

"Harlan has an alibi for at least two of the nights when the rapes occurred. A young lady he was seeing."

"Why didn't she come forward before now?"

"She's married and she didn't want her family to find out. But now that it looks like he might actually be convicted of these crimes, she's decided to come forward."

"And no one believes her?"

"The testimony of a lover isn't all that much above the testimony of a wife or mother, people others assume would lie to protect a criminal. Besides, the times of death established by the coroner aren't that precise. An hour or two here or there and there's a window in which Harlan could have committed those crimes."

Fletcher pulled a slip of paper from his shirt pocket and slid it along the table toward Nelson. "But you don't have to take my word for it. You can speak to her yourself. I told her to expect you."

Nelson picked up the paper, looked at it and handed it to her. She recognized the name and address immediately. This had to be some sort of joke. Now all she wanted to do was get out of there. She folded the paper and stuck it in her pocket and stood. "I think we've taken up enough of Mr. Fletcher's time."

Without waiting for Nelson, she turned and headed for the door. By the time Nelson caught up with her, she was already in the parking lot leaning against his car.

"Okay, what do you and Fletcher know that I don't know?"

She held the piece of paper in her fingers. "This woman that Jacobs was supposedly seeing, the one that can give him an alibi, is none other than Robert's sister."

Nelson pulled out of the parking lot and onto the street. Frankie's words echoed in his ears along with all the possible ramifications of that revelation. If Parker's sister could vouch for Jacobs, Parker had it within his power to drop the charges against him. So, why didn't he? Did he have reason to believe his sister was lying? He wouldn't know until he spoke to both the sister and Parker.

As he stopped for a red light, he focused on Frankie. She'd been dead quiet since they got in the car. That wasn't like her, unless she was brooding. "What are you thinking about over there?" he asked her.

She shrugged. "This mess just gets weirder and weirder. I can't believe Rita would even know someone like Jacobs. She's president of the town's arts council, for Christ's sake."

"How do she and her brother get along?"

"Like two pit bulls at a dog fight. Apparently Daddy

liked to set the two of them against each other in the quest for his affections and they haven't given up the fight even though Daddy's dead. But I can't imagine Robert would still prosecute a man who had an alibi just to get back at his sister."

Nelson stepped on the gas as the light changed. Frankie might not be able to imagine that, but he could. With crimes like this, prosecutors were under tremendous pressure to convict somebody. He'd probably get lambasted in the press and elsewhere for letting any suspect without an ironclad alibi go. Better to go to trial and blame the jury for letting him go if they came back with a not-guilty verdict. District attorneys, after all, had to get themselves reelected.

Nelson followed Frankie's directions to a large house set back from the street. He parked in the circular drive in front of the house and got out of the car. Frankie waited for him by the passenger door and the two of them walked up to the house together. Before they had a chance to knock, the door was pulled open by a fortyish-looking woman with a cinnamon complexion, wearing a blue shirtwaist dress.

"Ms. Hairston, Mr. Santiago, Ms. Forbes is waiting for you in the parlor."

So, Fletcher called ahead and added his name to the party list. He hadn't missed the fact that Fletcher had been totally surprised by his appearance alongside Frankie that morning.

They followed the woman through a tastefully decorated house to a small solarium at the front of the house. The sole occupant of the room, a tall, thin woman of indeterminate age, stood as they entered. "Francesca, how lovely to see you again."

Frankie stepped forward and accepted the other woman's embrace. "Good to see you, too, Rita."

When Frankie stepped back, Rita turned her attention on him. "Pleased to meet you, Mr. Santiago. Are you really Francesca's cousin?"

He couldn't imagine what difference that information could make to the woman, but managed to answer her with a straight face. "Yes."

"Well, do sit down. I realize this isn't a social call, but I have some iced tea and cookies if you like."

Frankie joined her on the settee, which looked much too feminine and delicate to support his weight. He settled into one of the wing chairs. He accepted the glass Rita handed him but declined the lemon cookies she offered. He didn't want to waste any more time with pleasantries. He wanted to know what this woman knew. "I understand you can give Harlan Jacobs an alibi the night Frankie was attacked."

Rita wore a multicolored caftan that drew more tightly around her body as she sat back and crossed her legs. At first he wouldn't have thought her outfit concealed much of a figure, but apparently he was wrong.

"Harlan was with me the night both Frankie and that poor Lopez girl were attacked. He wasn't capable of doing those things."

"What time was he with you?"

"Vinton, my husband, was out of town. Harlan came over that morning. We spent the day in my pool and the evening watching *Fahrenheit 451* on the

classic movie channel. He didn't leave until about
eleven o'clock. I remember because the news was
coming on and Harlan hated the news. Too much de-
pressing information for him. He was with me all
day, so you see he couldn't have been the one to hurt
you, Francesca. You know how sorry I am that you
lost the baby."

Rita addressed that last comment to Frankie, who
looked back at her with a surprised expression. "I didn't
know you knew."

"I didn't, until afterward. One of the doctors told
me. That didn't make me any less sorry."

"Thank you," Frankie said in the quietest voice he'd
ever heard come out of her.

More to distract her than anything else, he asked,
"Why didn't you give this information to your brother
right away?"

"I did. As soon as I found out that Harlan had been
arrested, I went to see my brother. He told me to stay
out of it. If Harlan really wasn't guilty, evidence would
come out to exonerate him, without me having to ruin
my good name by admitting to an affair with a handyman. What he really meant was that I wouldn't ruin his
good name by creating a town scandal."

"So you let it slide?"

She nodded. "Harlan didn't want me involved in it,
either. He knew the news would hurt my family and he
hoped he'd find some other way to prove his innocence."

Rita speared him with a scrutinizing look. "I see you
don't believe me, either."

Nelson shrugged. To his mind, it wasn't a question

of belief or disbelief. But it sure as hell was as unlikely a story as he'd ever heard. "How did you meet Jacobs?"

Rita laughed in a way that suggested she'd expected that question. "I hired him as a handyman. I had an armoire whose doors wouldn't stay shut. On his off times he used to do some repair work. One of my neighbors gave me his number. He saw this copy of the *Lord of the Rings* trilogy, the books, on my shelf. We started talking about how much we liked the film adaptations. It's such a silly thing, talking about how the director brought Treebeard and the other Ents to life."

She drew a long sip from her glass. "I'll admit it, I was lonely. My husband travels a lot for his business. I liked talking to Harlan so much, I started finding things for him to fix. After a while, I gave up the pretext of having him fix anything."

Nelson sipped from his glass, giving himself a moment to think before responding. If what Rita said were true, it would have been impossible for Jacobs to have attacked Frankie. In his mind, he'd always considered linking her attack with the others a bit of a stretch. All of the other attacks had been on college students, not teachers. Each of the other girls had been strangled and she hadn't been. No one, save her attacker, knew if she'd been raped, as well. The only thing that linked the attacks were similar fibers that no one could say accurately if they were from the same set of clothing or similar clothing. Brianna Lopez had been found the same night that Frankie was attacked, but the coroner speculated she'd been killed twenty-four hours before. As far as he knew, Jacobs didn't have an alibi for the day before.

But Rita was certain of Jacobs's innocence unsupported by anything she'd told them so far. Either she knew something he didn't or she possessed the righteousness of a woman who believed her lover couldn't have done that much wrong. If it were the latter, he could understand Parker's not wanting to put his sister on the stand. Such testimony would never hold up. To Nelson's mind, the woman was probably hiding something.

"How can you be so certain he didn't kill those other girls?"

"Let me ask you something, instead," Rita countered. "Why do you think it's taken so long for this case to come to trial? In this little town with virtually no crime to speak of, you'd think they could fit a mass murderer in before a year was up, wouldn't you?"

"You'd think."

"Harlan spent the first six weeks after his arrest in the hospital. He had a heart attack the night they arrested him and none of the treatments were working. He spent the next six months in and out of the cardiac unit. Only now is he strong enough to stand trial."

She paused, breathing deeply, in an obvious attempt to calm herself. "I know he didn't rape anybody. He was on medication for high blood pressure. You want to know what one of the side effects of most of those medications is? Erectile dysfunction. That's a fancy name for a common male problem, also known as impotence."

Chapter 10

"Impotence?"

That came from Frankie, who had remained silent for most of their time there.

Rita nodded. "As in 'unable to perform.'"

Frankie shook her head, clearly non-plussed. "Why didn't Jacobs's lawyer tell this to the district attorney?"

"He wouldn't even discuss those effects with his own doctor. There were other medicines he could have tried. He's a proud man. I doubt he even told his *brother*. Why would he want to share that with mine?"

"Maybe to save his own life?" Frankie ventured.

"Well, I broke Harlan's confidence and told my brother. You know what he said to me? That there was no way to tell whether at the time of the rapes that he was, since his physical condition changed that night. Or maybe the problem was he just couldn't get it up with me." Rita sighed. "The fact that I confessed to having an affair with Harlan hurt his case, not helped it, since no one can believe I would endanger my marriage if I wasn't getting at least a little something out of it."

"Then why didn't you refer to it as a friendship?"

"Because that's not what it was. Believe me, if he could have, we would have. Besides, sex isn't all there is to an affair, now, is it? There are intimacies shared that have little to do with physical acts. Confidences exchanged, hopes and dreams discussed. The kinds of things you do with your husband if he's worth the trouble. It wasn't friendship."

In the silence that followed, Nelson surveyed Rita's distraught face. Whatever she'd told them, she believed at least. If Jacobs was indeed impotent, that changed everything. That meant that for the past year, the real killer had been out there on the loose. The killings had stopped the night Jacobs was picked up—one more reason to think him guilty, since serial killers generally didn't stop killing on their own. They stopped because they got caught, they died or were incapacitated in some way, or they moved on to somewhere else. They didn't just quit. At this point, the only explanation Nelson could come up with was that the killer had been a student at one of the nearby colleges who'd gone home at the end of the school year.

Whatever. He wasn't going to solve that here. He placed his glass on the coffee table and stood. "Thanks for your candor, Ms. Forbes." He cast a pointed look at Frankie. "We should be going now."

Both Rita and Frankie stood. "I thank you for hearing me out. I'll walk you to the door."

Nelson allowed the two women to precede him. As they walked down the hall, Rita linked her arm with Frankie's. "Is there any chance of you and my brother getting back together?"

Nelson noticed Frankie didn't answer yes or no, but asked, "Why?"

"I know my brother can be a pompous horse's ass sometimes and we get into it, but I really do want what's best for him. You were good for him, Frankie. He wasn't quite so stuck up or full of himself when he was with you."

Now he knew why Rita had asked if he were really Frankie's cousin. She wouldn't have brought up this topic in front of a stranger or someone she believed to be Frankie's man. But if he were family, then it was all right.

Frankie shook her head. "I don't think so, Rita. But thanks for asking."

They reached the front door. Both women stepped aside and allowed him to open it.

"You have nice manners for a Yankee," Rita said.

"Thanks," Nelson said, and followed Frankie out of the door.

Neither of them said anything until Nelson pulled out of the drive and onto the street. He cast a glance at Frankie, who was sitting with her legs crossed and arms folded. "What did you think of that story Rita handed us?"

"Other than it sounds like the plot of a movie of the week—*The Socialite and the Sanitation Worker?* She definitely believes it." She sighed. "Where does that leave us if Jacobs was impotent as she says?"

"Truthfully, we don't know if he was. Her brother could have been right. There are plenty of men in the world who can't function unless what they're doing is illicit, dirty or dangerous. You'd be surprised at how many men can't make it with a woman unless she is at his mercy. Unfortunately, we don't have any way of knowing if this was true of Jacobs."

Frankie grinned. "Not so. When I spoke to Pink, she referred to him as 'pervert,' so he had to be over at the club doing something freaky."

She had a point there. "I'll check it out."

He glanced her way to judge her reaction, but she just shrugged.

"To what do I owe this newfound agreeableness?"

She shrugged again. "Despite what you think, I'm really not interested in getting myself killed, or worse. I'm perfectly content to let you go play with the women with the large boobies."

"Is that why you think I want to go there?"

"Maybe why you want to go there *alone*. But who am I to try to crimp your style?"

"What are you going to do while I'm gone?"

"I'll invite Rachel over and we'll practice our stripper techniques."

"You're not going to let this go, are you?"

"Nope. Then all I'll have to think about is who besides Jacobs could have killed those girls."

That was the question of the hour. Since he didn't have any answers, he said nothing. But maybe he would by the end of tonight.

* * *

Nelson arrived back at Tara about eight-thirty. Scanning the room, he saw the same crowd that had been there the previous night. At least Rachel's son didn't appear to be here, which relieved him of the decision whether to tell Frankie or not that he'd seen him.

He went to the bar and asked for Pink. The waitress asked if he wanted regular or something fancy. When he answered "regular" the woman handed him a key. He didn't bother to say that he only wanted to talk to her. In general hookers spoke to two kinds of men: johns, when they were collecting money, and pimps, when they were paying it out. People looking for information didn't rate, unless some quid pro quo was involved.

He found the room on the second floor, sat on the bed and waited. In another moment, Pink breezed into the room, took one narrow-eyed look at him and frowned. "You some kind of cop?" she accused.

"Used to be. Sit down."

Her mouth opened and closed. Clearly she wasn't expecting that bit of honesty from him. But she recovered herself, the broad smile returning to her face. "Well, tell Pink what you want, sugar. I like to settle the money up front."

"Tell me what I want to know, and I'll make it worth your while."

"Tell you? What are you talking about?"

"That guy Harlan Jacobs used to come in here? What do you know about him?"

She focused another narrow-eyed glare on him. "Someone came in here last night asking about him."

"I know. I was with her. Answer the question."

She shrugged dismissively. "He'd come in here every once in a while. No big deal."

"What did he want?"

"Mostly, he just sat at the bar. Once or twice he came up to one of the rooms we have up here. Some people like to be watched. And some people like to watch the people watching them. Kind of an interactive peep, you know what I mean?"

He nodded. "Go on."

"Well, the whole point of this is to get yourself off. Jacobs just sat there, like he was watching a movie. Weird."

"To your knowledge, has he ever slept with any of the girls?"

"I haven't taken an official poll or anything, but not that I know of."

"Thanks."

"That's it?"

"That's it." He stood, walked the few feet to where she still stood and pressed a single hundred dollar bill into her hand. He was sure that was at least twice what she would have asked for. "As long as you keep this conversation and the one last night between the three of us."

She took one quick glance at the bill before tucking it in the pocket of her robe. As he tried to slip past her, she blocked his way. "Sure there's nothing else you want? It sure would be nice to do a guy who doesn't have a pot belly and breath that smells like stale beer."

And who might have more than one of those hundreds in his pocket to share. That's the part she didn't add. "Not tonight, sweetheart." He slipped past her, went back to his car and drove back to Frankie's.

When he pulled up in front of the house, he noticed that the only light that appeared to be on was in the living room. But when he opened the door, Frankie was nowhere to be found. He checked the kitchen next, expecting her to be at the table with Rachel. The light was on, but the room was empty.

"Frankie?" he called.

"Down here."

He followed the direction in which her voice had come to an open door. He hadn't been aware the house had a basement. He loped down the stairs, surprised to find a room with a white padded floor and a variety of gym equipment. Frankie was sitting on the floor with her legs drawn up, a bottle of water in her hand. Her hair was braided into two pigtails. Without makeup she looked about sixteen. She was breathing heavily, and a layer of perspiration coated her chest.

"Nelson, this is Myron, Rachel's son and my occasional sparring partner. She pointed in Myron's direction with her water bottle. "Myron, this is Nelson."

Myron, who'd been sitting on one of the pieces of equipment, got up. "Hey, man," Myron said, extending his hand.

Seeing him up close, Nelson would put Myron in his early twenties. He was taller than Nelson by a couple of inches, with a wiry kind of physique, a shaved head and a bronze complexion. "Hey," Nelson echoed, shaking his hand.

"Now that you're here, I guess I can beat it." Myron glanced over his shoulder at Frankie. "Give me a buzz, anytime."

"I will," Frankie called back.

After Myron left, Frankie stretched her feet out in front of her and rested her hands on the mat behind her, giving him, for the first time, a full look at what she was wearing. She wore a white crop top under which a darker sports bra was visible. She wore a pair of spandex gym pants that rode low on her hips, leaving her entire midriff bare. "Couldn't you be accused of corrupting the morals of a minor in that outfit?"

"In the first place, Myron isn't a minor. In the second, I wasn't corrupting anyone." She nodded toward him. "How'd your date with the hooker go?"

"Very illuminating. Apparently Jacobs just liked to watch and he wasn't even good at that." Before she got a chance to ask him what he meant by that, he added, "Exactly what kind of sparring do you folks do?"

She sighed, crossing her legs at the ankle. "I kind of recruited Myron to be the tackle dummy for one of the classes I was asked to teach. The idea is that since most women are shorter than the men who attack them, reaching critical points for attack on a man's body— eyes, ears, throat—might not be possible. So we train women to get their attackers to the ground where they can basically kick the shit out of them."

"Okay."

She tilted her head to one side, studying him. "Okay, what?"

"You believe this method works?"

"I never said I thought it works. I said I was asked to teach it. Why?"

"If you really want to protect yourself, I'd suggest

you get a carry permit for a gun you can stick in your purse or tuck a stiletto in one of those braids."

"You want me to wear a knife in my hair?"

"No, not particularly, but it would be more effective. Statistically speaking, the bigger opponent wins. Period."

"Then you must lose a hell of a lot of fights."

He grinned. "I fight dirty."

"What, in your opinion, is wrong with this method?"

"Well, for one thing, don't you pay this guy to fall down? Do you think a real assailant is going to lie down that easily for you?"

"No. But the point is to get women to believe they can defend themselves. That has value, too."

"Only if it works."

She pursed her lips and glared at him. "There's only your word to say that it doesn't."

"Okay, I tell you what. You get me down on the ground for more than two seconds and I'll shut up."

She got to her feet. "It'll be my pleasure, just for the silence." She moved to one end of the open area. "Will this do?"

"This will do fine. How are we supposed to start?"

"Duh. You have to attack me."

Just for fun, he growled and lunged at her.

She shot him a droll look. "Not like a freaking grizzly bear. Grab my arm. Choke me. Something."

This woman had to be out of her mind. He'd said what he did to tease her, but she was dead serious. "If that's what you want. But turn around. Only an idiot would attack someone with no weapon and absolutely no element of surprise." And many an assailant relied

on a convenient wall to push you up against and take
what he wanted. They were out in the open.

"Fine. I'll pretend I'm walking down the street.
Minding my own business."

She took two steps forward. He leaned forward and
grabbed her wrist. She swung around and struck him
hard on the chin with the heel of her hand. He let her
swing follow through. In another second he had one arm
wrapped around her with both of hers pinned beneath.
He lifted her slightly off the floor so that she had no real
leverage to kick him, but she wasn't high enough on his
body for a good head butt. She kicked back at his shins
with her heels. It hurt, but not enough that any real assailant would let her go.

"What are you going to do now, sweetheart?"

"Tell me something. What exactly are you planning
to do with me in this position?"

He hooked his thumb in the waistband of her pants
and tugged downward slightly.

"Point taken." She rammed her right elbow into his
solar plexus. She didn't break his hold enough for
him to release her, but he leaned forward enough for
her to stomp his instep. She dropped down and swept
her feet from beneath him with one leg. He landed on
his back. An instant later she was beside him, her leg
extended over him. "From here I could stomp you
here, here or here." Her foot traveled from his throat
to his abdomen to his groin. "What are you going to
do now, sweetheart?"

He lifted his head to look at her. She was quick,
strong, aggressive—and he'd completely underesti-

mated her. If the necessity ever came, that would be in her favor. But that cocky grin on her face had to go.

He pushed her leg back toward her and swung his body over hers. Her leg was trapped between their bodies and his hands held her wrists to the floor. "You were saying?"

He'd noticed the beaded metal chain around her neck. In this position the chain pooled around her neck. Somehow she got the attached police whistle in her mouth and blew it in his face.

He rolled off her in mock pain. "Okay, round one goes to your whistle."

"Round one? You said if I could get you down for two seconds you'd shut up."

He leaned up on one elbow to look at her. She was lying on her back with her face turned toward him. A hint of a smile played on her lips. Her chest rose and fell rapidly from the exertion of her breathing. His own breath caught simply watching her.

To distract himself, he sat up. "Two seconds in which I wasn't listening to you lecture me on what you could to do me. The fact is you didn't do it."

She sat up, too. "You would have preferred it if I'd kicked you in the groin?"

"No, not particularly. But following through is more important than talking about following through."

"Fine, Santiago." She rose to her feet. "Have it your way. Get up."

It hadn't been his intention to egg her on, but that's what he'd succeeded in doing. He got to his feet. "It's late. I'm going to take a shower."

He walked past her. Something in her eyes told him

he should keep an eye on her, but he didn't. He wasn't aware of what she was going to do until a second before she did it. He felt the air behind him whoosh right before she landed on his back. But rather than fighting him, she tickled him. He tried to fight the upsurge of laughter rising in him, but couldn't. He tried to take a step, tripped and went down.

She rolled off him and onto her back next to him, laughing, too. "Oh, how the mighty have fallen."

"Now, that was fighting dirty."

She ran her hand along his arm from his biceps to his shoulder. "It's nice to know even tough, former New York City cops have a few vulnerabilities."

She smiled up at him, perhaps the first completely open gesture he'd seen from her. He brushed his thumb across her cheek. "Oh, I have all sorts of vulnerabilities when it comes to you."

He lowered his mouth to hers. Just like last night, she melted into his embrace, but this time she didn't push him away. His arm wound around her waist, pulling her closer, bringing her flush with his own body. Then a sudden shooting pain ripped through his groin and abdomen, making him curl in on himself. Vaguely he was aware of her scrambling away from him. He muttered a few words under his breath he was glad she wasn't still there to hear.

Damn. Nausea roiled in his belly for a moment, then receded. He pulled himself to his feet and followed her. After last night, he should have known better than to touch her. She'd as much as said she wasn't interested, whatever her reasons might be. But honestly, he hadn't been doing too much thinking before he'd kissed her.

When he got to her room, the door was closed. He knocked softly. "Frankie, can I talk to you?"

He half expected her to tell him to go away, so relief flooded him when he heard her say, "Come in."

She had her back to him when he opened the door. The clothes she'd worn were on a heap on the bed. She was wearing that big white robe again. From her movements he surmised that she was tying the sash.

"I just wanted to apologize. I'm old enough to know better—"

She cut him off. "It's not your fault. You only did what I was thinking of doing. Did I hurt you?"

"No more than when my youngest accidentally hit me with a hockey stick." He'd hoped to see some glimmer of humor in her, but there was none. He didn't understand her. She had no problem allowing him to attack her, even if it wasn't real, but a simple kiss freaked her out. "What happened?"

"I closed my eyes."

"And…" he prompted.

She did turn to face him then, an expression of entreaty in her eyes. What did she want from him? His understanding? His sympathy? She already had the latter, but he needed her help with the former.

"Don't you see? Every time I close my eyes, I see him. Jacobs or whoever in that mask. I don't even know if it's real, if the same man who attacked the girls came after me. I keep seeing this tattoo, a dagger, here, on the man's neck." She gestured to a spot on the side of her own neck, just under her ear.

"Did you tell this to Parker?"

She nodded. "I was having nightmares, too. He suggested I see a therapist. The man had me half convinced that it was just a hallucination brought on by the concussion. Jacobs didn't have any such tattoo, nor did anyone else in town that anyone knew of. He said I was just feeling guilty because I was alive and they were dead. He wasn't wrong about that. When I looked at those pictures, I knew that could have been me. If it weren't for Rachel scaring him off. Who was there to look out for those girls like she looked out for me?"

Her voice had risen to an emotion-filled crescendo, but the next words she spoke were quiet. "Do you want to know the real reason Robert and I broke up? I didn't think it was fair to ask him to stay with me when I pulled away every time he touched me. I haven't been with a man since."

She shook her head. "God, I don't want to feel this way anymore, not even knowing what's real. I don't even know what that bastard did to me."

She wasn't asking him for anything. He understood that. Just telling him how she felt. He'd wondered from the beginning why she had so much invested in Jacobs's guilt or innocence, and every step of the way he found more and more what that one night had cost her. Her need to know wasn't just to avenge the girls or to seek justice for herself, but for her own sanity, a way to put that night behind her.

He couldn't give her everything she needed, at least not tonight. But he could give her one thing if she let him, and he wasn't averse to trying.

A single tear trickled down her cheek. He brushed away the moisture with his thumb. "Do me a favor, Frankie?"

She looked up at him, confused. "What's that?"

He offered her a lopsided grin. "Try keeping your eyes open this time."

Chapter 11

Nelson lowered his head to kiss the side of her throat. He wanted her mouth, but that would have to wait. The chance of a repeat of the last time was still too strong.

"Nelson."

That one word from her sounded like a protest, but the way her fingers gripped his biceps suggested encouragement, not restraint. He took her lobe into his mouth, sucked on it and released it slowly. "Tell me you want me to stop and I will," he whispered against her ear.

"No."

He pulled back enough to see her face. Her expression told him nothing. "No what, sweetheart?"

"No, I don't want you to stop. I want to feel something."

His first impulse was to take her hand and show her

precisely how much something he had for her to feel. But her fingers had already gone to the sash of her robe, undoing it. He pushed the robe from her shoulders. It slithered down to form a pool at her feet. His heated gaze roved over her body. Damn, she was beautiful, more beautiful than he's imagined, even after seeing her in that skimpy outfit she'd worn last night.

He pulled her to him, letting his hands rove over her back and lower to caress her backside. Feeling her stiffen, he pulled back to look at her. Her eyes were closed and her teeth were clamped on her lower lip. With one hand under her chin, he tilted her face up to him. "Look at me, baby. It's me. I'm not going to hurt you."

She did as he asked. "I know."

He didn't know how she could be so certain about anything about him as those two words sounded. He ran his fingers along one of her braids. "Then why did you freeze up on me?"

"I didn't. Not the way you mean it."

Despite the slightly breathy quality of her voice, he didn't know if he believed her. She'd been so damn good at hiding things from him that he couldn't help wondering if she hid something from him now. He only knew he'd have to take it slow with her, even slower than he'd first intended.

He lifted her and laid her down on the bed. He lay down beside her, leaning up on one elbow. He touched the fingertips of his other hand to her belly. Her muscles contracted beneath his hand and she shivered. "Do you mind if I ask you something?"

"Now?"

He smiled at the incredulity in her voice. "Yeah."

She shrugged and lifted her hands, as if to say, "Why the hell not."

"I understand the part about the double bras." He trailed his fingers beneath her breasts. "But what was with the grunge look you had going before?"

"That was pretty bad, wasn't it?"

He nodded.

She shook her head. "I don't know. I just wanted to disappear, I guess. I didn't want anyone to notice me."

"Notice you sexually?" He slid his hand down her side to grasp her buttock in his palm.

She bit her lip and nodded.

He slid his hand upward to cover her left breast, using his thumb to strum her nipple. "I hate to tell you this, but it didn't work."

"It didn't?"

Her voice had a breathy quality to it that made him smile. "Nope." He let his hand stray lower to her belly. "Do you remember when we were in your apartment? You gave me a bit of a peep show."

"No I didn't."

"You took off your shirt and showed me your belly." His fingers splayed across her abdomen. "Here." He dragged his fingers downward. She sucked in her breath and her belly contracted, but this time he doubted that had anything to do with fear.

"I d-didn't know that."

"I didn't think you did." He circled his hand upward to cover her right breast, kneading the soft flesh, positioning her nipple for him to take it into his mouth.

"Peeping Tom," she accused, but there was a smile on her face.

"Yup," he agreed. "I've wanted you ever since." He flicked his tongue against the engorged tip, before drawing it farther into his mouth. A soft moan escaped her lips and she drew her legs up so that her knees rested against his thighs. He felt the restlessness in her body, the build-up of tension seeking release. She called his name, and this time there was no doubt that she did so wanting more from him.

His hand strayed down her body, over her rib cage, her belly and lower. He parted her legs and skimmed his fingertips over her. She bucked against him, obviously unsatisfied by his cursory touch. He gave her what she wanted, circling his fingers over her tender flesh. He felt the tension building in her, but also the frustration. He stroked the side of her face. "Just let it happen, sweetheart. Don't rush it and don't fight it."

She looked up at him, her eyes vague and darkened, her breathing labored. The scent of her arousal filled his nostrils. It took every ounce of strength he possessed not to shed his clothes and join with her. But this was her time. If this was all she wanted from him, he could deal with that. For the moment, all he really wanted was to please her.

He slipped two fingers inside her, using his thumb to stroke her. She arched against him and cried out. Her tongue darted out to lick her lips. This time he couldn't resist lowering his head to claim her mouth. Her tongue met his for a wild dance, an in-and-out imitation of the movements of his fingers.

This time when she stiffened it was with the on-slaught of her orgasm. Her body trembled and her legs tightened around his hand. After a while, she subsided, rolling toward him and burying her face against his chest.

He stroked his hand over her back. "What's the matter, baby?"

"Nothing."

He wasn't sure how to take that response from her, considering she was using his body to hide herself from him. "Don't lie to me, Frankie."

"I'm not." She rolled onto her back and gazed up at him. Rather than seeing the sadness, regret or confusion he expected to see in her eyes, she was smiling. "I'm just surprised. That's all."

"About what?"

"I didn't think I could feel that way again."

"What way is that?"

"Good. Really, much more than good. Exquisite, actually."

He tugged on one of her braids. "Glad I could be of service."

An impish grin lit her face. "You're not done yet." She looped her arms around his neck and pulled him down to her. As their mouths met, her fingers went to his shirt, trying to free him of it. He did the honors for her, yanking it over his head and tossing it aside. He sank back against her, reveling in the feel of her soft, bare flesh meeting his and the motion of her hands on his back.

Her hands slid down to cup his buttocks at the same time one of her legs insinuated itself between his. It was

KIMANI ROMANCE

An Important Message from the Publisher

Dear Reader,

Because you've chosen to read one of our fine novels, I'd like to say "thank you"! And, as a special way to say thank you, I'm offering to send you two more Kimani Romance novels and two surprise gifts – absolutely FREE! These books will keep it real with true-to-life African American characters that turn up the heat and sizzle with passion.

Please enjoy the free books and gifts with our compliments...

Linda Gill

Publisher, Kimani Press

Peel off Seal and Place Inside...

PUBLISHERS FREE GIFT SEAL THANK YOU

THE EDITOR'S "THANK YOU" FREE GIFTS INCLUDE:

▶ Two NEW Kimani Romance™ Novels
▶ Two exciting surprise gifts

YES! I have placed my Editor's "thank you" Free Gifts seal in the space provided at right. Please send me 2 FREE books, and my 2 FREE Mystery Gifts. I understand that I am under no obligation to purchase anything further, as explained on the back of this card.

PLACE
FREE GIFTS
SEAL
HERE

▼ DETACH AND MAIL CARD TODAY! ▼

168 XDL EF2E   368 XDL EF2Q

FIRST NAME	LAST NAME

ADDRESS

APT.#	CITY

STATE/PROV.	ZIP/POSTAL CODE

Thank You!

(K-ROM-08/06)

The Reader Service — Here's How It Works:

a double whammy that forced a groan from his chest, and his arms to close more tightly around her.

She broke the kiss. "Any chance you plan to take those pants off any time soon?"

"Maybe." He released her and rose from the bed. He watched her as she leaned up on her elbows to watch him shed the rest of his clothes. He retrieved the condom he kept in his wallet and sheathed himself.

She grinned up at him. "Now, there's a present for the teacher. Come here and give it to me."

He did as she asked, covering her with his body and thrusting into her. His body shivered with the pleasure of having her envelop him.

But she froze, her eyes squeezed tight and her body still. Figuring it was something about their position that upset her, he rolled onto his back, taking her with him. He hadn't intended for it to happen this way, but their bodies were still joined. He started to pull away from her, but her fingers dug into his shoulders making him still.

He felt the dampness on his chest before he heard her sniffle. He stroked his hand over her hair. "Baby, what is it? Talk to me."

"Oh, God, Nelson. It was real, wasn't it? It isn't a nightmare or a hallucination. It really happened."

Considering that her reactions to him were visceral and subconscious, not intellectual, he'd have to agree with her. "I think so."

Rather than his agreement appeasing her, she cried harder, sobs racking her slender body. Her pain tore at him, too, in ways she couldn't imagine. All he could do was hold her and try to comfort her as best he knew how.

Abruptly, she raised her head, wiped her eyes and looked down at him. "Make it go away, Nelson," she whispered. "Make it go away."

He wished he had the power to do that, to take away her pain. That wasn't in his power, but he knew what she wanted—the chance to replace the hurtful memory with a fresh one. The only problem was his erection had died an unhappy death the moment he realized why she'd frozen.

But she brought her mouth down on his and her body moved against his in a way that didn't fail to stimulate him. He broke the kiss and cradled her cheeks in his hands in a way that allowed him to see her face. "Are you sure, sweetheart?"

"Please."

That one whispered word was his undoing. He brought her mouth down and thrust into her slowly, a caress as languid as the kiss they shared. He withdrew from her just as slowly, only to thrust into her again, more deeply this time. Then she began to move, meeting his thrusts. A soft sound of pleasure escaped her lips, bringing a smile to his. He knew he couldn't be hurting her or mining painful memories if she could make a sound like that.

He stroked his hand over her hair, down her back, to grip her hips. Every movement she made drove him crazy, and it had been too damn long for him to have much finesse in his game. Perspiration coated his skin and his nostrils flared, drinking in the scent of their lovemaking. Slow and languid or not, he was going down, in flames or otherwise. He damn sure wanted to take her with him. His fingers grasping her buttocks, he thrust into her. She gasped and her fingertips dug into the flesh at his shoulders. Her body shuddered against his. He thrust into her one last time. His orgasm came as several electric bursts of pleasure set tremors throughout his body.

She collapsed against him, laying her cheek on his shoulder. They lay there like that a long time, their bodies damp, their heartbeats erratic, waiting to recover. Nelson scrubbed his hand up and down Frankie's back. "How are you doing?"

She lifted her head and offered him a lopsided grin. "I think I know what exhausted feels like."

He didn't doubt it. Their being together must have been a draining experience for her both mentally and physically. "And I think I know what you meant by exquisite."

"Really? I would have thought…"

She trailed off. In his mind, he finished for her. She would have thought that her revelation would have turned him off. Why she thought that he couldn't imagine. She had been there when he climaxed in her arms. But maybe her mind had been too preoccupied to pay him much attention.

"I think I hear your shower calling to me."

"Good, since it's calling to me, too. How about a bath instead?"

"Whatever you want, sweetheart. Why don't you go get it started while I make sure we locked up downstairs?"

"Okay." She kissed his mouth, then left the bed.

For a moment he watched her walk away, his gaze on her shapely backside. Then he went downstairs, checked the front and back door and secured the lock on the basement door. When he got back to the bathroom, Frankie was standing by the half-filled tub.

"Get in," she urged. "I need to see if this is too much water."

He couldn't say about the water, but she'd definitely gone too far with the bubbles. He wasn't about to argue with her about it at the moment, though. He got in and settled at the end of the tub nearest the door.

She got in the other end, facing him. "I should have a camera. Nelson the Barbarian ensconced in his bubble bath."

"We're back to that again?"

"That's been my nickname for you after the first time I met you. You were not exactly the friendliest wheel on the welcome wagon that night."

"I'm not usually at my best at large family functions. If you'll remember I was doing a good job of avoiding the festivities the second time you found me."

For a moment, he regretted bringing up the subject, figuring she'd question him on his lack of familial devotion—or worse, question why he hadn't helped her the first time. If he had, she probably would have put all this behind her by now.

Instead she smiled sympathetically. "I know how you feel. There's a maze on my parents' property that makes for a few good hiding spots. There's a manmade pond I like to escape to."

"Your family is that bad?"

"That boring. There should be a test—how to tell if you are a dead bore. If you know Peter and Margaret

Hairston and actually like them, then you, too, are a dead bore. My brother is okay, though."

She grew silent after that, looking away from him. For the first time he noticed how she was sitting, with her legs drawn up and her arms wrapped around them. A defensive posture that allowed her to share the same tub with him without them touching in any way. There was no way she could be comfortable with the faucets at her back. The only explanation was that she was avoiding him. "Is there any chance you intend to come down here with me?"

She sighed, resting her chin on her knees. "You don't need to treat me like a piece of porcelain, Nelson. I'm not that delicate. I'm not going to break. I've been more weepy in the last few days than I have been my whole life—except when my mother forced me to take ballet. Most of the time when someone gets to me I respond by irritating them right back. Surely you've noticed that."

"On occasion."

"If you want to know what I'm feeling right now, it's mostly relief. Finally, I can accept the truth of what happened, which I was afraid to do before. I just wanted to put it out of my mind, which I'd succeeded in doing for the most part until I knew I had to come back here."

She sighed again. "Before tonight you weren't afraid to touch me."

"I was just trying to avoid that knee-jerk reaction of yours."

"I already apologized for that."

"No, you asked me if I hurt you. I don't remember hearing an apology."

"Okay, then, I'm sorry. But the point is, if you'd wanted me, you would have just grabbed me and been done with it. You don't have to treat me any differently now."

"Then why are you scootched down at the other end of the tub?"

"I just needed a moment to regroup, I guess."

Which he supposed for her meant being as alone as the situation allowed. "Then get your ass down here, Pocahontas." He leaned forward to grasp her wrist and pull her toward him, sloshing water and suds over the side of the tub.

Laughing, she settled against him with her back to his front. "You are cleaning that up, mister."

"Maybe." He wrapped his arms around her waist and nuzzled her neck. "Do you mind if I ask you a question?"

"Depends on what it is."

"Did you put all these bubbles in here on purpose?"

"Actually, no. I just wanted to scent the water, but my hand slipped. Why?"

"I didn't take you for the frilly bubble bath type, either."

"Good thing." She shifted slightly, linking her fingers with his. "Do you mind if I ask you a question?"

"Depends on what it is."

She freed one hand to smack him on his thigh. "Don't be a wiseass."

"What is it, baby?"

"Assuming Jacobs is out of the picture, what are we left with?"

He should have known the case was still uppermost in her mind. "I don't know. According to Don, they cleared everyone else they looked at, mostly anybody who had cause to wear that sort of coveralls. Then again, they focused on Jacobs fairly early. He was registered at the county office as a sex offender. They just couldn't figure out where he might have taken the girls."

"What do you mean?"

"There had to be a crime scene. It wasn't their dorm rooms or the woods. That's just where they were left. They searched his home and the sportscenter where he worked."

"I remember that. The police closed the building one day and I couldn't get an explanation from anyone, not even Robert, as to why. But that was back in February, right after Kerry was killed."

"As I said, he was the prime suspect almost from the beginning."

"We have to get him out of jail."

"Who, Jacobs? You think if Parker wouldn't listen to his own sister, he's going to take the word of a hooker?"

"Well, once you put it that way, no. But I would hope he'd listen to me. The man I keep seeing had a tattoo. Jacobs doesn't."

"Even so, Parker can counter that with what the shrink said."

"Are you saying that Robert is deliberately trying to prosecute a man he knows or at least suspects may not be guilty?"

"No. I'm saying prosecutors like to win. Why should he turn loose someone who can almost guarantee him a conviction without conclusive evidence someone else committed the crime? In his shoes, I wouldn't."

"This is completely frustrating."

"I know." And having her locked so intimately with

him was frustrating in another way. But despite what she said, he intended to take his cue from her. Maybe she read his mind or maybe she felt the same restlessness he did, but she lifted one of his hands from the water, kissed his palm and put his hand over her breast.

Frankie woke the next morning, still in the haven of Nelson's arms. She smiled to herself. Last night her dreams had been troubled, but nowhere near as gruesome as most of her nightmares. Compared to what she usually endured, she'd actually gotten a good night's sleep.

His hand on her back stirred, letting her know he was already awake. "Hey," he said.

She shifted so that she could look up at his face. "Hey." She smiled, still a bit drowsy. "Have you been up long?"

"Not too." He brushed one of her braids from her face. "Hungry?"

"Not too." She let her hand wander over his broad chest. She loved his body, all muscle and sinew, and in the endowment department she certainly couldn't complain. More than that, she enjoyed this closeness with him. It seemed like forever since she'd simply lain in a man's arms and felt contented.

He hugged her to him. "How are you this morning?"

She shrugged, not knowing exactly how to answer him. Physically she felt fine, more than fine. After they got out of the tub last night, he'd carried her here and made love to her again. That time there had been no flashes of memory to mar the experience. Even now, the pleasure he'd given her still resonated in her body. But she knew that's not what he referred to.

The previous night had been an emotional one for her. She'd finally admitted to herself that her memories weren't aberrations or some trick of her mind, Jacobs wasn't the man who'd attacked her, and, as she now believed, more than likely raped her. That last image that rushed up on her as Nelson had entered her was of herself, on the floor of her living room, her skirt up and that man on top of her, his masked face close to hers. From that brief flash she didn't get the sensation of having been penetrated, only the feeling of trying to fend him off. But was this her destiny? To remember in bits and pieces a night she'd rather forget?

"Sweetheart?"

Obviously she'd taken long enough answering his question to concern him. She smiled up at him, not wanting him to worry. "I'm fine."

He cast her a skeptical look, but before he could question her, the ringing of a cell phone caught both their attention. Since she didn't have that ring tone, she knew it must be his phone. She remembered him leaving his pants by the side of the bed. "I'll get it." She leaned over the side, unclipped the phone from his belt and handed it to him.

Only then did she notice the look of concern on his face. Obviously from the tone he knew who was calling. Whoever it was, he spoke to them only in rapid Spanish. Deciding to let him have his privacy, she went to the bathroom to wash up.

Looking at herself in the mirror above the sink brought a mixed bag of assessments. She did look more well rested than she had in a long time. Her hair, on the other hand, had escaped the elastic bands she'd fastened on the ends of her braids. Consequently, the lower third of each braid, the part that had gotten wet in the bath, had started to curl in odd ways. She'd need to wash her hair if she expected to do anything with it that day.

That could wait, however. She'd heard the agitation in Nelson's voice, even if she didn't understand the words. If there was trouble, she wanted to know what it was—now.

She went back to her bedroom to find it empty. She went to his room next. He stood by the bed, putting things back into his suitcase. The grim set of his features told her she hadn't been mistaken about the nature of the call. "Nelson, what's the matter? Is everything all right?"

He turned to face her, the worry in his dark eyes clear for her to see. "My kids were in a car accident. I have to go home."

Chapter 12

She went to him and wrapped her arms around him. If she knew anything about Nelson, it was how much his children mattered to him. "Oh, my God, Nelson. Are they okay?"

One of his arms closed around her, but it was a distracted embrace at best. "I don't know, Frankie. I don't know. The hospital called my mother and she called me. She'll know more once she gets there."

"What do you need me to do?"

He set her away from him. "Get ready to go. There's a flight to New York in an hour."

"You don't need to be worrying about me right now, Nelson. Go home to your family."

"Don't argue with me, Frankie. I'm not leaving you here alone."

She didn't want to argue with him or make things worse for him. She went back to her room, threw whatever she could think of in a bag, showered, dressed and managed to fix her hair in some semblance of order. She took her bag downstairs, went to the kitchen and brewed coffee. When it was done she poured a cup for each of them.

"Are you ready?"

Frankie nearly jumped hearing Nelson's voice behind her. She grasped both cups and turned to face him. "I made some coffee. I thought you could use some."

"Not now. Make sure everything in here is off, okay?"

"Sure." By the time the word was out of her mouth he'd already left the room. She poured the coffee out, turned off the coffeemaker and unplugged it. She left all of the other appliances as they were. She picked up the phone and dialed Rachel's number. They would need a ride to the airport. Rachel might as well take whatever was left in the refrigerator. She didn't know if she'd be back before the perishables spoiled.

After she hung up with Rachel, she went out to the living room. Nelson was coming down the stairs, his bag slung over his shoulder. As he approached her she said, "I asked Rachel to drive us to the airport. Myron will park the Ferrari in Rachel's garage if you give him the keys."

She thought the idea of that beautiful, expensive car being driven by another man might get a rise out of him. All he said was "Fine."

Luckily there wasn't much traffic to the airport and the flight left on time. By the time they were halfway through the two-hour flight, Nelson hadn't said two words to her that weren't absolutely necessary. Instead he spent his time staring out the window, ignoring her. After last night, she would have sworn they'd forged some sort of bond between them, the nature of which she couldn't codify or give a name to. She only knew her feelings for him had deepened considerably. She'd assumed his had, too, but perhaps she was wrong. Maybe he just saw her as some pathetic woman he took pity on, and since he got sex out of it, what they hey. Whatever he thought of her, she wanted to give him back some of what he'd given her. She laced her fingers with his. "Nelson, it will be all right."

He didn't look at her, but his hand squeezed hers. "I can't lose my kids, Frankie. I can't. Not like this. I was supposed to be with them."

And if it weren't for her, he would have been. "Why didn't you tell me?"

"Would it have changed anything?"

Knowing she was taking him from his children was the one thing that might have put her off, but she didn't see any point in telling him that now. "I'm so sorry, Nelson."

He did look at her then. "I'm not blaming you. I just wish she'd call."

Frankie assumed the she in question was his mother. Funny, but she'd heard him talk about his grandmother, his ex-wife and his kids. Until today, she'd half assumed his mother wasn't alive or at least not in New York since he never spoke of her. But that was neither here nor there. "What would you prefer, that your mother was seeing to your daughters or calling you?"

"As you say, point taken. That doesn't make it any easier."

She didn't suppose it did. The plane dipped, signaling a loss of altitude. A second later the seat belt light came on. They would be landing soon. Hopefully they would find out more then. For Nelson's sake, she hoped it would be good news.

It wasn't until they were on the ground, walking through the terminal, that Nelson's cell phone rang. He paused right where they were, in the middle of the baggage-claim area and retrieved his phone with a hand that trembled. He knew by the ring that it was his mother calling. Without preamble, he said one word into the phone, *"Digame."* Tell me. He wasn't usually rude to his mother, so she'd have to forgive him this one time.

As he listened, he let go of Frankie's hand and pulled her to him, mostly to protect her from the crowd of people passing by, disgruntled because they were in the way. He could feel her looking up at him, but he didn't return her gaze, concentrating instead on what his mother was saying. When the conversation ended, he thanked his mother and snapped the phone shut.

"Well?"

Burying his face against her neck, he let out a heavy, relieved sigh. "They're all right. Dara's fine except for a cut on her forehead. Bonnie hurt her arm on the dashboard, but it isn't broken. They're all right."

Her arms wound around his neck. "Thank God." She hugged him tighter. "But I have one question."

He pulled back enough to see her smiling face. "What's that?"

"Is this the right time to tell you 'I told you so' or should I wait until later?"

Before he had time to respond, an unfamiliar male voice inquired, "Miss Hairston."

Both he and Frankie turned toward the man who'd spoken to find a liveried driver holding a sign with her name on it.

"Yes," Frankie said.

"I'm Jenkins. Anderson sent me. The car is just outside."

The man gestured over his shoulder to the outside of the building where a white stretch limousine was parked at the curb.

Frankie stiffened in his arms. "I'm going to have to kill an old man."

He would have asked her what she meant by that, but she pulled away from him and put her bag in Jenkins's waiting hand. "Thank you."

He nodded. "This way."

Once Jenkins opened the door for them, Frankie slid in first, scooching over for him to enter after her. He sat in the corner and pulled her to him with an arm around her shoulders. "Who is this you want to do in?"

She rolled her eyes, letting him know she wasn't serious. "Anderson, my mother's butler. I called him and asked him to send a car. A regular car."

Not seeing the problem, he prompted, "And?"

"And he must have told my mother I was here—which I had not intended to do. Only she would try to embarrass me with such pretentiousness."

"If it's any consolation, the girls will probably love it."

The driver slipped in behind the wheel. Nelson gave him his mother's address in Queens, where she'd taken the girls once they were released from the hospital. The driver nodded and disappeared behind the rising privacy screen.

Nelson turned back to Frankie, who was sitting next to him with her arms folded and her foot swinging, the only real show of nervousness he'd ever seen in her. "What's the matter, sweetheart?"

"It just occurred to me that I'm going to meet your daughters."

"Is that a problem?"

She glanced up at him. "You're kidding, right?"

He shrugged, having no idea what she was talking about. "Again, what's the problem?"

"Oh, nothing. They probably just hate me already."

"They don't hate you. They don't even know who you are."

She turned slightly to face him. "Didn't you tell me you were supposed to be spending this time with them?"

"Yes."

"Tell me they didn't beg you not to go. Tell me they didn't call you every day to ask you to come home."

He chuckled. "Something like that. How did you know?"

"Don't forget, I was a young girl once desperate for Daddy's attention. In my case, it would have helped if I were a golf ball or a good cigar, but believe me, I've been there. So if you don't mind, just leave me at the nearest gas station. I'll hitch a ride from there."

He brushed his knuckles across her cheek. "I can't imagine you turning chicken now."

"Tattoo-sporting assassins are nothing compared to teenage girls."

He knew she wasn't serious, not entirely. He knew his girls could be a handful and that their precociousness might be a topic for the family grapevine. He doubted that's what really bothered her, though. It seemed too intimate to be introduced to his daughters so soon after the intimacies they'd shared last night.

He couldn't change what happened between them, nor did he want to. Neither could he say where, if anywhere, this thing between them might lead. More than likely, they would go their separate ways now that she had found out what she wanted to know. Harlan Jacobs wasn't guilty, whether the district attorney chose to believe it or not. Either way, Frankie wasn't much use to him as a witness anymore.

He'd go back with her to pick up his car and retrieve his gun from where he'd left it—between the mattress and box spring in his room—and go home.

But for the time being, while she was here with him, he would play that by ear. For the moment, though, he knew what he wanted. He tilted her face up with a finger under her chin. "Don't worry. I'll protect you," he whispered, before lowering his mouth to hers.

Nelson's mother lived in a small, detached house in a quiet neighborhood in Queens. Like all the women in his family that Frankie had met, she had black hair, hazel eyes and a slender figure. When she opened the door, she cast a speculative look at Frankie before focusing on her son. "*M'ijo,* I thought you said you were out of town with a client." Focusing on her again, Nelson's mother added, "You're Matt's sister, right?"

"Guilty as charged," Nelson said, "but she's also a client. Can we come in first or do you plan to grill us out here?"

"I'm sorry." She stepped back to allow them to enter. "The girls are in the li—"

That's as far as Nelson's mother got before a twin cry of "Daddy" sounded behind her. The two girls brushed past Frankie and their grandmother to get to their father. They threw themselves at him as if he'd just returned from a year's long campaign at war, each of them talking over the other, rather than a three-day trip. Under the circumstances, that was understandable. So, too, was the way he hugged them to him. The only words Frankie made out from their conversation were "Come into the living room and we'll tell you what happened." Of the three of them, the only one to pay her any attention was Nelson, who nodded in a way that indicated she should follow.

She had no intention of doing that. The girls needed a moment with their father. Nelson's mother probably wanted a moment with him, too. If she'd thought about it, she probably would have waited outside in the car, considering that no one in the house really required her presence.

She turned to Nelson's mother. "Is there somewhere I can freshen up, Mrs. Santiago?"

The older woman cast her an assessing look before smiling. "Please call me Jeannie. There's a bathroom at the top of the stairs."

"Thank you, and please call me Frankie."

"Will do. If you need anything, let me know."

Frankie headed off toward the stairs on the left side of the house. While she walked, she looked to her right to the living room. Nelson was seated on the sofa with a daughter on either side of him. He had his arms around them and each had her head on his shoulder. Nelson the Barbarian was apparently a pushover when it came to his daughters.

She hurried the rest of the way up the stairs to a pink-and-white-tiled bathroom. She didn't really have any need to come in here, but she washed her hands, stalling. While she did so, she surveyed her image in the mirror above the sink. Her hair was slightly askew and anyone with eyes could tell her lips were kiss-swollen under the recent application of lipstick. No wonder Nelson's mother had given her that look. She probably suspected they'd spent the past fifteen minutes doing just what they'd done—making out in the back of the limousine. Thank goodness the ride hadn't been any longer, or she'd have to worry that her clothes were on inside out or backward, too.

She knew he'd kissed her that first time, at least in part, to shut her up. She also knew his ardor had stemmed, at least in part, from his relief that his daughters were all right. But the kiss had taken on a life of its own, apart from any considerations except their own mutual desire. Even this morning, before his mother called, she hadn't given much thought to what the future held for them. She'd needed him and he'd been there for her in so many ways. If that's all he'd offered her, she could have lived with that. The ring on his finger told her he considered himself belonging to another woman, even if that woman didn't want him.

But that kiss said things weren't over yet—at least not from his end of it. She wasn't sure how she felt about that. Every damn thing in her life was a hand-me-down—from her parents to her brother's apartment to the furniture in her own house in Atlanta. Did she really need another woman's secondhand man complicating her life? Well, he hadn't actually made any promises in that direction, either, had he? He'd only let her know that he still wanted her. Despite her better instincts, she still wanted him. So what was the harm? She was a big girl. She'd be able to walk away when the time came.

She adjusted her hair, but there was little she could do about the rest of her appearance. Truthfully, she didn't care what Nelson's mother thought. She knew her exploits were probably fodder for the family gossip mill already. Ever since the two families had been joined by her brother's marriage to Nina, it was as if everyone had forgotten how to shut up. But Nelson's children did concern her. They were both at tender ages, they both apparently adored their father, and like most children of divorce, they probably hoped their parents would get back together, no matter how far-fetched a prospect that was.

She refused to do anything to insinuate herself into that mix. Whatever happened between her and Nelson when they were alone was one thing, but while they were with his daughters she intended to keep her distance.

While she descended the stairs, she noticed Nelson waiting at the bottom for her. As she neared the last few steps, he held out his hand to her. "We're going to get going," he said.

She glanced to her left to see the living room empty. "Where are the girls?"

"I told them about the car and they went outside to check it out. We'd better hurry up before they discover the liquor cabinet in the door."

"I'm ready. Where's your mom?"

"With the girls. Why do you think I'm worried about the liquor cabinet?"

She laughed and preceded him outside. Jenkins opened the car door as she reached it. Nelson's mother and his daughters were sitting at the back of the car so she slid in facing them. Nelson's mother was in the process of kissing her grandchildren goodbye.

When she was finished she focused her gaze on Frankie. "It was nice seeing you again. I hope we see more of you."

Since Frankie couldn't make any promises about being seen again, she said, "It was nice seeing you, too."

"I hope whatever Nelson is helping you with works out."

"Thank you."

Jeannie smooched each girl again. "You two behave yourselves," she admonished before getting out of the car.

Frankie watched her get out. When she focused on the girls again, they were both staring at her—Dara with interest and Bonnie with unconcealed hostility.

"Is this really your car?" Dara asked.

"Of course not," Bonnie interjected before Frankie

got a word out of her mouth. "People don't own limousines, they rent them."

Frankie fought down the urge to inform her that her parents did indeed own a limousine, just not this limousine. She didn't see any point in antagonizing the girl. "No, this isn't my car."

"It's cool, anyway," Dara said. She pointed toward the television screen mounted to the ceiling. "Can we watch a movie?"

"If your father says it's okay."

"If I say what's okay?" Nelson asked as he got into the car. Clearly he intended to take the seat next to her, until Bonnie grabbed his arm and pulled him over to sit between her and Dara.

Not too subtle. Frankie crossed her arms and tried to keep the smile off her face. Her gaze met Nelson's. The expression in his eyes was a silent apology for his daughter's bad behavior. She shrugged. She'd already decided she didn't want to be in the middle of that, anyway. "Dara wanted to know if they could watch a movie."

He looked down at Dara, who like her sister had snuggled up against him. "We live ten minutes from here."

Dara made a comically sour face and folded her arms. "All right."

Frankie's gaze traveled from Dara to Nelson and then to Bonnie. The three of them made a handsome family. Dara shared Nelson's eye color and hair texture, but not his features. If she looked like her mother, Nelson must have married a beautiful woman. Bonnie wore her hair straight and long. She had her father's bone structure, but her eyes were the hazel color she shared with her female relatives on her father's side.

They were both beautiful girls, but it was easy to see which was the more intractable one. "By the way, Mom wants you to call her," Bonnie announced with particular glee. "She's still in the hospital."

She didn't know why, but until that moment, she hadn't considered who had been driving the car.

"Why is she still there? Your grandmother told me she just bumped her head."

Bonnie shrugged. "I don't know, Dad. Maybe you should go over there and find out."

Frankie stared out the window. This was going to be a fun day.

Chapter 13

Ten minutes later they pulled up in front of Nelson's house, a two-story brick building almost twice the size of his mother's. It was set back from the street by a row of hedges and expansive well-manicured lawn. A long drive that ended at the garage lay to the left side of the house. The driver pulled up as far as he could and stopped. While they waited for the driver to come around, Frankie looked around the property. The hedges were nicely trimmed and the few trees standing on the lawn looked as if they'd seen a good pruning. Rows of well-tended flowers had been planted beneath the front windows. She hadn't expected him to live in a cave, but neither did she expect the Cleaver family home, either. It reminded her how little she knew about him.

"What do you think?" Nelson asked.

Luckily, the driver picked that moment to open the door for them.

The interior of the house proved just as surprising. The front door opened onto a large living area to the left. At the back of the room was a staircase that led to a gallery on the second floor. To the right was obviously a home office, as she could see the corner of a desk with a computer on top of it through the open door.

"Who's hungry?" Nelson asked as he set their bags down by the door.

"Me," both girls said.

Frankie could do with something to eat herself, since they hadn't eaten all day, unless you counted the stale and cold sandwich neither of them had touched on the plane. Though she and Nelson hadn't discussed anything about coming to New York except making sure his daughters were all right, she figured she'd call a taxi and go home after the meal. She'd had enough of being the fourth wheel on a tricycle.

They settled on ordering pizza, since there was nothing worthwhile in the fridge. The only person dissatisfied with the choice was Bonnie, who claimed to be on a diet. Frankie had the feeling that if they had ordered cottage cheese and bowl of lettuce, Bonnie would have been in the mood for pasta—whatever it took to gain her father's notice, even if it were in a negative way.

Once the pizza arrived, Nelson served each of them a slice. Bonnie looked around the dining room and frowned. "Dara has the most pepperoni."

"Who are you?" Nelson asked. "The pepperoni police? Eat your pizza."

"That isn't fair. We should all have the same."

Dara said, "She never eats them, anyway. She says they make her fat."

Nelson turned his head toward his younger daughter. "You stay out of it."

"Yeah, dweeb," Bonnie said. "You stay out of it."

A muscle flexed in Nelson's jaw. "Okay, here's what we're going to do. Dara, you take your food into the living room and put on whatever movie you want, within reason. Bonnie, I don't care what you do as long as you do it in your room. Don't come back until you're ready to apologize to your sister. Now, both of you, go."

Both of the girls opened their mouths as if to protest, but neither said anything. Bonnie grabbed her plate and stomped off toward the stairs. Dara slumped off in the opposite direction. Nelson put his elbows on the table and rested his forehead in his hands. "And to think I rushed home to this." He straightened and regarded her. "I'm sorry."

"Don't apologize to me. They're the ones who are mad at you for making them miss you and they're taking it out on you."

"No kidding."

"Is Bonnie usually that, um…"

While she searched for an appropriate word, he said, "No. Just the last few days. She's always been a bit melodramatic, but lately…" He shook his head.

"Sixteen is a tough age." And if she weren't mistaken, Bonnie had more on her mind than simply her father's absence. Frankie recognized attention-seeking behavior. She'd done enough of it herself to know it when she saw it. But she wondered if Nelson did.

"Yeah, for the parents. I figure if I can make it until she's twenty one without having a nervous breakdown we'll be all right."

"Can I come back now, Dad?"

That call came from Dara in the living room. Frankie laughed at the unintentionally comical look of exasperation on Nelson's face.

"Sure, sweetheart."

Dara bounced back into the room and flopped into her seat. "Can I ask you something, Dad? And you have to promise not to get mad."

"What is it?"

"Are you going to check on Mom?"

"Your mother has Uncle Ted to look after her."

"He's not really our uncle," Dara said to Frankie as if confiding a secret. "But it's not the same thing as you looking after her."

In a patient voice Nelson said, "I'll call her after we finish eating."

"That will take forever since you haven't eaten anything yet."

When Nelson looked to her, Frankie could only shrug. She didn't doubt the girls were interested in pushing their parents together to see if something sparked, but that didn't mean they weren't truly worried.

Nelson let out a sigh of capitulation. "Fine. I will go see your mother. But you are responsible for calling your mother to tell her I'm coming."

Frankie cast a look at Nelson, wondering why such

a warning was necessary since he and his ex-wife seemed on good-enough terms to talk.

Dara answered the question for her. "Dad and Uncle Ted are not allowed to be in the same room together."

"Why not?"

Dara shrugged, then cast an expectant look at her father, as if she might finally hear the truth of the matter. Frankie wouldn't mind hearing it, either.

Nelson leaned close enough to Frankie to whisper in her ear. "I would only have hit him once if he'd had the good sense to stay on the floor."

Frankie bit her lip to keep from laughing. If Dara was curious before, she would be more so with that reaction from her. "I see," she managed to say with some effort.

"Hey, no telling secrets," Dara protested.

Nelson tossed his napkin onto the table and stood. "Frankie, can I speak with you for a moment?"

"Sure." She stood as Nelson pulled out her chair and followed him to the front door. "What's up?"

He turned to face her and ran his hand over her hair. "I know this is putting you on the spot, but would you mind staying with them?"

"Come again?"

"You expected to come with me?"

"Actually, I was planning on going home. I figured you'd call when you were ready to go back."

"I should only be gone an hour. I know they're old enough to be left on their own, but after this morning, I'd really rather not do that."

She poked him in the chest. "Aren't you the one who

promised to protect me? Now you want me to stay here with your daughters by myself?"

He caught her finger, turned her hand over and kissed her palm. "That about covers it. Besides, Dara likes you. Bonnie's holed up in her room. What's the worst that can happen?"

He was wrong about part of that. Dara didn't like her; she just didn't perceive her as a threat. "When you come back and find me tied up in a closet, don't say I didn't warn you."

With a hand on her arm, he pulled her closer. "I'll owe you one."

"No, you'll owe me about thirty-five for this."

"We'll see." He pulled her closer still and covered her mouth with his for a brief kiss. Pulling back, he set her away from him. "I'll be back as soon as I can."

He pulled the door open and slipped outside. Frankie closed the door behind him, leaning her back against it for a moment. Honestly, she didn't mind staying with the girls. Dara was sweet and Bonnie, well, Bonnie reminded her too much of herself at that age for her behavior to really bother her.

If anything, Frankie was tempted to call her own mother and apologize for the way they'd left it last time. Her mother's machinations were annoying, not fatal, but Frankie had lit into her in a way she hadn't since she was Bonnie's age. Frankie knew it was the stress of returning to Atlanta that had driven her to overreact, but her mother didn't know that. Maybe instead of going home, she should pay her mother a visit and explain.

Frankie sighed and pushed off the door, but something made her look upward. Bonnie was standing at the railing to the gallery above, her arms folded and a hostile look in her eyes. How long had she been standing there? Probably long enough to see her father kiss Frankie goodbye. Damn. Frankie had no idea what to say to the girl, but it didn't matter. Bonnie turned, went back to her room and slammed the door.

Once Nelson got to the private hospital he found the appropriate room door and knocked.

A soft voice called, "Come in."

He pushed open the door, surprised to find Sandy the only occupant of the room. He knew Ted wouldn't be there, but maybe one of her sisters or her aunt. He hadn't anticipated this scenario, and for a variety of reasons didn't particularly want to be alone with her. In the garish light of the room she looked pale and tired, and there was a bandage at her temple. Her hair was plaited into one long, dark braid, a style, to his knowledge, she rarely wore. He came to stand at the foot of her bed. "Where's Ted?"

She shook her head, rolling her eyes. "Why do you want to know? Planning to take another swing at him?"

"That was years ago, Sandy. I didn't think he'd leave you here completely alone."

"He knew you were coming. I sent him to the cafeteria. Is that why you really came here? To find out what Ted was doing?"

"The girls wanted a progress report. They're worried about you."

"I see. And what about you? Were you worried?"

She had to be kidding. "You made sure I no longer had that right."

She huffed out an annoyed sigh. "If you're going to be here, Nelson, would you please sit down? You're making my neck hurt."

"I should go, then. Just let me know what to tell the girls."

"Tell them I'm fine and that I'll be home tomorrow morning. But don't go. Actually, I'm glad to have you here alone for a few minutes. I need to talk to you about something."

He pulled the room's one chair over to the bed, figuring she wanted to discuss something about the children. "What is it?"

"Ted and I are getting married in three weeks."

He'd known that had to be coming one of these days, but the fact that she'd waited so long did surprise him. So did the fact that neither of his children had managed to blab that news to him yet. "Why didn't you tell me sooner?"

"We just decided. I haven't even told the girls yet. I would appreciate it if you didn't, either."

He wouldn't dream of it. He knew that both Bonnie and Dara harbored secret hopes that their parents would get back together despite the presence of "Uncle" Ted in their lives. He knew Sandy had never done anything to encourage this fantasy, but it hadn't occurred to him until that moment that his still wearing his wedding ring might have. "You had five years in which to marry the guy. What's the rush?"

"I didn't marry Ted because I didn't see any need. I didn't care about the piece of paper and you were the girls' father. If they needed or wanted anything, you were always there for them. I didn't see any point in confusing things with any stepdad nonsense."

"What changed?"

"I'm pregnant, Nelson. My new child deserves to have a father, too."

Only then did he notice the way in which her hand rested on her stomach, protectively. "How far along are you?"

"About two months. That's why they kept me overnight. I had some spotting. The doctors don't think it's anything but they want to err toward caution."

Lacking a more thoughtful reply, he said, "Congratulations."

"Thanks." She shifted slightly. Her mouth opened as if she were poised to say something more, but she hesitated.

"Tell me."

"Regarding all this, I need to ask you a favor."

"What's that?"

"I want you to give me away."

He burst out laughing at the totally unexpected request. He'd thought she was going to ask him to take the girls so she could honeymoon without them. "How hard did you say you hit your head?"

"I'm serious, Nelson."

"Okay. Then my answer is seriously no. Why don't you ask your father? I'm sure he'll agree this time."

"I'm sure he would if I asked him, but I'm not going to. I wouldn't give him the satisfaction."

She said that with the sort of steel in her eyes and her voice that he knew she meant it. Sandy's father's refusal to participate in or pay for their wedding had been a deliberate and public snub of him. Though Nelson had been annoyed at most by the older man's poor behavior, Sandy had truly been hurt. In the end, Sandy's father had only succeeded in driving a wedge between himself and his daughter.

"Think about it, Nelson. It makes sense. It will be a family celebration. No matter what, you and I will always be family."

"And you wouldn't mind rubbing your old man's nose in it by not asking him."

"There is that, too."

Although there were a million other things he'd rather do, like get zapped with a thousand-watt cattle prod, he said, "Let me think about it."

She nodded. "All right. I promise to live with whatever decision you make."

He stood. "I'd better get back to the girls."

"Kiss me goodbye?"

He moved closer to the bed, leaned down and kissed her forehead. "Take care of yourself."

As he pulled away, she grasped his left hand. Her fingertip touched his wedding band. "Isn't it way past time you took this off?"

If he'd felt a perverse necessity to wear the ring, she'd possessed a perverse need never to acknowledge she knew he wore it. Why did she bring it up now? "Why?"

"Dara doesn't wear perfume and that's not Bonnie's scent tickling my nose."

He grinned because he couldn't help himself. "She's my cousin."

She cast him a skeptical look. "Whatever you say, Nelson. You take care of yourself, too."

He turned to leave, but something Rita Forbes said popped into his mind. "Was I just not worth the trouble?"

Her brow crinkled. "What do you mean?"

"It's something someone said to me recently—why she drifted into an affair. It was too much effort to get her husband to notice her."

She sighed, looking down at her hands. "You were worth the trouble, I just didn't have the stamina."

Now it was his turn to ask. "What does that mean?"

"Two. Four. Nineteen ninety-nine." She drew the numbers in the air with her finger with slashes in the appropriate places. "Do you remember that day?"

As if it were yesterday, but he didn't see the connection. "Of course."

"That's the day I lost you, the day you found out about your father. You changed, not me. You changed toward everyone, except maybe the girls."

What had she expected? He'd discovered on that day that everything he believed about himself was a myth. That had rocked him in ways that he'd never even expressed to her. So, he'd needed time to cope? Wouldn't anyone? "I thought the vows said till death do us part."

"Weren't you dead to me? You shut me out completely. I held on for two years hoping my husband would come back, that man whom I loved and whom I thought loved me. We'd been through so much together, Nelson. And I also know how much you didn't want to be like the men in your family, only around for the short haul. I didn't want to let you go, but I'm human, Nelson.

If I hadn't left, you would have hung in there forever. But that wasn't enough for me. I still needed someone to make me feel like you used to."

"Ted," he said, with more animosity in his voice than he intended.

"Yes, Ted. I know you don't believe this, but there was nothing going on between us while you and I lived under the same roof."

"Nothing physical."

She nodded in a way that told him she got his implication—that they had been emotionally involved long before she left. "I had to make a choice and I made it. If it's any consolation, that was the hardest decision I've ever had to make."

It wasn't, but he appreciated her honesty after all this time. Perhaps if they'd had this conversation years ago, they could have saved themselves a lot of aggravation. Then again, he doubted he'd really been ready before now to address it. He couldn't think of anything that had happened in his life recently to account for that shift in him, aside from Frankie's entrance into it. Maybe some of her courage was rubbing off on him. Considering that she'd been terrified to be left alone with his daughters, it was time he got back to her. That wasn't the only reason he wanted to see her, but it was a good reason to get him out the door.

"I'd better get back to the girls."

She offered him a knowing smile. "The little ones or the big one?"

"They're all little."

"Bring them by the house tomorrow afternoon. All of them."

Now, that would be an event to sell tickets to. The one trait both women shared was an agile tongue—and the willingness to use it. "We'll see."

Nelson went back to his car, started the engine and sat back. He looked down at his left hand resting on the steering wheel and the ring he still wore. He couldn't remember the last time he'd taken it off or if he had taken it off since the day Sandy put it on him. But with the clearing of the air between them, he no longer felt the need to taunt Sandy with its presence. He'd never understood her side of what happened between them. He'd assumed there was only one right side of it, his side. He'd considered the business with his father on a par with his work—which she never asked about and which, for her benefit, he never talked about at home. He hadn't realized how helpless she must have felt reaching out to him and hitting a brick wall.

Whatever, that was over. They all had their choices to make. For now, his choice was to take off the ring, but it wouldn't slide over his knuckle. Judging by how little give there was, he doubted soap and water would help. Just his luck, he was going to have to have the damn thing cut off.

Maybe it was just as well. If he came home without his ring the girls would surely notice and question him about it. Come to think of it, so would Frankie. The girls he could tell to mind their own business; Frankie wouldn't be put off so easily. Since he had no idea how to explain to her the shift in him, he'd rather keep it to himself for the time being.

He put the car into gear, headed out of the parking lot and drove for home. Hopefully, it would still be standing when he got there.

Chapter 4

Chapter 14

For the fourth time in the past fifteen minutes, Frankie checked her watch. Nelson said the trip would only take him an hour, but he'd been gone more than two. Bonnie hadn't come out of her room. Dara, after talking Frankie's ear off and pigging out on popcorn and soda, had fallen asleep with her head in Frankie's lap. Worse yet, Dara had left the remote on the coffee table, which Frankie couldn't reach. One episode of the *That's So Raven* marathon, and every brain cell in her head would probably turn to mush.

So far Bonnie hadn't deigned to make an appearance, not that Frankie really wanted the girl's company. But at least if she showed herself there was the off chance the girl would hand her the remote.

But where the hell was Nelson? Despite his claim that there was no chance of reconciliation between him and his ex-wife, she suspected Nelson still had strong feelings of some kind for her. An indifferent man didn't keep wearing a wedding ring, no matter how wrong-headed he thought his wife was in divorcing him. Most divorced men were more than happy to move on. Some had already moved on, which was the cause of the divorce in the first place.

Either way, as Frankie saw it, it was none of her business. She'd only slept with the man, not pledged her undying love. She didn't deny his long absence rankled—and he would pay for that. But he wasn't her man to keep tabs on. Then again, she wasn't the freaking baby-sitter, either.

The sound of a key turning in the lock of the front door cut short her musings. Frankie hadn't heard Bonnie's door open or the sound of her feet on the stairs, but she launched herself at her father the moment he got the door closed behind him.

"Dad, how's Mom?" she said with an emphasis on the last word, as if to remind all present that such a person existed.

Nelson hugged her back. "She's fine. They're only keeping her overnight." His inquisitive gaze shifted to settle on her. "What were you guys up to before I came in?"

Bonnie cast a worried look at her over her shoulder.

Now Frankie understood Bonnie's haste to get to the door. She wanted to give her father the impression that she hadn't spent the entire time sulking in her room. Frankie didn't see any point in ratting Bonnie out. "Just a little girl talk."

He looked down at Bonnie. "Is that so?"

She nodded vigorously.

"I see," he said, in a way that suggested to Frankie that he wasn't fooled. Bonnie seemed not to notice.

Nelson kissed his daughter's forehead. "It's time you got yourself into bed, young lady. Girl talk is over for tonight."

Nodding, Bonnie pulled away and practically skipped from the room, probably relieved that her father hadn't come home a moment earlier and that Frankie hadn't ratted her out. "Good night, Aunt Frankie," Bonnie called as she headed for the stairs.

Oh, please. "Good night," Frankie called back, but her eyes were on Nelson as he walked toward her.

"I'd better put this one in bed myself." He scooped Dara from her lap. "Don't go anywhere. I'll be right back."

She nodded, but the moment he disappeared up the stairs, she gathered the popcorn and cups from the table and took them to the kitchen. She poured out the cups in the sink and was in the process of emptying the bowl into the trash when she heard Nelson come up behind her.

He wrapped his arms around her and nuzzled her neck. "I thought I asked you to stay where you were."

"You did, but I wanted to clean up."

He took the bowl from her hands and placed it on the counter. "Seriously, did Bonnie spend the whole time in her room?"

No way was she getting in between father and daughter. She turned in his arms to face him. "You'll have to take that up with her."

"I will, right after I take this up with you."

His mouth closed over hers, silencing the word of protest that sprang to her lips. Whatever thoughts she had scattered as she gave herself up to his kiss. Her arms wrapped around his neck as his arms closed more tightly around her waist. She didn't pull away until one of his hands strayed downward to grasp her buttocks.

He looked down at her with an expression of concern in his eyes. "What's the matter, baby?"

"I'd prefer that we didn't do that where your daughter could walk in on us. She's already got me painted as the slut who's sleeping with her father."

He brushed a strand of hair from her face. "Did being with me make you feel that way?"

"Of course not, but I'm a grown-up. I don't see the world in black and white. Girls Bonnie's age do. We've left New York together, what? Three days ago? I may not be a cheap date, but apparently I'm an easy one."

"There is not a damn thing easy about you, Frankie."

She shrugged. "I've got to go. If I'm going to make it to Westchester before the old people go to sleep, I need to leave soon."

"Why don't you stay here tonight and I'll drive you home tomorrow."

Frankie shot him a droll look. "Did we not just discuss that?"

"I was planning on giving you my bedroom while I risked my sacroiliac on the lumpy sofa in my office."

Honestly, she'd figured as much. Despite the kiss he'd just laid on her, she figured him as too circumspect a man to flaunt his sex life in front of his daughters.

"Maybe you'd better show me to this bedroom before we get ourselves in any more trouble."

His bedroom was the first door on the left at the top of the landing. When they got to the door, Nelson flicked on the light. The room was large, dominated by heavy wood furniture, particularly a king-size bed with dark blue bedding. "You've got your own bathroom in here with enough towels if the girls haven't stolen them."

She stepped over the threshold and turned to face him. "Thanks."

"See you in the morning."

That's what he said, but he made no move to leave her. For one electric moment their gazes locked. She knew what was in his mind, because it was in her mind, too, and in her body—a tempest of want unsatisfied by the fact that she was trying to do the right thing.

Nelson broke the stalemate, stepping far enough into the room to kick the door closed behind him. He reached for her and pulled her to him. For a long time he simply held her, his hands roving over her back in a soothing fashion. She rested her cheek against his chest and her fingers curled around his arms, nestling into the sensual embrace. After a moment she heard Nelson chuckle.

"What's so funny?"

"How things have changed. The last time I had to sneak around to be with a woman, it was so her parents wouldn't find out. Now I have to worry about my kids." His hand strayed over her hair, setting off tiny sparks along her scalp. "I'm sorry, baby."

She lifted her head from his shoulder to look up at him. "For what?"

"Dragging you back here. Leaving you with the girls. I know you were intent on seeing Parker today."

Harlan Jacobs had spent nearly a year in jail. He'd keep another day. "I was mentally sticking a voodoo doll of you with pins for taking so long…."

"It hadn't occurred to me when I made the promise to be back in an hour that I was going to hit rush hour traffic on the way out there."

"It's all right, really. But I do want to get back tomorrow."

"Not a problem. I've already asked my mother to drive us back to the airport whenever we're ready. I thought you wanted to see your mom, though."

"I'll call her instead and see what flights are leaving tomorrow morning."

"Fine." He grinned down at her. "By the way, there's something I've been meaning to ask you all day."

Her eyes narrowed, considering him. "What's that?"

His finger traced the path of her scoop neckline. "Where did you get this dress?"

Despite Nelson's directive to hurry, she'd dressed with care that morning. She knew she'd be meeting Nelson's family. She didn't mind embarrassing herself with outlandish outfits, but she didn't want to embarrass him. The short-sleeved, salmon-colored dress she had on fit tight at the bodice and flared into a long skirt that ended mid-calf. "A gift from my mother. Why?"

He lifted one shoulder in a shrug. "It doesn't suit you."

His hand drifted down to cover her breast. Her breath caught and escaped slowly on a sigh. She covered his hand with hers as a means of restraint. "Nelson, behave yourself."

His hand stilled, but his thumb strummed against her nipple. "I am behaving myself, or I'd already have you out of that dress and whatever else you've got on under it, and you know it. By the way, what do you have on under there?" He hooked a finger under her neckline in a way that exposed her cleavage and the peach-colored lace bra she wore. He rubbed the backs of his fingers along the swell of her breast. "Have mercy."

She affected a disgruntled groan, but truthfully she liked him like this, both playful and intent, or at least the look in his dark eyes was intense.

"What?"

She shrugged. "I was thinking that you and Dara are the only two people in your family I've met with such dark, dark eyes. Does that come from your father's side of the family?"

"Something like that." And suddenly the playfulness was gone and only the intensity remained. "Now, I know it's time for me to let you sleep if we're going to start picking leaves off each other's family trees." He kissed her briefly in a way that satisfied neither of them and set her away from him. "I'll see you in the morning."

This time there was no hesitation in him. He opened the door, stepped out into the hall and closed the door behind him.

For a moment, Frankie stood in the center of the floor where he'd left her staring at the door. She'd once accused him of being able to clear a room. Tonight she wasn't doing so bad in that department, either. At first, all she could wonder was what exactly did she say to cause that reaction. Then she remembered a conversation she'd had with her sister-in-law, Nina, after her brother had gone missing. Some punks had actually waylaid him trying to steal his motorcycle. But Nina had been convinced that, after their first fight during the marriage, he'd left her.

According to Nina, all the men in her parents' generation abandoned their women by one of the three *D*s: death, divorce or desertion. She didn't know which of the three choices Nelson's father might be guilty of, but she was certain now it was one of them. Which made it insensitive of her to bring up the topic in the first place. "Way to go, Frankie," she said aloud.

Shaking her head, she pulled out her cell phone and dialed her mother's number. Time to see how many folks she could alienate in one day.

Margaret Hairston answered on the third ring. "Hello."

Lacking any better intro, she said, "Hi, Mom."

"Francesca is that you?"

"How many daughters do you have?"

"Two, including your sister-in-law."

Frankie shook her head. She'd have to give that round to her mother. But Frankie wasn't interested in fighting. She just didn't want to leave her mother with the impression that she was deliberately slighting her by not visiting while she was in town. "About the car—"

"Before you light into me about that, it wasn't my idea. That was all that was available on such short notice."

"I was going to say thank you."

"Oh." There was a brief pause. "Are you all right?"

Frankie almost laughed at the implication in her mother's words: if she wasn't being contentious there must be something wrong with her. "I'm fine, Mom." Frankie inhaled, drawing in strength. "I have some things to tell you that I need to say in person, but I just wanted you to know that I'm okay. I have to go back to Atlanta in the morning, that's why I didn't come by. We only came in because Nelson's daughters were in a car accident."

"I heard. How are they?"

"Fine."

"And Nelson?"

Frankie sighed. She knew what her mother was asking—had anything developed between the two of them. Even if Frankie wanted to confide the details of her relationship with Nelson she had no words to describe it. She appreciated his protectiveness and his acerbic humor. She admired his devotion to his family, including the woman who divorced him. Her body quickened every time she thought about being in his arms last night. Were it not for his daughters, she was certain she'd be in his arms right now and loving every minute of it. If she didn't know herself better, she might worry about losing her heart, but thankfully she did. "He's fine, too," she said finally.

"Mmm hmm" was her mother's only response.

Frankie sighed. She was definitely going to have to work on being less transparent. Or maybe she wasn't the problem. "How did you find out about the accident?"

"Nelson's mother called me this afternoon."

Which probably meant after they'd picked up the girls. Terrific.

"If you ask me, it's about time, and not because of the inheritance. You're a beautiful young woman, Frankie, that is when you're not dressing like the Scourge of Scarsdale."

Frankie supposed that was the closest to a full-out compliment as she was ever going to get from her mother. "Thank you."

"Whatever it is you're up to, be careful."

Something about her mother's tone made her question whether she was talking about her being with Nelson or the reason she was going back to Atlanta. For the first time she wondered how much her mother knew or if she knew anything "I'll call you when I get back to the city."

Frankie disconnected the call and returned her phone to her pocket. For once she'd had a completely civil conversation with her mother. What was next? World peace? Probably not quite yet. In the interim, a nice hot shower would have to do.

After he left Frankie, Nelson went to the bathroom down the hall and splashed some cold water on his face. It didn't do anything to cool the anger that burned in him at the moment, the same rage that overtook him every time he thought of the man who'd donated half his genetic makeup to him. When Frankie asked about his father, undoubtedly she knew nothing of him, only the man who'd married his mother and given him his last name, but little else. Though Effraim Santiago had walked out on her six years into their marriage, his mother still kept their wedding picture on her piano as if he were some beloved gone missing. Maybe he had been at one point; Nelson had been too young to remember anything but the fighting.

Thank God Frankie hadn't ventured into his mother's living room, or she would have known he'd lied to her. Knowing what he did about her, he wouldn't tell her the truth. And with Frankie that meant nipping any conversation as it began at the bud. She was far too inquisitive and perceptive to let her get a good hold on a subject. He hadn't planned on leaving her the way he had tonight, but all things considered it was probably better that way.

He dried his face, folded the towel and put it back where it belonged. Now he had another female to contend with. He'd noticed the light on under Bonnie's door. He didn't know what had gotten into her the past few days, but he couldn't miss her attempts to focus his attention on her. She wanted something from him, though he wasn't entirely sure what. He supposed it hadn't helped much for him to come home with Frankie in tow, another person to distract him from her.

Looking back, he probably should have taken Frankie to her mother's and spared her Bonnie's rudeness, but there was nothing he could do about that now. But he did intend to find out what Bonnie's problem was. Tonight.

He went to her door and knocked. "Who is it?" she called back.

He answered her as he had when she was a child, figuring a dose of humor might serve him better than a straight answer. "It's the plumber. I've come to fix the sink."

Bonnie pulled the door open a second later. "That is so old, Dad," she said, but there was a smile on her face.

"Can I come in?"

She shrugged, but she moved to the side to let him in. "Don't fuss because it's messy."

Nelson looked around his daughter's room, decorated in a warm pink and white. If there was anything out of place, he couldn't identify it. Bonnie was the only child he knew who never had to be told to clean her room. Dara, on the other hand, could sometimes be a little piglet.

Bonnie closed the door and turned to face him. "So what do you want to talk about, Dad?"

Nelson smiled to himself. He recognized that "everything is so cool and I am so not nervous you showed up in my room for no reason" tone of voice that hadn't fooled him once. Since there wasn't a chair in the room that would survive him sitting on it, he took a spot on the edge of her bed. "Sit."

She did so hesitantly, sitting as far away from him as possible without making the distance between them seem abnormal. "What do you want to talk about?"

"First, if you wanted to stay up here in your room in a snit, that's fine, but don't try to convince me that's not what you did."

"She told you that, didn't she?"

"*She* has a name and *she* didn't tell me anything. *She* said I should talk to *you*."

"Oh."

"Aside from that, according to Dara, you've been a real, and I quote, tremendous pain in the ass."

"Dara's not supposed to say *ass*."

"Neither are you. So what's the deal?"

Bonnie shrugged. "I don't know."

Nelson ground his teeth together. If he had a dollar for every time she said that he'd out-Trump Trump. Knowing his daughter, there were only a few possible sources for her sour mood. "How are you getting along with your mother?"

Bonnie shrugged. "Okay, I guess. She only has time for Uncle Ted now and she sleeps a lot."

Given Sandy's pregnancy that news didn't surprise him much. Since he'd promised not to say anything, he didn't, but he was grateful his daughter wasn't sophisticated enough to figure it out for herself. Or maybe she considered both her parents too old and dried up for babies to be a possibility. That also explained why Bonnie hadn't turned to her mother for advice in his absence.

"What about that boy who came around here, Flake?"

Bonnie rolled her eyes, but there was a hint of a smile on her lips. "His name was Blake, Dad. And he's history."

Not that Nelson considered that a bad thing, but he noticed the quiet way Bonnie had spoken that last sentence. It was a big deal to her. "What happened?"

"We are definitely not going there, Dad. Just forget it."

Yeah, right. If Bonnie really didn't want to talk about it, she'd have said he was a jerk or made something up. "I want to know."

Bonnie sighed. "If you must know, he dumped me. For some stupid girl with three rings in her eyebrow. *She*—" Bonnie paused as if searching for the right words "—doesn't say no."

Nelson exhaled, not realizing until that moment he'd been holding his breath. There were so many worse things she could have said, though suffering one's first heartbreak was bad enough.

"Come here, sweetheart," he said, though he was the one to move closer. He put his arm around her shoulders. "I'm sorry."

She leaned her head on his shoulder. "Why are guys such jerks?"

"You want the short list or the long one?"

"Da-ad," she protested, but he could hear the humor in her voice.

"Can I ask you something?"

She shrugged.

He'd probably be sorry to open this can of worms, but the one time he'd seen Bonnie with this boy she'd seemed to really like him. "Why did you say no?"

"Isn't that what I'm supposed to say?"

"Yes, but why did you?"

"I told him it was because if you found out you'd kill me, kill him and then come back and kill me some more."

Damn straight. "But…"

"But the only reason why he even brought it up was because his cousin was ragging on him saying he wasn't a man because he hadn't done it yet. His cousin is twenty-three and he already has two kids he doesn't support." She sighed. "You're the one who always said that I shouldn't say yes until I'm ready."

"Who'd have thought you paid that much attention to what I said?" He ruffled her hair. "I'm still sorry."

"Me, too."

"I've got to go back to Atlanta with Frankie tomorrow. Are you going to be okay?"

She nodded. "I'll be nice to Dara, too," she said, as if she expected that to be his next question.

"You owe Frankie an apology, too."

"Why, because she's your girlfriend?"

"Because you put her in the position of having to lie for you. And she's not my girlfriend."

"I saw you two kissing."

Despite what Frankie said, that thought hadn't occurred to him. How was he supposed to explain the politics of a sexual relationship to the woman/child that was his daughter? "It's complicated."

He kissed her temple and stood before she thought of any other questions to ask him. As he walked to the door, he said, "Get some sleep. No watching television all night." He'd just gotten the door open when she called to him. He turned to glance at her over his shoulder. "Yes?"

She was leaning back, both hands braced on the bed beside her. "You know, Mom has Uncle Ted. I guess it wouldn't be such a bad thing if you had someone, too."

Nelson shook his head. Maybe his little girl was growing up after all.

It wasn't until after Frankie took a long, soothing shower that she realized two things: Nelson had brought up her bag and left it just inside the door, and she'd neglected to pack anything vaguely resembling pajamas. She'd planned on spending the night either in her own apartment or at her parents' house. At home she wouldn't mind sleeping in the nude, and at her parents' house she already had adequate sleeping attire. She didn't think Nelson would mind her borrowing one of his shirts under the circumstances. She got a T-shirt from one of his drawers, tugged it on and got into bed.

Despite her fatigue sleep didn't come. She checked the clock beside Nelson's bed. She felt like she'd been awake for years, but it was still only a little past eleven. Robert would still be up, watching the nightly news. She didn't need to see him face-to-face to give him the information she'd discovered. She got out her cell phone and dialed his number.

"Frankie, where are you?" he asked once he recognized her voice. "I've been calling your house all day."

"I'm back in New York. Family emergency." She didn't figure he needed to know whose family. "I'll be back tomorrow. That's what I w—"

He cut her off before she could tell him what she and Nelson had found out. "I wish you'd let me know before you left. As it turns out, I won't be needing you to testify."

"Why not?" Frankie asked, hoping he'd finally come to his senses and believed his sister.

"For one thing, there isn't going to be a trial. I thought I should tell you before you heard it somewhere else. Harlan Jacobs is dead. He killed himself in his cell last night."

Chapter 15

Sitting in the aisle seat this time on the way back to Atlanta, Nelson squeezed Frankie's hand. She'd spent most of their time in the air staring out the window, pensive, quiet. Remembering the trip to New York, they seemed to have switched their moods as well as their seat assignments. "What's so fascinating out there?"

She turned her head to look at him. "Nothing, really. I was just thinking."

That's what he was afraid of. When she gave him the news that morning that Jacobs was dead, part of him had felt relief. That definitely took her out of the picture if there was no longer a trial in which to testify. He would have thought that knowing her role in this was over would have made things easier. But it didn't. In his mind, that could only mean trouble. His plan was still to take her home, collect their things and drive back. How co-operative Frankie would be was yet to be determined.

He rubbed his thumb across her knuckles. "What were you thinking?"

"For one thing, Jacobs's suicide doesn't make any sense. If he knew his brother had contacted us and that we believed Rita's story, why, after all this time, would he suddenly decide to kill himself? Wouldn't he have at least waited to see what we found out?"

Nelson shrugged. "Maybe he didn't know." That's one question Nelson hadn't bothered to ask. "Haven't you ever snuck behind a loved one's back to do something for their own good?"

"Me? No. I usually sneak right in front of people's faces. Saves a lot of wear and tear on having to admit you're responsible later."

"Even if he did know, he also didn't want Parker's sister involved. Maybe this was his way of making sure she wasn't."

"That's if he really did kill himself in the first place."

That was the conclusion he'd dreaded her reaching. If someone had helped Jacobs commit suicide, that was all the more reason why he wanted to keep her out of it. Let the local folks sort it out, if they were so inclined. But the way Frankie relayed the information Parker had given her, the fact that the man died by his own hand had so far gone unquestioned.

But he knew Frankie's concern centered less on fer-reting out the guilty party than preserving her own safety. His only hope was that an appeal to logic would mollify her. "Think of what you're suggesting. Anyone

who might have killed Jacobs needed not only motivation but access. They don't let just anyone stroll into jail
in the middle of the night."

"I know that. Maybe I'm just grasping at straws, but
nothing about this feels right."

It didn't feel right to him, either, but he couldn't say
what precisely about the situation made him feel that
way. "I take it you want to make Parker our first stop."

Frankie shook her head. "There's someone I need to
see before that."

Myron met them at the airport, driving Nelson's car.
It didn't escape Nelson's attention that Myron was
wearing a blue work shirt and pants made of the same
type of fabric discovered at the crime scenes. A patch
over his breast pocket contained the logo of the garage
he worked for and his name written in red script letters.

Myron had been wearing a similar dark shirt the
night in the club, but the room had been too dark for him
to notice much other than that. As they drove, Nelson
eyed Myron in the rearview mirror. The kid was certainly strong enough to have committed the murders, but
assuming what Frankie remembered about her attack
was true, Myron was one thing the killer was not—
black. They dropped Myron off at his job before heading
off to Frankie's true destination—Rita Forbes's house.

Instead of being greeted by the maid, the door was
opened to them by a light-skinned black man of average
height and cultured appearance. Nelson pegged him as
Mr. Forbes before the man said a word.

"Francesca. What brings you here?"

Despite the benign expression on his face, there was something in the man's eyes that said if he didn't know about his wife's infidelity before, he did now. Nelson felt for him. In his own way, he'd been there, too.

Frankie said, "I was hoping to see Rita."

"She's in the parlor. I'm sure you know the way there."

Alvin Forbes moved off as they headed down the hall, perhaps wisely deciding not to join them.

Rita was sitting on a settee by the window, staring out at the remnants of afternoon sunshine. When Frankie called her name, she took a moment to dab at her eyes before rising to greet them. Or rather to greet Frankie. He might as well have been a piece of furniture for all either woman noticed him. That didn't bother him. He had nothing to say to her, anyway. Not that he didn't feel for her, but he didn't know her well enough to be of any use.

While the two women settled on the sofa, he sat in the chair he'd taken before. For a while he glanced out the window at the azure, cloudless sky, tuning out the women's conversation until Rita said, "Harlan did not kill himself. You've got to know that Frankie. After you left him, his brother went to see him. The sheriff told me it was the first time in a long time Harlan had seemed to have any hope. Why would he take his own life if he thought you would help him?"

"I don't know," Frankie said in a calm voice.

"The papers are calling him the murderer, as if his death proves he was guilty." Rita pulled in a deep breath. "Alvin knows. Until this point he didn't have any idea."

In Rita's voice he detected both disappointment and anger. She'd thought he'd known and suffered in silence, which probably pleased her to some degree. Her anger probably came from her husband's cluelessness about her unhappiness.

"What are you going to do?"

"I don't know. Alvin's only concern seems to be if the neighbors get wind of it. But I will be at the funeral whenever it's arranged."

Frankie nodded and stood. "I'll keep in touch. You take care of yourself."

Rita stood and embraced her. "Thanks for coming." For the first time Rita looked at Nelson. "Both of you."

Nelson followed Frankie's lead out of the room. Once they were back in the car, Frankie rested her elbow on the door frame and leaned her cheek against her palm. "This just gets better and better."

He laid his palm on her thigh. "She got to you?"

Frankie nodded. "I'm no fan of adultery. Seems like you should be able to finish with one man before you start on another. But she's in real pain, whether in some ways she brought it on herself or not. I would never tell her this, but Robert suspected that not all of Alvin's business trips were related to his business."

Nelson didn't know what to say to that, so he said nothing. He started the engine and put the car in gear. "Off to Parker's?" he asked.

She shrugged. "Why not? How much worse can this day get?"

"I thought I told you I didn't need you to rush back" was the first thing Robert said to Frankie when they turned up in his office.

Frankie had called from the road to find out if Robert was in his office. His secretary had warned her he was on his way out the door to a court appearance, but she might be able to catch him if she hurried. They'd pulled up in front of the building five minutes later. Robert had been in the process of loading files into his trial bag when they came in.

Now he looked from her to Nelson then back to her, as if assessing the possibility of ousting them both from his office. He sighed and his shoulders drooped, as if in defeat. "I'm late for court."

She slipped into one of his visitor's chairs while Nelson stood in roughly the same spot he'd taken before. "We just came from your sister's house."

"Then I can imagine the stories she's been feeding you. And before we go any further, let me tell you I checked on Jacobs already. He was alone in his cell two nights ago. He had no visitors except his own brother. Just like I told you over the phone. The man killed himself."

She said nothing at first, taking a moment to assess the man in front of her. He seemed almost happy to report those facts to her. From someone else, that emotion might not have surprised her. If Jacobs were truly guilty, any reasonable person might well feel that justice of a kind had been served. But she knew Robert better than that. He took no pride in dealing criminals their just deserts; he liked to win. For him, Jacobs's death offered no real victory, at least not a legal one. His only triumph was in getting rid of the one man who could damage his reputation. She'd always known Robert was shallow and self-absorbed, but this degree of callousness she hadn't expected.

"What if he wasn't guilty?"

Robert offered a brief, scoffing laugh. "Rita really got to you, didn't she?"

She'd already acknowledged that to Nelson, but not in the way Robert meant. "Would it change your mind to know he was incapable of committing the crimes?"

"According to whom?"

"A woman who works at a club called Tara."

"You want me to take a hooker's word for it?"

"Who better to know? All I'm asking you to do is look into it."

Robert snapped his briefcase shut. "Look, Frankie, the man is dead, the case is closed and I've got to go. I trust you and your friend can see yourselves out of my office." He rounded the desk and left.

Frustrated, Frankie looked at Nelson. He wore a lopsided grin. "This really must be one hell of a boring town."

"Shut up," she said, but couldn't keep the laughter from her voice. At the moment she was having a hard time figuring out why she'd wasted so much time with Robert herself. "What do we do now?"

"How about some dinner?"

Her stomach rumbled her acquiescence, but her heart wasn't in it. They drove to a restaurant near her house. Yet most of the good Southern cooking still lay on her plate by the time Nelson finished his.

"I think I'd better take you home," Nelson said, eyeing her plate. "We'll regroup tonight and figure out what we're doing tomorrow."

That sounded like a plan to her, considering that she

was tired and disheartened by all that had happened. Maybe one night not thinking about those girls would do her some good.

But when they pulled up in front of her house, the first thing she noticed was that her porch light was on, not the way she left it.

"What's the matter?"

"You didn't leave the porch light on, did you?"

"I don't even know where the switch is. You sure Rachel didn't turn it on for you?"

"She never has before."

"Wait here."

Hearing the ominous tone of his voice and seeing the hard look that came into his eyes, for once she was going to do as he was told. She watched silently as he got out of the car and headed up the front steps. At the top, he stooped down, for what purpose she couldn't tell. When he stood up, he circled around one side of her house, emerging a few minutes later on the other side. At least he hadn't found anyone lurking in her bushes. But what had he found?

He didn't answer that question when he walked back to the car a few minutes later, motioning for her to roll down the window. As she did so, he said, "Give me your keys."

She handed them to him. "What's going on?"

He didn't answer her, just motioned for her to roll the window back up. He was gone before she complied. Obviously, he intended to check the house before he allowed her to enter it. That was fine with her, but did the man have to be so cryptic? He probably thought so, since thus far keeping her in the dark had proved the only way to get her to do what he wanted.

But truthfully, if there was any danger to be found, she didn't want him in there, either. She didn't want him risking his safety on her account, though that's the deal he'd agreed to when they started this. She wanted him whole, in one piece and in her bed tonight, even if that arrangement wasn't permanent. She'd deal with that when she had to. Thankfully, that time wasn't now.

When she noticed him coming back for her, she switched off the engine and got out of the car. She tossed his keys to him. "So what was so exciting up on my front porch?"

"Some Romeo sent you flowers."

Was that a note of jealousy she heard in his voice or was that her imagination working overtime? "Some Romeo? There wasn't a card?"

"It wasn't addressed to me."

When she saw the flowers she didn't have to guess who'd sent them. Two dozen roses arranged in a faux crystal vase sent from a florist in Atlanta. "They're from Robert, probably as an apology for being rude this afternoon. That's what he usually sends when he gets on my nerves."

Nelson lifted the vase. "I didn't think you'd be the type to be won over with flowers."

"I'm not." She pushed open the door and held it for him to enter.

"Where do you want these?"

"I'd say the trash, except I don't see the point in

letting beautiful flowers go to waste. How about the dining room table."

She followed Nelson to the other room. Once he set the flowers down, she removed the plastic covering, including the card, and tossed it into the garbage in the kitchen. That done, she turned to face him.

He stood with his back against the counter, his arms crossed. "Feel better now?"

"No." She walked toward him. As she did so, his arms opened to welcome her. She stepped into his embrace and wrapped her arms around his neck. She laid her cheek on his chest as his arms closed more tightly around her.

For a long moment, she simply enjoyed being held by him, basking in the warmth of his big body, inhaling the woodsy remnants of his cologne mingled with his own natural scent. One of his hands rose to tangle in her hair. His breath fanned her cheek as he leaned down to whisper, "How about now."

She gave a contented *mmm* of an answer, not quite trusting her voice. If anyone had told her a week ago she'd seek comfort in this man's arms, or any man's arms for that matter, she'd have told them they were nuts. She'd never leaned on a man for anything, not even Robert. At the moment, it didn't seem like such a bad deal.

"Ready to call it a night?"

She pulled back enough to see his face. The intense expression in his eyes belied the smile on his lips. He wanted her, which was okay since she wanted him, too. But something in her, maybe as a reaction to the intimacy they'd shared, couldn't resist teasing him. "I always thought barbarians just clubbed you over the head and dragged you off to their lair. Must have been mistaken."

"If that's what you want…" He trailed off as he bent to lift her over his shoulder.

She shrieked and hit him. "You know I didn't mean that."

He swatted her backside. "Keep still before you make me drop you." Once they got to her room, he set her down slowly, letting her body slide down his own. His mouth found hers even before she gained her feet. His tongue plunged into her mouth, seeking hers.

With a sigh, she gave herself up to his kiss. If the embrace downstairs had been about quiet intimacy and succor, this one was about heat and pent-up passion. They tore at each other's clothes until they all lay strewn on the floor. She lay on the bed and pulled him down on top of her.

Bracing his forearms on either side of her, he leaned down to trail a path of moist kisses along her throat and shoulder. She squirmed beneath him, wanting, needing more.

"Easy, baby," he whispered against her ear.

Slowly, he moved down her body, pleasuring her with his hands, his mouth, his tongue. Finally he settled between her thighs, hooking her legs over his shoulders. He parted her with his fingers and brought his mouth down to her. His tongue circled over her sensitive flesh, making her moan and buck her hips against him. He drew her clitoris into his mouth and sucked hard, and she gasped at the sheer pleasure of it. Already, she wasn't far from coming. Her legs shook with tiny tremors and her belly quickened.

When he slid two fingers inside her, she lost it, bucking against him, calling his name, as ecstasy exploded inside her. Only once she started to subside did Nelson lie down beside her and pull her to him. She wound one arm around his back and buried her face against his neck.

One of his hands stroked her back. "Are you all right?"

She smiled. "I am so much more than all right."

He chuckled and hugged her to him. "Think you can handle some more?"

"Bring it on, baby. Bring it on." She ran her hand down his body to circle her fingers around his shaft. Hearing his answering groan brought a smile to her lips.

His fingertips skimmed her cheekbone and he regarded her through half-closed eyes. "You're enjoying yourself."

She was, but not entirely the way he meant. She sure didn't mind knowing her touch could arouse him the way his did to her. But more than that, she felt as if she were reclaiming a bit of her sexual identity, coming back into herself. She was no delicate flower in bed, as she had been with him the first night they were together. It gratified her to know that that side of her was still intact. Her grin turned impish. "You want me to stop?"

"Hell, no."

Chuckling, she lifted herself onto her knees, leaned over him and took him into her mouth. His breath sucked in and his hips rocked toward her. She took him deeper into her mouth and sucked hard. He groaned again, this time carrying her name with it. She smiled again, relishing having this big, strong man at her mercy.

But his hands went to her shoulders. "I want to be inside you."

She didn't mind giving him what he wanted. She got a condom from her nightstand and rolled it onto him. Straddling his body, she took him inside her, her body shivering at the intimate contact.

"Come here, baby," he said, drawing her down to him with his hands low on her back. She lowered her mouth to his as their bodies set a slow, sensual rhythm. His tongue met hers for a dance as languid and heady as the rest of their lovemaking.

When they finally drew apart, she sat up, bracing her hands on his chest. Both their bodies were moist with perspiration, and when she inhaled she breathed in the stimulating aroma of their lovemaking. His hands covered her breasts, to mold the soft flesh in his palms. He leaned up to take one nipple into his mouth and then the other, then both together. It was too much. She moaned his name and her fingertips dug into the flesh at his shoulders.

He sat up, bringing their bodies flush. She wrapped her legs around his waist and buried her face against his shoulder. His hands roved over her back and lower to grasp her hips to position her so that he could thrust into her. But the time for slow and easy had passed for both of them. She met each of his thrusts with one of her own, taking him deeper inside her body. Beyond all thought and reason, she called his name as her orgasm overtook her, arching her back and sending wave after wave of pleasure coursing through her. And then his arms tightened around her and his body shuddered. He groaned his own release out next to her ear.

For a long moment, they clung together, recovering. One of his hands tangled in her hair, pulling her head back so he could look at her. "Are you all right?"

The look in his dark eyes didn't tell her if he was concerned for her or fishing for compliments. Considering he was a man, it was probably the latter. "That was...I don't know if there's a word for how good that was."

He tucked a strand of her hair behind her ear. "I agree with you, but that's not what I was asking."

His concern touched her more than she thought it would. She buried her face against his neck. "I'm fine, Nelson. I told you that you didn't have to worry about me."

"You let me worry about what I'm going to worry about."

"Yes, sir," she teased.

He swatted her bottom. "We'd better get some sleep if we plan to get anything done tomorrow."

She nodded. Her body was sated and tired. But as they settled beneath the covers, sleep didn't claim her. Once she was certain Nelson slept, she got out of bed and headed down to the kitchen. Maybe a cup of tea would make her drowsy enough to fall asleep.

She brewed the tea and drank it at the kitchen table. But when she went to dispose of the tea bag, the sight of Robert's card in the trash caught her eye. She hadn't bothered to read it since she assumed it was some clumsy attempt to get her back. He'd never mentioned renewing their relationship, but she knew him. She knew he didn't believe that Nelson was her cousin. She'd seen it in his eyes that afternoon. Even if he had no interest in her, seeing her with another man was enough to spark the competitiveness in his nature. If he couldn't win, he'd make damn sure no one else did, either.

Her impression of him deepened once she read the one sentence written on the card in Robert's handwriting: *Maybe you should ask your friend why he really left the NYPD.*

Chapter 16

Nelson woke early the next morning to find Frankie still asleep in his arms. Her head rested on his shoulder, her mouth slightly open and her leg draped over his. Her hand rested low enough on his belly to be a distraction. He moved it farther up, to his chest, and left it there. She mumbled something in her sleep but didn't waken.

He leaned down and placed a single kiss on her forehead, a symbol of his affection for her. *Affection* wasn't the right word for what he felt, though he didn't have one to replace it in his mind. He wasn't ready yet to call it what he probably should: love, or the beginnings of it, anyway.

He wasn't afraid to admit she got to him in ways even Sandy never had. Raised both Catholic and very conservatively, Sandy had expected him to be the man, always, the final arbiter in their lives, the pants wearer. Frankie, on the other hand, he had to fight at every turn, and in a crazy way, he preferred that. Sandy wouldn't have thought twice about him entering a dangerous situation for her protection, but he'd seen the expression on Frankie's face as he got out of the car. She was worried for him, not herself. He should probably be offended by her insinuation that he couldn't take care of himself, but he wasn't.

As Frankie's hand drifted lower on his body, it occurred to him that Sandy would never have been the aggressor in bed, either, and fellatio ranked as the eighth deadly sin. He wondered briefly if Sandy enjoyed the same type of relationship with Ted as she had with him, but he doubted it. There seemed to be egalitarianism between them that had never existed in his marriage to Sandy. Besides, there was no way in hell the Sandy he'd married would ever have lived with him sans the "piece of paper" as she called it.

Obviously, she'd changed and found what it took to make her happy. Even now, he found himself stuck in neutral, unable to go back and afraid to move forward. He understood that now. That's what the whole ring thing had been about. As long as he clung to the past he didn't have to face what came next.

He wasn't sure what the future held, but he knew it would never include the woman in his arms if he didn't come clean with her. Not that he wanted to, but he knew if he didn't tell her, her son-of-a-bitch ex-boyfriend would. He hadn't exactly lied to her when she asked him if he read the card, but he hadn't been honest, either. He should have known the minute Parker referred to him as Frankie's friend, not her cousin, that the man had checked him out and found out whatever dirt he could. There wasn't much, but what was there was enough.

She stirred in his arms, whimpering, her hands balling into fists. Probably another of the nightmares she told him about had her in its grip. He shook her shoulder to wake her. She responded by lashing out at him, striking him. He didn't want to hurt her, but, damn, she was strong. Since all else failed, he rolled over on top of her, trapping her hands between them. Still she struggled underneath him.

"Frankie, wake up," he said in a sharp voice. "It's me, Nelson."

Instantly, she stilled. Her eyes opened, the expression in them vague and terrified until her gaze focused on his face. She let out a sigh of relief mixed with another emotion he didn't understand. Her eyes drifted shut. "I'm okay now. You can quit smothering me."

He eased off of her onto his side so that he could look down at her.

She put her hands in her hair and tugged. "God, I thought these things would be over by now. Isn't that how it's supposed to work? You face the thing you fear and all the goblins go away?"

He scrubbed his hand over her stomach. He heard the frustration in her voice laced with a kind of self-deprecating humor. "You thought you'd sleep with me a couple of times and your nightmares would go away? I'm flattered."

She lifted one hand and hit him on the shoulder. "No,

Mr. Egotist, I was just starting to feel so, I don't know, normal. Normal for me, anyway."

"Every wound takes time to heal, baby. You know that. I wouldn't mind so much if your idea of recovery wasn't socking me in the jaw every morning."

Her wide-eyed gaze flew to his face. "Did I hurt you?"

"Maybe a little." He pointed to the spot where she'd struck him. "Here."

She cast him a skeptical look. Smart woman, since she hadn't really hurt him at all. Still, she took his face in her hands and brought his face down to kiss his jaw. "Better?"

"Mmm. And I've got a few other spots that need attention, too."

Later, after they made it out of the bed and into the shower, Nelson went back to his room to dress. Neither of them had discussed what their plan of action would be. He supposed that conversation awaited once he arrived in the kitchen. Though it was still before seven, he dialed Don's home number. He might not get another opportunity to call without her overhearing him, and he didn't want her to know what he was up to until he'd explained it to her. Knowing her loyalty to those around her, she probably wouldn't believe what he suspected, anyway.

Don picked up on the fourth ring and issued a sleepy "Meyer."

"Sorry to wake you, but I need some more of your expertise."

Don groaned, accompanied by the sound of rustling sheets. "In other words, you need another favor."

"Something like that."

"Shoot."

"What do you know about Myron Gibbs?"

"The kid that lives across the street from Ms. Hairston? He paying her too much attention?"

Nelson snorted at both Don's reference to a man in his mid-twenties as a kid and the assumption he heard in Don's voice that the call for information had been fueled by jealousy. Nelson hadn't bothered to feed Don the cousin story, and when the older man had assumed a more personal reason for his involvement, Nelson hadn't bothered to correct him. He figured Don would be more willing to help a friend's woman than to offer assistance to a woman who'd blackmailed said friend into cooperation.

In answer to Don's question, he said, "Nothing like that. I was just wondering if he was ever looked at in terms of the murders. I saw him at Tara the other night, which means he could have known a couple of the girls."

"I see."

What Don had enough tact not to ask was what he'd been doing out there, which saved him from having to disclose that Frankie had been with him. "Was he looked at?"

"I don't know. The only two people who'd ever been considered seriously were the first girl's boyfriend and Jacobs. Now that the case is considered closed, a few folks might be more willing to talk. Call me back this afternoon."

"Will do." Although Don agreed to help, Nelson also heard in his friend's voice the sort of skepticism of one roped into a fool's mission. He recognized that tone. It was the same one he'd used when trying to convince Frankie not to come here in the first place. She wasn't wrong, though, and he doubted he was, either. Still, he was grateful for whatever assistance Don was willing to give him. "Thanks, buddy," he said, and disconnected the call.

Frankie was brewing coffee by the time he made it down to the kitchen. She glanced at him over her shoulder. "And they say women take a long time getting ready. You don't even have an excuse since you don't exactly color coordinate."

It was the second time she'd ragged on him about his black-on-black wardrobe. "Does that bother you?"

"Not at all, though the color does bring out the blood-shot in your eyes."

He chuckled as he accepted a mug of black coffee from her. He was certain she hadn't gotten much more sleep than he had, but neither her eyes nor her manner reflected that. She wore a pale peach sundress that molded to her curves. He wondered why, given the shapeliness of her legs, she didn't prefer shorter skirts. Like most of the other dresses he'd seen her in, this one ended at her calves.

"What? You don't like?" She turned around in a way designed to foster compliments not criticism.

"It's a little long."

She shook her head, tsking. "Short skirts divide the body, making the wearer look shorter. You should know that."

That was also at least the second time she'd made some reference to his height. "Let me ask you something. I am taller than average height for a man, while you are shorter than the average height for a woman. So why do you keep ragging on me about it?"

"Because I've heard every short joke there is and want to share?"

He doubted that. In fact he suspected this entire thread of conversation was merely a diversion for what needed to be done. Since, for once, she seemed loath to do the honors, he would.

He leaned his back against the counter and met her gaze. "Aren't you going to ask me?"

"Ask you what?"

"Like the note said. Why I left the force."

"I hadn't planned on it."

"Why not?"

"For one thing, I don't like being manipulated. For another, whatever the reason, I'm sure it's far less sordid than Robert tried to imply. He just wants to stir up trouble. Last, if you wanted me to know, you would have told me."

He couldn't argue with any of her points, but he knew she had to be curious. On top of that, it galled him that Parker knew what she didn't. But given her willingness to discuss the subject, he had to assume that she hadn't been trying to delay the conversation. Instead she'd been waiting for him to bring it up himself. In some ways he was glad he had. "I put a suspect in the hospital."

She didn't seem surprised or react much in any way. "I take it that's a no-no these days."

"Pretty much."

"So you decided to leave?"

"It wasn't so much my decision." It had been that or

face being brought up on departmental charges, if not criminal ones as well.

"Did he deserve what you did to him?"

"He deserved more than what I gave him."

"Too bad you didn't get to finish."

He couldn't help cracking a smile at that. "I forget what a bloodthirsty wench you are."

She grinned at him. "Bloodthirsty, yes, but never a wench." She cast him a long, assessing look, probably trying to figure out if there was more to the story than he'd told her. There was, and he would have elaborated if the phone hadn't rung, depriving him of his chance to.

While she went to answer the phone, he went to the front window to look out. Honestly, part of him was relieved not to have to tell the whole sordid story. There wasn't any real need for her to know, and telling her would lead to questions he'd rather not answer.

Movement across the street caught his eye. Rachel Gibbs was hanging her clothes on the line in her yard. His first thought was, hadn't the woman heard of dryers? Then again, some people paid good money for detergent that made their clothes smell like they were dried in the country air. Rachel Gibbs had the real thing.

He shook his head at the direction of his thoughts and turned to face Frankie as she walked into the room.

"Guess who that was? Harry Brandt of all people."

The name sounded familiar, but he didn't immediately place it. "Who?"

"The first girl's boyfriend. The one who was originally suspected in her murder. He called me when we first got here, but we had other fish to fry at the time."

"What does he want?"

"To tell us whatever the police weren't willing to listen to when he said it the first time."

"That might prove interesting. I take it you've arranged a meeting."

"I have. He attends Tyson University, about an hour from here. He gets out of class at twelve-thirty. He'll meet us then."

And hopefully, he'd have a new direction in which to point them, since the one Nelson was headed on was one that was sure to upset Frankie.

Frankie had met Harry Brandt only once, after one of her team's home games. She knew his reputation as a campus Lothario better than his face. Still, she scanned the meager crowd outside the student center hoping to catch a glimpse of him. He was already fifteen minutes late to meet them and she could tell by Nelson's demeanor that he'd given up expecting Brandt to show.

"Just ten more minutes," she said to Nelson, hoping to placate him by putting a time limit on their wait.

He shrugged in a way that said it was her time to waste.

Annoyed herself, Frankie sighed. What did this kid hope to accomplish by keeping them waiting? If he was so anxious to tell his side of the story, wouldn't he be here?

Then she heard her name being called by a masculine voice. She took a couple of steps in that direction, craning her neck for a look at Harry.

He rushed up to her, out of breath, smiling in a way

that exposed twin dimples and shining blue eyes. A day's stubble on his chin did nothing to detract from his country-boy good looks and lent to his starving-student appeal.

He kissed her cheek, a familiarity she wouldn't have allowed if she'd been asked. "Sorry to be late, but I was detained," he said in a way that suggested it hadn't been schoolwork that had kept him.

Further annoyed, she snapped, "I thought you wanted to talk to me about Diana."

Whether naturally or by design, his expression grew contrite. "I do. And I do take this seriously."

"I'm glad." Her annoyance faded. Just then she felt Nelson come up beside her to drape an arm around her waist. Never before had he touched her in the presence of someone they hoped would help with the case, not even his friend Don, whom she assumed knew the truth of things. The fact that he did so now, in the presence of this young Adonis, bespoke a certain possessiveness. Or at least that was the easy answer. She couldn't imagine that little peck Brandt had given her was enough to warrant Nelson asserting his position.

Either way, any other man would have gotten a subtle elbow in the ribs for such Neanderthal behavior, not that any other man she'd been with would have resorted to physical assertions of position. In a similar situation, Robert would have issued some comment designed to wither the other man, but physicality was beyond his limits. Still she wondered at her own lack of response. Maybe for the first time a man's protectiveness didn't seem out of place. She wasn't sure she trusted Brandt, either, and for reasons that had nothing to do with sexual politics. If nothing else, Nelson's gesture reminded her to be on her guard.

Focusing on Brandt, she said, "Harry, this is Nelson Santiago." She didn't bother with the cousin story since Nelson had already blown that.

"Hey," Harry said, extending his hand toward Nelson.

But Nelson's hand rested on Frankie's hip and he declined to move it. Harry eventually got the message and put his hand in his pocket. "There's a coffee shop around the corner, if you like."

The coffee shop was fairly empty despite the midday hour, probably due to the fact that only those daring enough to brave summer session were on campus. They took a booth by the window with Frankie seated on the inside next to Nelson and Brandt across from them. Both she and Nelson ordered coffee; Brandt a cheeseburger with fries and a Coke.

When their order arrived, Nelson said, "Have you got something for us or not?"

Brandt, who'd just taken a bite from his burger, swallowed and coughed. Frankie couldn't blame the kid, considering that Nelson had been shooting death-ray stares at him since they sat down.

"What did you want to tell me?" she said, more to smooth the way than anything else.

Brandt made a quick recovery, smiling at Frankie in a way she found disconcerting but couldn't say why.

"What I've got for you is the name of the man who killed Diana and the other girls."

Frankie glanced at Nelson. His expression remained

the same, giving away nothing. Focusing on Brandt again, she asked, "What do you mean?"

"Like I tried to tell the police, some guy had been harassing her for weeks, following her around, sending her flowers."

"She told you this?"

He took a sip from his glass, then wiped his mouth with his napkin, giving the impression he was either trying to draw out responding for maximum effect—or stalling for time. "She was frightened of him. Wouldn't you be if someone were stalking you?"

"I'd kick his teeth in, but that's just me." She smiled to herself, seeing Brandt's complexion pale just a little. He hadn't been expecting that from her, but then again, why should he? "Did she tell you who it was?"

"No. She wanted to handle it herself." Smart girl. Despite his swimmer's physique, Frankie doubted Brandt would offer much in the handling-of-things department. "Then how do you know who he was? Is?"

"I saw her with him once. I knew the guy, not his name, but where he worked. I had to get my car towed once and he was the guy that picked it up."

"And the police never checked this guy out?"

"I think they were starting to, but then their attention got diverted elsewhere."

Frankie sipped from her cup, using it as an opportunity to scrutinize Brandt. She hadn't paid much attention to him the first time she'd met him, but something about his demeanor seemed off. Maybe it was that stupid kiss, or she, by association, was developing some of Nelson's natural wariness, but she didn't trust him and moreover she didn't doubt his only goal was to manipulate her into doing what he wanted.

But what exactly did he want? If he hoped she'd convince Robert to reinvestigate the case, he could go on hoping if he liked. Whatever sway she might have held with Robert had evaporated. "Why are you telling me this?"

Brandt shrugged. "It's kind of around that you are looking into what happened to the girls. I figured you might get someone to listen where I couldn't. And because of who the guy is. I tracked him down myself."

Brandt paused again. This time Frankie was sure it was for dramatic effect. Whoever Brandt thought it was, she wished he'd just spill it already and stop wasting her time. "Who?"

"That's another reason I thought I should tell you. You know, so that you'll be careful. He lives across the street from you. His name is Myron Gibbs."

Chapter 17

Myron Gibbs. Nelson hadn't expected to hear any other name and Brandt didn't disappoint. While Nelson admitted his own suspicions lay with Gibbs, he didn't trust Brandt, so his accusation was tainted, too. First off, Brandt didn't strike him as the devoted beau determined to find his lover's killer. More than likely he would have forgotten Diana Hill existed ten minutes after the funeral if he hadn't been accused of her murder. For another, the strongest emotion he read off the man was animosity toward Gibbs. Whether that stemmed from Gibbs stalking, as he called it, his girlfriend or some other motivation, Nelson couldn't tell.

Besides, the actions Brandt described could merely be the actions of a man courting a woman. What made it stalking was whether the woman wanted the man's attention and how far the man was willing to go to get it. It didn't sound like Gibbs had crossed the line, especially since the woman in question wasn't apparently ready to enlist anyone's help in putting a stop to it.

Despite Brandt's facade of struggling student, his mannerisms and speech bespoke Southern gentility and some degree of wealth. From what he'd read about Hill, her family wasn't screaming poverty, either, which was probably part of her appeal. How would a man like Brandt take a man like Gibbs, both poor by comparison and black, pursuing his woman, especially if she wasn't turning him away?

Although Nelson had anticipated Brandt's revelation, clearly Frankie had not. She blinked and her mouth worked, though no sound came out. "You expect me to believe Myron Gibbs murdered all those girls?" she asked finally.

There was such incredulousness in her voice that Nelson feared Brandt would clam up in response. If there was more to this, Nelson wanted to hear all of it. "What makes you suspect Gibbs is capable of this?"

The glee on the other man's face told Nelson this is what Brandt had been waiting for—the opportunity to drop whatever bombshell came next. "He has a record, you know. Lewd conduct or something. He served six months in Cranford. That's a juvenile facility in Gwinnett County."

He didn't add the words *for those of you who don't know,* but it was in his tone—a supercilious smugness that made Nelson want to deck him. Such a record probably should have been expunged or at least sealed if Gibbs had been young enough for a juvenile court to mete out his justice. Nelson wondered whether Southern charm or Southern cash had smoothed the way for that discovery. Then he decided it didn't matter. The idea of this man using either to defame another man soured the taste in Nelson's mouth. He'd bet Brandt's closet held a few skeletons in it, as well, which might explain how he knew how to look for them—or hide them.

Whichever the case, Nelson needed time to check out Brandt's story, as well as take care of a few other matters. He grasped Frankie's elbow. To Brandt, he said, "If you think of anything else, let us know."

Frankie said nothing, following him to the car without a single peep. Even after he'd pulled out onto the main road she remained uncharacteristically silent. He reached over to squeeze her thigh. "What are you thinking?"

"No matter what he says, I know Myron didn't do it."

He heard the conviction in her voice and wondered at it. He might be her friend, but could anyone voice for what was in another's character? At one time, he hadn't thought himself capable of certain things until he found himself doing them. How could she be so sure about a man she'd known less than a year?

He asked her that, but she took so long answering him that he thought she wouldn't. Finally, she turned to him, her teeth clamped on her lower lip. "I guess I don't want to believe it. That would mean that every 'memory' I've had was a false one. That would mean I'd been around a man who'd hurt me and never sensed it. I know my instincts are off, but I can't accept that they're that off."

To some degree, neither could he. She was a sharp woman. Then again, he'd never quite bought the idea that her attack and the other crimes were related. He had his own suspicions where that was concerned. Hopefully, he'd know more when they got back to her house. For now, he didn't want to get her mind moving in that direction until he could prove something.

"Did you know that Myron was at Tara the night we were there?"

Her eyes narrowed. "No I didn't."

"That's probably because you were busy scoping out ways to get yourself in trouble."

He hadn't expected her to deny that, and she didn't. She grinned. "Well, there is that. But showing up at a strip club doesn't make you a murderer, unless you count good taste."

"He was wearing a set of coveralls." He let that hang there a minute, giving her time to mull it over.

She sighed. "So now you think it's Myron for sure?"

"I'm not saying that. The only thing I'm sure of is that Brandt has it in for him—why, exactly, is anyone's guess."

She tilted her head in a sideways nod. "I suppose. What's our next move?"

"I need to take care of a few things at the house. Then I'll put in a call to Don Meyer. He's checking out a few things for me."

He stopped talking, mostly because he realized she wasn't listening to him. She'd turned her head to stare out the window, her teeth worrying a spot on her lower lip. He'd learned to recognize that look. She was planning something. He had no idea what, but decided the direct route was his best option. "What are you up to?"

"I was thinking Rachel would probably know if Myron were involved in this."

"How do you figure that?"

"You can't keep many secrets from the woman who does your laundry. I can't imagine anyone killing those girls that way without it getting messy. Rachel would have noticed if he came home with blood on his clothes."

He couldn't argue with that so he didn't bother.

Frankie pulled out her cell phone and punched in a number. "Rachel, I'll be home in about fifteen minutes, can you come over then?" He didn't hear Rachel's end of the conversation, but Frankie ended by saying, "See you soon."

"You plan on asking her flat out if she thinks her nephew is capable of murdering those girls?"

She cast him a disapproving look. "Trust me to have a little more finesse than that."

There was something about the way she said the word "trust" that made him question it. "What do you mean, 'trust you'?"

"You don't think Rachel will say one word if you're in the room, do you?"

He supposed not, but he didn't mind. He had his own information to check out, and if Frankie was busy with Rachel, that was all the better for him.

Rachel was waiting on the porch when they pulled up in front of the house. Why Rachel didn't just go in, Frankie didn't know. When she reached Rachel, she relieved her of the Pyrex baking dish she carried. "Is this more peach cobbler?"

"Just made it this morning."

"How about some coffee to go with it?"

"I was counting on it."

She supposed Rachel had figured she hadn't been invited here on a social call. That was fine with Frankie, since asking Rachel if she suspected that Myron was involved in the murders would be hard enough without her friend having false assumptions about why she was here.

Once the coffee was made and both women were seated at the table, Rachel said, "You want to ask me what I know about Myron and them girls."

Frankie wasn't entirely surprised by Rachel's statement, but wondered why she'd figured that out. "How did you know?"

"I figured someone would get around to it eventually." Rachel sipped from her cup. "Besides, you've got such a long face on you, I figured it had to be something bad."

"I saw Harry Brandt this morning. He claims Myron was stalking Diana Hill."

"Stalking my behind. He knew the girl. She drove her car into some ditch on one of the back roads and he towed it back to his garage. They struck up a friendship, I think. If it was more than that, I don't know. There are things a son doesn't tell his mother. Mostly, I think he felt sorry for her. She had broken things off with Brandt, but he'd fixated on her like some men do. 'If I can't have you, no one will.' Brandt was one of them spoiled rich kids, always causing trouble, thinking they're entitled to whatever they want. If anyone was stalking that girl, it was Brandt."

Although she thought she knew the answer, she asked. "Why didn't Myron tell that to anyone?"

"And bring himself under police scrutiny? It took those boys forever to get up the nerve to arrest Brandt in the first place. No one wanted to anger his daddy, I guess."

"But you thought Brandt was responsible."

"I did, like everybody else. Until that second body showed up. He couldn't have dumped it from a jail cell." Rachel sighed, shaking her head. "I told Myron not to have anything to do with that girl, but he never could stand for anyone picking on a woman. When he was fifteen, he got into a fight with one of his classmates because the boy was picking on his own sister. The boy's family had the nerve to press charges and Myron was the one who was punished."

Frankie shook her head at the way life worked sometimes. At least that explained Myron's record. "Is that why you figured I was going to ask you whether Myron was involved?"

Rachel nodded. "Besides, I knew someone was trying to pin this on him. A couple pairs of his overalls disappeared from my wash line."

"Is that why you came running when you heard the noise at my house?"

Rachel smiled. "The idea of catching that sucker might have made my feet move a little faster, but I would never have let anyone hurt you if I could prevent it. Too bad I scared him off by making so much noise on that step. I had Myron fix it after that."

Frankie sipped from her cup, mulling over what Rachel said. If Brandt couldn't have dumped that body from a jail cell and Rachel's words were more than a mother trying to protect her family, neither man could have been the killer. So where did that leave them? Back at square one.

While Frankie went to the kitchen with Rachel, Nelson went up to his room to boot up his laptop. He subscribed to an information service, the type that provided background data—the kind of stuff most people thought was either private or protected, but in reality was neither. He'd sent in a request for details on Parker the moment he found out that Frankie had been involved with him. Nelson probably could have gotten a cursory report in twenty-four hours, but a thorough check like he wanted took time. When he logged on, the information was there waiting for him.

He skimmed over most of the personal data. Parker had attended Howard for both undergrad and law school. He'd never been married. He'd worked for the Gwinnett County prosecutor's office straight out of law school. His record was impressive enough for him to advance in the office.

But Nelson was more interested in his financial records. He didn't have to dig too deeply to confirm his suspicions. Parker's bank accounts were nearly dry, his house carried a second mortgage and his credit cards were to the max or close to it. Yet he had no visible means of debt: no investments that soured, no old folks in a home, no child-support payments or other items that might eat up cash. Robert Parker was up to his neck in something. Nelson contemplated the possibilities: boozing, drugs, whoring or gambling, and settled on the last one as the most likely culprit, only because the others were less easy to hide.

Whatever the case, he couldn't help wondering if Parker's offer of marriage was in part or wholely motivated by a desire to get his hands on her family's money.

Hearing the downstairs door close, he turned off the computer and went to find Frankie. She was still seated in the kitchen at the table. The expression on her face told him nothing. "What did Rachel have to say?"

"According to Rachel, Brandt was the one stalking Diana Hill. She'd broken things off with him, but he didn't want to let go. Myron befriended her, or maybe it was the other way around, so he knew her, but he had no reason to kill her or the other girls."

Nelson slid into the seat opposite her. "Baby, most of the time there's no reason for these crimes. The victim fits the profile of the type of woman the killer has objectified in his mind. Most of the time the only rhyme or reason is that they fit the pattern."

"I thought you said that this kind of killer doesn't stop, either, but this one did."

"Okay, so this one doesn't fit the profile," he said, expressing a little more of his frustration than he intended. If neither man on their radar was responsible, someone else had to be. If he had command of the investigation, he'd reinterview everyone connected with these girls, everyone who had access to the campus. He couldn't believe that so many girls could have been murdered without anyone seeing anything. But as it was, the police considered the case closed. No one was interested in what he might have to say.

"Let's go see Don," he suggested. Maybe whatever the older man had found out would point them in a new direction.

Don's house was on a block lined with maple and magnolia trees. A low white fence marked the perimeter of his property. A knock on his door yielded no answer. Nelson tried the knob and the door opened. Stepping inside, he called Don's name. That surprised him, considering that Don's car was in the drive. "Don," he called again.

He motioned for Frankie to stay where she was. Pulling his gun from his waistband, he moved farther into the house, calling Don's name as he went. He searched the downstairs, finding nothing. He eased up the stairs, his back braced against the wall. All the upstairs doors were closed, save one. A flickering light emanated from that one room. He headed toward that room, hoping to find Don there, hopefully unharmed.

What he found when he reached the room surprised him. Don sat in a wing chair perpendicular to the door holding a half-full tumbler in his hand. The flickering light Nelson had seen must have been the images dancing on the opposite wall, an old and grainy home movie of a young girl at a piano recital. He recognized the resemblance immediately, although as far as he knew Don didn't have any kids.

"You can put the weapon away," Don said in a voice

as flat and grainy as the film. "I'm fine. Or as fine as I'm going to be today."

Nelson eased the gun back into its holster. Only then did he notice the decor of the room. The walls had been painted a pale pink. A twin-size canopy bed occupied one corner of the room. A white antique-looking dresser and matching nightstand rounded out the room. It was a room for a young girl, perhaps the one on film. The only objects that seemed out of place were the chair Don sat in and the man himself. "What are you doing in here, Don?"

For a long time, Don said nothing. The only sound in the room was the dull cacophony of the movie player. "Don?"

"Most guys don't have the stomach to do what we did. The good ones, the ones that last, almost always have a sister or mother or…child, someone affected by what these bastards do."

"I know." When he was a cop, Nelson himself had been drawn to sex crimes due to a need to understand the sort of mind of a person who committed such crimes.

"I got so lost in that. Once I found out about Jacobs's past, I couldn't let it go. I hounded those boys to go after him. I even followed him myself sometimes when I was off duty."

"What are you talking about, Don?"

"Jacobs. His autopsy came back today. He didn't kill himself. Someone trussed him up to make it look that way, but the medical examiner found he died from a broken neck."

Whoever it was must have assumed that the authorities would see Jacobs's suicide as an admission of guilt and not look into it any further. Maybe it hadn't occurred to this person that an autopsy in such cases was often mandatory.

"Do they know who did it?"

"They got one of the guards on duty to admit he'd been paid to do it, but not by whom or for how much. He's got a sick kid who needs treatment, and he needed the money."

"What has that got to do with you, Don?"

"We used to call her Stevie. She was only twelve years old when some bastard came along and took her. She was walking home from her piano teacher's house when she was grabbed right off the street. They didn't find her body until a month later. The things he did to her shouldn't happen to a dog."

Don wiped his sleeve across his face. "I was a cop already then, but I made it my mission to get these scumbags that prey on children off the street, but never did I have someone locked up who didn't deserve it. Not until now. That man is dead because of me."

Even if Don had pushed the police to look at other suspects, they'd been the ones to pick him up. Parker was the one who saw fit to prosecute him. Whoever really killed those girls was desperate enough to further hide their crime by making someone else look even guiltier. They might have succeeded, too, had they been less inept. But that made him wonder, why now? Maybe they'd heard about Frankie's refusal to testify and needed to confirm Jacobs's guilt. He said as much to Don.

"It's not public knowledge, but the district attorney

no longer had a case. Not that he had much of one to start with."

"Then help me find out who really did this."

Don wiped his sleeve across his face again. "Where's Ms. Hairston?"

Good God, he'd forgotten Frankie downstairs. She was still waiting for him by the front door, her arms crossed, her foot tapping impatiently. When she saw him, she asked, "Is everything all right?"

"In a manner of speaking. Come in."

Don joined them a moment later, looking not much the worse for wear. "Why don't we go in the den," he suggested.

Nelson wasn't surprised to find Don had set up a similar chart to his on a big movable easel. Of course, Don's contained more information than his, news clippings and file reports he lacked.

"Can I get anyone a drink?" Don asked.

Frankie settled on a beer, while both he and Don preferred Scotch. For a long moment, none of them said anything. Nelson studied Don's flow chart, hoping the additional information would jog something in his brain. In truth, if the police had recognized that Jacobs wasn't the killer, there was no real need for he and Frankie to do anything. The police would be looking for the real killer. He also knew Frankie would never be satisfied with that and Don needed something to do.

Don was the first to speak. "By the way, I didn't turn up anything on that Myron kid. No priors, no arrests, not so much as a speeding ticket. He wasn't even on the police radar until I started asking about him."

So much for not needing to do anything. If the police needed a new focus, they may just have provided them with one.

"What about Harry Brandt?"

He should have known Frankie wasn't quite finished with that bone yet. Honestly, neither was he. There was something about Brandt that got to Nelson, a certain disingenuousness that suggested he had something to hide. It might not be murder, but murder wasn't the only crime.

"He's been a troublemaker since he was born. Just a for instance, he got picked up a couple of years ago, wandering around the back roads, drunk out of his mind and stark naked. He said he was looking for his keys. I remember it was a couple weeks after Halloween. The only clothing they had to fit him was a Batman costume from the lost and found. Daddy got him out of that scrape and every other one. The family owns half the town, and what they don't own they control. The boys around here waited so long to pick him up, building their case, hoping the charge would stick."

But the appearance of the second body sunk it. Then Brandt being the killer didn't make any sense. There was nothing to suggest that more than one man had killed the girls. Besides, most of these guys acted alone. They didn't trust anyone or believe anyone else could be as clever as they were. Whoever had killed the girls must have been somewhere laughing at the cops and D.A.'s office for locking up and prosecuting the wrong guy, that is, until the suicide. He wondered if the killer knew the police were once again involved.

For some reason, Nelson's gaze was drawn to the wall to the dates of each murder written in dark black ink. He focused on the days of the murders, the first of December, the first of January and so on. For some reason, a picture of Sandy from her hospital bed on the day he'd found out about his father etched its way into his consciousness. "Maybe he was finished," Nelson said.

"What do you mean?" Don asked.

"It's a date." Nelson picked up a marker from the table and wrote on the wall beneath the pictures 11/14/04. If you count the one month without a killing as a zero, that's what you get. What day did you say Brandt was found wandering around?"

"A couple weeks after Thanksgiving."

"The fourteenth?"

"Could be. I don't know for certain. You think he killed them because of something that happened that night."

Nelson shrugged. It was the most logical conclusion he could come to. For some reason, Brandt could have focused his rage on these women that night.

"What about the stab marks? Why six of them each time?"

Both he and Don turned to face Frankie, who'd spoken. He had no answer for that. He was sure that number figured in somewhere, but how he couldn't guess.

"Maybe there was a sixth girl that figures in this somehow. Maybe one he couldn't take his revenge on for whatever reason."

Nelson shrugged. They would probably never know unless they figured out what happened that night.

"Frankie," he said, "Do you think any of the girls might know?"

"And not have gone to the police? I doubt it. The whole campus was pretty shaken up by the murders. We had girls as well as cops patrolling the campus and no one saw anything. But if there's any gossip going around, Julia would know it."

"Then let's find out what she knows."

Chapter 18

Unlike most of the students at Excelsior College, Julia was a full-time resident of the area. Her address and phone number were listed in the phone book. Even though Frankie had lived in the town for years, she'd never explored much of it. When she called to ask Julia if they could come over, Julia had given them directions, but she'd seemed hesitant about the visit. Once they stopped in front of the house, Frankie thought she knew why.

Given Julia's vivacious personality and flair for fashion, Frankie never would have expected Julia to live in this backwater area in a tiny house that had clearly seen better days. A lawn of overgrown grass ringed the house. A bowed and sickly maple tree bent low toward the structure. The shed at the back of the property looked no more sturdy.

Nelson drew her attention by saying, "I'm half expecting Jane Pittman to come out and ask us to set a spell."

Frankie looked up at him, but she said nothing. During the trip, neither of them had said much, though she sensed an excitement in him she hadn't seen before. He probably figured they were on to something. For everyone's sake she hoped he was right. She was ready for this to be over with. She knew Nelson couldn't spend forever on this. He'd already done for her what he'd promised. Aside from that, she was ready to get on with her life, as well. She wanted to be able to put this behind her. She knew she couldn't do that until she knew who attacked her and why. Was it part of the campus killings as nearly everyone believed, or for some other reason as Nelson suggested? She had to know, and she hoped Julia could tell them something to lead them in the right direction.

There was no immediate answer when Frankie knocked on the door.

A second knock brought a frazzled "I'm coming." But it was Harry Brandt who opened the door a moment later. It took a second for Frankie to register both his presence and the import of the object he held in his hand: a big black handgun that was pointed right at her.

"I figured you two might make it out here eventually," Brandt said. "But not so soon. Come in, but I'll take your weapon first, if you don't mind." He extended his hand toward Nelson.

Frankie hadn't realized Nelson had drawn it until he dropped it into Brandt's waiting hand. Brandt stuck the gun in his waistband. He stepped back. With a flick of his wrist, he motioned them inside. "Julia is waiting for you."

At first, Frankie did nothing, sure Brandt intended to kill them the moment he got them inside. No matter how isolated this place was, no good could come from killing people on the doorstep. Then she heard Nelson whisper in her ear, "It'll be all right."

She couldn't see how Nelson could guarantee that, since he'd given up his only weapon.

"No talking among yourselves. Move it."

A prod at the small of her back from Nelson got her moving. But she hadn't taken two steps before a shove from Nelson sent her flying forward. She lost her footing on the carpet and went down hard. Ignoring the pain in her knees, she flipped over to see what was going on behind her. Nelson had Brandt against the wall. One of his hands pinned Brandt's gun hand to the wall, the other held his own gun under Brandt's chin.

"Drop it," Nelson said, "or they'll need a tweezer to pick your brains out of that wall."

The gun clattered to the floor. Nelson kicked it away, in her direction. She scrambled to pick it up.

"Are you okay?" Nelson asked.

"I'm fine," she said, though her left knee smarted. She stood up and for want of anything else to do, stuck it in the back of her jeans.

"Go see to Julia."

She found the other woman in the living room, her arms and feet bound to a chair that probably belonged in the kitchen. A piece of duct tape covered her mouth. Frankie pulled off the tape and Julia winced. Frankie saw why a moment later. Her swollen lips oozed fresh blood from a cut at the corner of her mouth. No doubt Brandt was responsible for that.

At first, Julia dragged in several long breaths. Then she fastened a pitiful gaze on her. "I'm so sorry," Julia said. "He showed up here after you called and I couldn't get rid of him."

Frankie didn't know what to say to that. Julia made Brandt sound like an unwanted houseguest rather than a man who had come here intending to harm her. "What's going on here, Julia?"

Tears spilled from Julia's eyes. Frankie ignored them at first, long enough to untie Julia from the chair. The bonds were loose, as if Julia had been working on them or they had been tied in haste.

Once her hands were freed, she brought her arms around and buried her face in her palms. Frankie wrapped her arms around the girl and let her cry out her misery on her shoulder. She turned her head slightly when she noticed movement behind her—Nelson bringing Brandt into the room. Brandt's arms were behind him, secured by what, Frankie didn't know or care. Nelson pushed him into a seat. For once Brandt looked subdued, sullen. She supposed being so easily bested by an unarmed man could do that to a guy.

Julia sat back and stared at Brandt. "You didn't have to hurt them. All they did was laugh at you."

"Those bitches got what they deserved. My only mistake was in thinking you were different."

Julia's eyes went wide, as if reacting to being slapped. Her mouth worked, but no sound came out.

"Tell me what happened," Frankie said. Julia looked

down at her. She could see the ambivalence in Julia's eyes. Should she speak or shouldn't she? Frankie wondered why she owed Brandt enough loyalty for that to be an issue. That was a question that would have to wait for later. "Tell me," Frankie whispered.

Julia shrugged as if to say it didn't matter anymore. "Five of us went down to Tara. Me, Diana and the other girls. We'd go down there sometimes, either us together or with other girls. We'd get a little drunk, find some horny men and have a little fun. That night, we got more wasted than usual. We left when Kerry was getting off shift, so we offered her a ride home, too." Julia sniffled. "We were about halfway home when Harry cut us off. He was furious because he'd heard that Diana was there."

Julia didn't say how Harry Brandt had heard, but Frankie assumed it was because he'd showed up there himself. "I told them not to do it. I knew his temper. But they were determined to teach him a lesson for bothering Diana. They pinned him down and took his clothes. They threw his car keys in the bushes someplace. They left him there with nothing but his car. Once we got back in the car, Kerry used her cell phone to call the police to report the poorly endowed naked man wandering around on the road."

And later that night he was further humiliated by the police picking him up. No doubt he endured a severe ribbing at their hands. She glanced over at Brandt. Even now his rage showed in the mottled color of his skin. She supposed the only thing keeping the man in his seat was Nelson's presence and the fact that while Julia spoke, Nelson had quietly called the police.

"He made me do it," Julia sobbed, drawing her attention. "He told me he'd do to me what he'd done to the other girls if I didn't help him."

"Shut up, you stupid cow," Brandt screamed. "I knew I couldn't trust you to keep your mouth shut."

Frankie turned back to Julia. "What do you mean you helped him?"

"The second body. I'm the one who dumped it. When the police picked him up he was on his way here. I didn't know what to do. I couldn't go to the police. I knew what he'd done. I was a party to it. But I couldn't live with Kerry's body being in the shed behind my house. Her body was already in a plastic sheet. I waited until nightfall, then I dumped her in the same spot he'd left Diana, the spot where we'd left him that night. It didn't occur to me that doing that would prove his innocence."

For all its viciousness, Brandt's plan for retribution was a pretty straightforward one, which left Frankie with one question. "Why didn't any of the girls figure out what he was doing?"

"A couple of them did. They didn't live long enough to tell anyone besides me about it."

Frankie shook her head. "If you knew what he'd done, how could you help him?"

Fresh tears brimmed in Julia's eyes. "Because he's my brother, the only member of the family to acknowledge me. I'm the family's dirty little secret, the bastard child of the city councilman and a domestic from the wrong part of town. My father pays for my schooling, my clothes, whatever I want, as long as I keep my mouth shut and stay in my part of town where I can't sully his good name. Harry is the only one who ever gave me the time of day. After my mother died, I had no one. No one."

Speaking for herself, Frankie would rather be alone than have a murderer for a relative. Then again, she'd always had people to love and care for her, even if they didn't get along. She had no idea what poverty or loneliness or privation could do to a person. And though she hadn't said so, Frankie suspected a good deal of fear was in the mix as well, if she'd thought to warn the other girls about Brandt's temper.

Frankie stood. The sound of sirens in the distance reached her. It was over. She'd gotten most of what she'd come back to this town to get. No closure for herself, but at least the girls' killer stood a chance of remaining behind bars. She glanced over her shoulder at Nelson. She had no idea what the future held for them, either. He'd probably want to head home in the morning, but at least they'd have tonight. For now that would have to be enough.

Hours later, after the police had grilled them on what they knew and when they knew it, Nelson got into bed and pulled Frankie to him. Her warm nude body relaxed against his. She sighed, seemingly with contentment, but he wasn't taking anything for granted. He stroked his hand down her back to give her bottom a squeeze. "How are you feeling?"

"A little tired. My knee feels better. Next time you're going to throw me to the floor, give me a little heads-up, okay?"

He heard the humor in her voice and smiled. "I did not throw you to the floor. You tripped."

"Details, details."

She waved her hand in the air dismissively. He caught it and brought her palm to his lips. They could joke about it now, but he'd never had such rage as when Brandt had come to the door with a gun trained on Frankie. The only thing that had saved the bastard from a real beating was the fact that he was incapable of putting up much of a fight.

He kissed her palm and laid her hand on his chest. They'd already agreed to go home in the morning. He needed to get back to his work and his family and she didn't want to spend any more time here than necessary. But if he'd thought about it before answering, he'd have asked for one more day. There was so much he needed to tell her, so much to settle before they went back to the real world of their lives. Most of all he needed to know if there was a future for them. Neither of them had expressed their feelings, whatever they were. There hadn't been time. But as sure as he knew his own name, he knew he was in love with her. But before he had any right to expect her to return his feelings, she had to know the truth about him, the whole truth. Even this morning that had seemed like a scary prospect. Now the scarier prospect was losing her.

He leaned down and kissed her temple. "Baby, there's something I need to tell you."

She opened her eyes and looked up at him. "Now? I was just lying here contemplating you ravishing me."

He doubted that was true. Up until the moment they'd come up to bed, she'd been speculating on both Julia's fate and Brandt's. Julia would no doubt be prosecuted as an accomplice, though her fear of Brandt would be a mitigating factor. He'd heard from Don Meyer that Brandt should have been a better housekeeper. Several bags of evidence were removed from that shed, probably enough to convict him.

He pressed her cheek against his chest. "I'm sorry," he said, this time referring to the one subject he really thought might be on her mind.

"What for?"

"Brandt isn't the one who attacked you. If we go home tomorrow, we may never know who did or why."

"I can't dwell on that anymore. I'm whole, I'm here. I have to go on." She sighed. "If you don't mind, what I'd really like to do right now is forget." She leaned up and pressed her open mouth to his.

The drive home the next day was uneventful. Nelson was glad that Frankie slept for most of the trip, as she had done the way up. Not only had the whole affair taken a lot out of her, it gave him time to think. Once he got a decent night's rest, he wanted to finish telling her about his past and make her understand how deep his feelings for her had grown. He wasn't sure her feelings mirrored his own, or if they did if she'd be willing to admit that. All he knew was that he had to try.

The sun was beginning to set by the time they pulled up in front of his house. Before they even got out of the car, the front door opened and Dara and Bonnie spilled out. He didn't know what they were doing here, but he was glad to see them. He glanced over at Frankie. He shrugged to let her know he hadn't expected them, either.

He barely got out of the car before they launched

themselves at him. He scooped them up in a kind of group hug. "What are you two doing here?"

"That's my fault."

Sandy stood in the drive facing him. With her face devoid of makeup and her hair pulled back into a ponytail, she looked as young as the day he first met her, or she would have were it not for the troubled expression on her face. "I need to talk to you."

He set the girls down. "Sure."

Frankie chose that moment to get out of the car. He'd wondered what would happen if he got these two women together. Now he'd have his chance to find out. For a moment the women sized each other up.

Frankie was the first to speak. "I'm Francesca Hairston," she said, extending her hand.

"I'm Sandra Blake, the girls' mother."

"I kinda figured that."

Nelson suggested, "Why don't we go inside."

Sandy nodded and turned toward the house, but Frankie cast him a look he couldn't begin to decipher. For all her transparency, there were times when he had no clue what she was thinking or how those thoughts reflected on him. When Sandy turned toward the house, she did also. He was left to bring up the rear with the girls.

Once inside the house, he shooed the girls away and turned to Sandy. "Why don't we talk in the kitchen while I make some coffee?"

"Fine." Sandy preceded him to the back of the house. When she reached the kitchen she turned to him. "I'm so sorry to burst in on you like this. I wouldn't have, if I'd thought you wouldn't be alone."

"It's not a problem," he said, mostly because he sensed genuine distress on her face. In truth he would have preferred to continue to be alone to hash out things with Frankie. "Why are you here?"

"I was hoping you could watch the girls, just for the day."

"Why?"

She wrung her hands and averted her eyes. "I lost the baby."

"When?"

"Yesterday morning. Luckily the girls were with my parents. My father brought them back this morning. The girls told me you were coming home today."

And she couldn't send them back without her parents getting suspicious as to why she would need to. He tilted her chin up to see her face. "Are you okay? You didn't drive over here, did you?"

She stepped back, out of his grasp. "No, of course not. Ted dropped us off."

"You still don't trust me around him? How am I supposed to give you away if we can't be in the same room together? Or did you change your mind?"

"No. The wedding is still on. I just need a little time to get myself together without the girls around."

"As I said, that's not a problem. Do you need a ride home?"

"Ted's on standby. He can be here in fifteen minutes."

"Whatever you want."

She leaned up on tiptoe and kissed his cheek. "Thank you."

This time he stepped away from her. There was no

need for her to thank him. She was and always would be the mother of his children. If nothing else, he owed her a bit of civility and understanding, even though he'd denied her that in the past. Besides, it was time for a little peace in all their lives, an absence of rancor. Now all he needed to do was make things right with Frankie and everything in his life would be as he wanted it. Even without the need to drive Sandy home, that part about making things right with Frankie was still a big if.

Frankie rushed back to the sofa, where she was supposed to be sitting, and propped her feet up on the coffee table for good measure. Although snooping on others wasn't entirely out of her character, trying to hide the fact that she'd been doing so was. But after watching Nelson with his ex-wife, a woman he supposedly didn't care about for, she'd prefer he didn't know she'd seen them together. More than that, she preferred that he didn't know the feelings of gut-churning jealousy that had clenched her stomach.

Frankie detested that emotion as useless, so it annoyed her to feel it in the first place. She hadn't expected Nelson to have married a troll, but did the woman have to be so tall, slender, gracefully feminine and stunningly beautiful despite wearing no makeup and with her hair in a ponytail? Couldn't she have one physical flaw, like maybe a hump back or a wart on the end of her nose?

"Where are the girls?" Sandra asked once she breached the living room area.

"They went upstairs." Bonnie had disappeared the

moment her parents went into the kitchen, making Frankie wonder if there wasn't some vent in the house somewhere where she could listen to every word. Dara had hung around a few minutes more.

Sandra went to the bottom of the stairs and called up. "Girls, I'm going."

Sandra returned to the living room as the sound of two doors opening preceded the sound of the girls' feet on the stairs. "We're not going with you," Dara asked, clearly disappointed.

Sandra put her arm around her daughter's shoulders. "No, I have a few things to take care of. I'll be back for you some time tomorrow."

"All right," Dara said, sounding somewhat mollified, but not much.

"You girls behave for your father," Sandy continued. "Now, both of you, scoot."

The girls embraced their mother and kisses were exchanged before the two girls headed toward the stairs. Sandy looked after them for a while, then turned to her. "He's a good man, you know."

Momentarily fazed by the abrupt change of focus, Frankie said, "I beg your pardon?"

"Nelson. He's a good man."

She had no idea why Nelson's ex-wife would say that to her, of all people. She blurted out the first words that came to her mind. "Then why did you divorce him?"

"I didn't fall out of love with him, if that's what you think. I couldn't take what he wanted to do with his life, jumping from one dangerous thing to the next." She shrugged in a way that made Frankie wonder what more there was to that story. "I guess I didn't have the right temperament for sitting home waiting to see if he'd come back safe. I don't know."

If she were looking to Frankie to provide her with an answer, she was out of luck. It seemed a bit frivolous to her to abandon a man over a few nights' worry. Then again, she'd never walked in those shoes to judge their fit. She did know one thing: she'd love for this uncomfortable conversation to be over with.

The sound of a car honking outside proved to be her reprieve. "There's my ride," Sandy said. She hurried to the front door and went out. Frankie didn't bother to watch her go. She was just glad she was gone.

But where was Nelson? Considering that his children were here, she should probably go home, anyway. They had some things to hash out between them, but that wouldn't be accomplished with the girls here.

Oh, who was she kidding? After seeing Nelson and his wife together, the way he'd looked at her, held her. If that was the behavior of a man over his wife, she'd eat her favorite practice ball.

She knew when she was in over her head. She needed to call in the big guns. She called the number for her mother's garage, waited five minutes for the chauffeur to show up and silently slipped out of the door.

Chapter 19

Nelson walked into the living room and knew something was wrong. There was Dara and Bonnie, but no Frankie. Unfortunately, a client he couldn't ignore called him on his cell phone and chewed his ear for fifteen minutes while a five-minute conversation would have sufficed. He'd figured his girls had enough sense to keep Frankie occupied for a minute while he was busy. Then again, Frankie was a grown woman. Wherever she'd disappeared to was her own choice. "Where's Frankie?"

The sheepish expression on Bonnie's face confirmed it. "She left, Dad. I saw her get into a car and drive off."

"And you didn't think to mention this to me. How long ago was this?"

"Five minutes."

Damn. He didn't know what to make of Frankie's hasty departure, but something made her leave. He doubted Sandy might have said something to her on her way out, but you never knew. Or had she seen the scene in the kitchen and misunderstood?

Either way, it was his fault for not making it clear to her what he felt for her. He'd allowed her to seduce him into forgetting all concerns but the physical last night. He'd been stalling, plain and simple, since he didn't know what he'd do if Frankie refused to give what they had a chance.

He had to go after her. That much he knew. But there were two things he needed to do first before he could really claim her as his own. He went to the girls' bathroom that sat between their two bedrooms and shut the door. Maybe the thick, gooey bubble bath Dara preferred would help get the damn ring off his finger. He slathered the gel on his fingers and tugged. The ring flew off and out of his grasp, hitting a framed photograph that stood on the shelf beside the sink. He retrieved the ring, then looked at the picture. He remembered when this shot was taken, a year or two before the divorce, at some carnival. All four of them had made funny faces for the camera. One of the last times all four of them were together as a family.

The fact that the glass frame was now cracked held some irony he didn't, at the moment, want to contemplate. He had one more stop to make before seeing Frankie. He hoped it wouldn't take long.

Riding up the drive to her mother's house, Frankie knew she'd made a mistake. The annual party her mother hosted to benefit some children's disease Frankie couldn't even pronounce must be tonight, since a row of expensive cars and limousines lined the drive. Damn! She didn't need this, but it made no sense to turn back. Maybe she could slip in unnoticed and ride out the rest of the event in her room. Yeah, and maybe while she was at it she could invent a vaccine for avian flu, too.

Her plan was shot to hell the moment she walked in the door. Her mother awaited her in the foyer. Margaret Hairston cast her a disapproving, hands-on-hips glare. "I admit I was shocked when Anderson told me you'd called for a car, but I was reasonably sure you'd be dressed properly for the occasion."

For a moment she pondered how Anderson knew she'd called for a car, until she remembered Anderson knew everything that went on in this house. "I would have been if I'd remembered your do was tonight. Actually, I came to see you."

"Oh." Genuine surprise showed on Margaret's face, which wasn't surprising since they didn't enjoy the sort of relationship where one might simply pop in on the other. "Come in, then."

Neither woman said much as they made their way to the upper landing and the master bedroom beyond. Margaret led her to the small, camelback sofa in her dressing room and sat. "Come tell me what's the matter. Does it have anything to do with Nelson?"

Frankie slumped on the sofa next to her mother, half expecting her mother to give her the standard lecture on proper posture, but no such lecture came. "Am I that transparent?" she asked finally.

"Not really. But nothing puts that particular variety of hangdog expression on a woman's face like trouble with a man. What did he do?"

That was just the problem. He hadn't done anything—or at least the one thing she wanted him to do, which was to take off that damn ring. "He's still in love with his ex-wife."

And that's a problem?"

"Well, yeah."

"Because you're in love with him."

"I haven't known him long enough to be in love with him."

"Nonsense. You haven't known him long enough to validate your feelings, maybe. But if you didn't love him, you wouldn't be here. You'd have cut your losses and run."

Frankie sighed. She had to admit that she'd have left any other man eating her dust by now. She was no glutton for punishment. "Okay, so I love him. What now?"

"How do you know he's still in love with her?"

"Aside from still wearing her ring? There's the way he looks at her."

"You've actually met this woman?"

"This afternoon, when we got to his place. She was there to drop off his daughters."

Margaret said nothing to that, only stared into space pensively.

"Well?"

"What do you think of her?"

Frankie shrugged. "She's no Cruella DeVil, if that's what you're asking. I actually liked her, what little I saw."

"But…"

"But, she still has feelings for him, too. As she put it, she didn't divorce him because she didn't love him anymore, but because she couldn't live with him putting himself in constant danger anymore. Then the usual yadda yadda about having to answer to her if I hurt him."

"And you bought that? What she really means is she couldn't control him and she doubts you'll have any better luck."

In an odd way, she had the feeling Sandy was giving her the go-ahead to be with Nelson. Even if that were true, Sandy wasn't the problem; Nelson was, so she didn't bother to contradict her mother. "I don't want to control him, any more than I want him to control me."

"You just want him to love you."

Frankie nodded, since her mother voiced the thought that was in her own head. Frankie didn't resist as her mother sloped an arm around her shoulder, drawing her closer. She rested her head on Margaret's shoulder as Margaret stroked her hair. Frankie hadn't indulged such mothering since she'd been a young child, but she accepted it now, feeling the need for comforting from some quarter. "What do I do now?"

"You have to make a decision. Is this man worth fighting for? You say he's still in love with his ex-wife, but he risked his life for you. How do you know you're not misreading what you saw? Frankly, it surprises me you haven't asked the man straight out what his feelings are. You have no problem getting into other people's faces."

True, but she'd never really had to fight for anything in her life. Not really. Even though she might complain about it, her family's wealth opened many doors. She'd never even wanted much of her own out of life. She had two homes full of other people's furniture, never feeling the need to make either place truly her own. What she wanted most from life was to simply be. Now that she'd found the one man who understood that about her, could she simply let him go? Not in this lifetime. Frankie sat up, a new feeling of resolve invigorating her. "Thanks, Mom."

"No, thank you," Margaret said in a somber voice. "I've always wanted us to be closer. I've always wanted you to feel free to come to me. I know I've made some mistakes with you. I've always tried to rein you in."

"Without much success," Frankie teased, wanting to lift her mother's mood.

"Well, I'm afraid we're alike in that way. My mother couldn't do much with me, either. She gave up on me, but then she didn't share my experience of losing a child. I never wanted to go through that again. It made me more cautious than I should have been."

Tears swam in Margaret Hairston's eyes. Frankie had never considered that even now, all these years later, the pain of that loss could still be so fresh for her mother. What must it have been like thirty years ago, or all the while she was a young girl? Frankie didn't want to contemplate that level of sorrow, nor have her mother relive it. "I can forgive you for everything else, but charm school? They must have invented that as torture for little girls."

Margaret brightened. "Are you kidding? That was my best fun all week—the call from the headmistress telling me what stunt you'd pulled that time. You were even more inventive than I was." Margaret swiped at the moisture on her cheeks. "Enough of that. I've got a surprise for you, anyway. I was saving it for your party, but you may as well have it now."

Frankie knew her mother referred to the formal party that would mark her thirtieth birthday. She'd also resigned herself to not getting out of the family tradition. She'd been putting off finding a dress, however, but she suspected she wouldn't have to worry about that, considering that her mother went to the closet and extracted a long garment concealed by a pink garment bag.

Margaret unzipped the bag. "I figured you wouldn't get around to shopping."

From her vantage point, all Frankie could see was a hint of burgundy satin material. She rose to her feet for a closer inspection. The sleeveless gown had a sweetheart bodice and straight skirt.

"What do you think?" Margaret asked.

"It's lovely," Frankie said. Finally her mother had gotten her taste in clothes right.

"Why don't you put it on and join the party?"

"I'm not exactly in the partying mood. Besides, don't you have to get back to your guests?"

"Not a soul down there is more worthy of my time than my daughter. Besides, Andrew Branson is downstairs. Isn't he the one that spread the rumor that they shouldn't let you play girl's soccer since you were really a boy?"

"In fifth grade, Mother. I'm over that now." Though his meanness had been particularly painful since she'd had a crush on him at the time. She hadn't seen Andrew in years.

"Nothing makes a woman feel better than looking fabulous and crushing the ego of some small-minded man."

Frankie laughed. "Okay, okay, you sold me." Anything beat sitting around wondering what Nelson was doing at that moment or the dread that what lay ahead was the one fight she really wasn't up to.

When Nelson's mother opened the door to him, she looked him up and down and inquired, "Who died?"

He couldn't blame her since the only times she saw him in a suit at were funerals. "Can we talk for a minute?"

"Of course." She stepped inside to let him enter. He waited by the entrance of the living room for her to join him.

"Stop with the formality," she chastised him. "This has always been your house and always will be."

He knew that, but he wanted to impress on her he hadn't come for a friendly chat. He figured she knew that when she added, "I'll tell you what you want to know."

She walked ahead of him to sit at one of the corners of the sofa. He took a spot at the middle, perching on the edge of the cushion with his fingers steepled. Now wasn't the time for mincing words, so he didn't bother. "Why didn't you ever tell me?"

"It isn't the sort of thing a son needs to hear from his mother. In retrospect, I should have told you, anyway. Being the kind of man you are, I should have known you'd ferret out the truth. I'm sorry for that."

To his mind, she had nothing to be sorry for. The only reason he asked her now was a need to have all of the pieces of his life fit together, to make some kind of sense so he could put them in proper perspective and move on.

"Why did you keep me?"

"I didn't even know about you until it was too late to do anything about it. And then, you could have been your father's son. I didn't know and I didn't want to know. I only hoped you'd come out looking like me so it wouldn't matter. But luck wasn't with me."

No, he'd come out looking exactly like the man who'd attacked her. "You could have given me up for adoption."

"I could have. I had thought about it, even made arrangements in the event that what I hoped for didn't come to pass. I didn't think I could raise the child of the man who'd hurt me. But when they put you in my arms, I didn't see his face. I saw life. I saw hope. Your father and I had been trying for a year with no success. But you were here. You were whole and healthy. What did it matter how you came into our lives? Your father said he'd support whatever decision I made, but in the back of my mind I knew our marriage died that day."

Not knowing what else to say, he whispered, "I'm sorry."

"Do you think I blame you for any of this? You didn't make me any promises. I blame the man you see in the picture across the room. He's the one who swore before God to stand by me for better or worse. Well, sometimes that worse can be pretty bad. He stuck around long enough to make our lives miserable. He wanted to turn me against you, but when he finally realized he couldn't do that, he left. And all because of his stupid machismo. Some other man had touched his woman, which tainted me in his eyes. After you were born, he never touched me again."

Which meant, on top of everything else, he'd probably been cheating on her as well. Nice guy, his father. "So why do you still have his picture on your piano?"

She shrugged. "As a reminder of sorts. I put up with your father much longer than I should have, hoping someday he'd come to his senses. After he was gone I vowed never to let a man come between me and my son."

What man? To his knowledge, his mother hadn't so much as looked at another man since his father left.

"Don't look so shocked, *m'ijo*. Your mother is still an attractive woman. I don't even have a gray hair on my head the colorist can't hide. It was a long time before I was even interested in men, but did you honestly think your man-hungry Aunt Jackie would let me slide all these years without foisting one of her castoffs on me?"

He supposed not. Honestly, he hadn't considered it since he'd thought his mother had been pining away, not using the photograph as a remembrance of past hurts. He looked down at his newly bare finger. At least he came by it honestly.

"Do you mind if I ask you a question?"

He offered his mother a sympathetic smile, though he couldn't fathom what she'd ask. "Of course not."

"Why now? You've known for years. Why did you wait until now?"

He gave her the only honest answer he had. "I wasn't ready to deal with it before now."

She patted his knee. "No, I don't think you had to deal with it before. But there's a new woman in your life, one who won't settle for easy answers or allow you to wallow in a pool of your own self-pity. She's good for you."

He smiled. "I know."

"Then you'd better go find her and settle things." At his surprised look she added, "Bonnie called. She thought you were mad at her for letting Frankie leave."

"Good God, is nothing in this family secret?"

Jeannie shook her head. "Not much. But know this. You're a good man, Nelson, a good father. I've always been proud of you. Lord knows, I don't begrudge any woman whatever decisions she makes under the circumstances I was in, but you have always been a blessing to me."

"Thanks, Mom."

Jeannie patted his shoulder. "Go on, now," she chided. "You'd better not keep her waiting."

No. He wouldn't make that mistake again.

A half hour later, with her gown in place, her face made up and her hair pinned into an elaborate style atop her head, Frankie descended the stairs with her mother. Margaret had even lent her some of what her brother, Matthew, referred to as her battle jewelry, pieces so expensive as to be housed in a separate vault rather than the one at home.

Her father was waiting for them at the bottom of the stairs. He greeted his wife with a kiss to her cheek. "I was just about to round up a search party for you." Turning to Frankie, he said, "And who's this with you? Have we met?"

"Peter, behave," Margaret chastised.

"Now, why should I do that and ruin all my fun? But you do look beautiful, pumpkin."

"Thanks, Dad," she said, grateful the design of her coiffure prevented him from ruffling her hair, too. The furniture in the front room had been moved aside to accommodate dancing. A four-piece band was playing a sultry ballad. She didn't notice Andrew Branson's approach until he was almost on them. For an instant, she shared a knowing look with her mother. Margaret immediately whisked her husband off toward the bar, leaving Frankie alone to meet with her former nemesis.

"Frankie, is that you?" were the first words out of his mouth.

"Does that surprise you?"

"You look...incredible," he said with equal awe and surprise.

"Shocked to find out I'm really a girl?"

He had the good grace to blush. "What can I say? I was eleven years old. I didn't know much about girls or soccer for that matter. Am I forgiven?"

"Of course." Now she had the pleasure of calling him on his prior bad behavior.

"Then dance with me."

Frankie shrugged, having no reason to decline. "All right." She took the arm he extended toward her and allowed him to lead her to the floor. Although he was an attractive man with stylishly cut black hair and green eyes and his conversation as they danced was pleasant enough, she had no desire to spend more time with this man when her mind was on another. As soon as the song ended, she excused herself and headed toward the back of the house. Once outside the glass doors that led onto the stone walkway, she slipped off her heels. Many of the guests had found their way outside already to lounge on furniture placed strategically on the grounds. It was a warm night with a light breeze that loosened tendrils of her hair to float around her face.

She brushed them back as she headed toward one of her favorite hiding places, at the center of the maze at the far end of the lawn. Once she reached her destination, she wished she'd had the foresight to bring along some sort of blanket. Sitting on either the stone bench or the grass beside the little man-made pool would ruin the dress. She picked the grass as the lesser of two evils, pulled up the hem and dangled her feet in the water.

Her earlier conviction of fighting for Nelson's love paled. She stared down at the water as she made small splashing movements with her feet. If he cared for her, why hadn't he at least tried to reach her after she stole away not telling him she was leaving, let alone where she was going? She didn't expect him to come after her, though her parents' house was one of the few places he knew of to look for her. But if it had worked out the other way, she would at least try to catch him on his cell phone. If she really wanted to be morbid about it, maybe she should wonder if he noticed that she'd left at all.

"Is this a private party or can anyone join in?"

The sound of Nelson's voice startled her to her feet. He stood with his hands in his pants pockets, his expression unreadable. Of course, the suit he wore was black, as was his shirt, but his tie was in a pattern of bright colors. He looked so good to her that her mouth watered. The first thing she said to him was "What are you doing here? How did you find me?"

"It wasn't easy. I kept getting lost by the goose statue with the waterfall."

"How did you know about this place?"

"You told me you liked to come out here to hide from your mother's friends. Your brother told me how to get here."

It surprised her that he even remembered that comment. "That's like the blind leading the blind when a man asks another man for directions."

He said nothing for a long while, as anticipation built in her belly. Part of her wanted to shout, "He came for me," but the other more rational part wouldn't allow her to lift her hopes just yet. For all she knew, he was simply angry with her for ditching him the way she did. What he said next seemed to confirm her last suspicion.

"Why did you run out on me?"

"I didn't run out on you. I needed some time to think."

"Did you come up with anything?"

As the saying went, it was go time. She wasn't sure what his answer would be or if she was ready to hear it, but the time was now. She turned slightly so that she could face him more squarely and met his gaze. "Over the past few days I've come to care for you a great deal, more than I thought I would. Maybe I'm deluding myself, but I don't want to let that go just yet."

"Then what's the problem?"

"You are. Or rather your past is, but it's not really the

past, is it? You're still tied up with it—your ex-wife. I saw you two together. I can't compete with that."

"It's not a competition."

"You know what I mean. I'm not willing to be third string, to come after your wife and your kids."

"My ex-wife."

"Whose ring you still wear."

"Wore." He held up his left hand, which was devoid of any jewelry. "I finally got it off."

Frankie blinked, not trusting her eyesight in the dim light of the moon. "What do you mean *finally?*"

"The first time I tried to take it off was the night we came back to New York after the accident, but it wouldn't budge. I probably should have taken it off years ago, but the reason I didn't had nothing to do with still being in love with Sandy. It had more to do with punishing her for abandoning our marriage. After a while it became an excuse for not moving on with my life. For a long time, that didn't matter to me. Then I met you."

He shook his head. "I have never known a more stubborn, determined, pain-in-the-ass woman in my life, nor one as compassionate, giving or kind. This all started because you weren't willing to help put an innocent man in jail. It's just my luck that I fell for you, Frankie. I've fallen in love with you. But that's all I have to offer. I can't give you any fancy mansions or liveried butlers to do your bidding. I know you balk at that, but it's a part of you, too. All I have is my love. I hope that's enough."

She stared at him a long moment, absorbing all he'd said. A moment ago she'd been wondering if he'd noticed her absence and now he was telling her he loved her. It was too much. "Do you realize that's the most you've ever said to me at one time?"

He grinned. "Probably. And just so you know, what you saw was Sandy telling me she'd lost the baby she was carrying, another man's baby. One she plans on marrying in two weeks. She dropped off the girls so the two of them could spend some time alone together."

"I'm sorry, Nelson."

He shrugged as if dismissing the subject. "Is that all you want to say to me?"

She smiled. "No. I was sitting here wondering how I was supposed to get over you, since you hadn't even tried to call me to find out where I was."

"I already knew where you were. I called your mother. She told me you were on your way here. Hence…" He hooked his thumbs in the lapels of his jacket.

Frankie gritted her teeth. Her mother had known Nelson was on his way here all along. Yet, for once, she hadn't interfered, allowing Frankie to make up her own mind about what she wanted. Maybe there was some hope for them yet. But in the meantime, Nelson was waiting for a response.

She tilted her head to one side. "If you must know, I love you, too. I didn't want to admit that to myself. I've never felt for anyone what I feel for you. It's kinda scary."

At last, he closed the distance between them. But he didn't touch her, except with his fingertips to brush back an errant strand of hair. "Have I told you how beautiful you look tonight?"

There was no awe or surprise in his voice, only the

undercurrent of masculine appraisal. That pleased her. "No you haven't, but you can go ahead if you want to."

Finally he pulled her to him to embrace her with his hands moving on her back in a soothing motion. In her bare feet, the top of her head didn't reach his shoulder. "Boy, you're short," he teased, holding her tighter, probably so she wouldn't hit him.

She didn't mind, though. She was in his arms, where she wanted to be. He could tease her all he wanted. Her arms wound around his back, holding him to her. "You know, no one but my brother and me ever comes out here," she said with a hint of suggestiveness in her voice.

He drew back to look at her, a sly smile on his face. "Are you suggesting a friendly roll in your parents' grass?"

"Pretty much, all except the *friendly* part. I think we can come up with a better adjective than that."

"Absolutely not." He gave her waist a squeeze, tickling her. "One day soon I'm going to have to ask your dad for his permission to marry you. He's more likely to say yes if I haven't be debauching you in his backyard."

For a moment she simply stared at him. "You know I thought you were teasing me before when you said you were a throwback."

"I'm serious, Frankie. I had one marriage where the in-laws were a constant source of irritation. I'm not looking for another one."

She doubted his mother was the problem, which meant his wife's family had made trouble for him. "You don't have to worry about that with my family. They've been trying to give me away for years."

He gave her waist another squeeze. "Let's get out of here, then."

She nodded and followed him back to the house. Once inside, she left Nelson on the main floor to go upstairs and change. If Nelson worried about her father's reaction to finding out they'd made love in the garden, finding out she'd seduced him in her bedroom would have to be worse, and in her present mood she wasn't making any promises about keeping her hands to herself. But there would be time for that later.

Smiling to herself, she walked into her bedroom. She flicked on the light, and out of habit locked the door behind her. She didn't immediately go to her closet to change. She wanted to savor the moment a little. She never expected to be in the position in which she found herself—in love with a man who loved and appreciated her for who and what she was as opposed to what she could bring him. She wandered to the French doors that led to her balcony, to give herself another breath of night air and another moment of solitude. Her mother's rose garden was directly below this balcony. A long spiked fence surrounded it, ostensibly to keep trespassers from stepping on the flowers, but Frankie knew better. The fence had been placed there to keep her in. Not that it ever had. Tonight she had no desire to sneak out, only to savor the breeze and the scent of the blooms.

She opened the doors and stepped out. Below her she heard the sound of music and the laughter and conversation of her parents' guests. She felt no sense of alarm until the cold steel of a blade pressed against her throat

and an arm banded around her, dragging her backward
into the shadows where her attacker lay in wait for her.

"Remember me?" A hoarse voice rasped against her
ear. "I'm not going to let you off so easy this time."

Chapter 20

Despite herself, Frankie shivered and her eyes squeezed shut. Her heart beat wildly and it was an effort to drag air into her lungs. The man's voice was unfamiliar, but his scent wasn't. He smelled of tobacco and whiskey—stale, as if the last time he'd consumed either of them had been a while, but the stench of each remained. Why hadn't she remembered that before? Why the hell was this happening to her once again?

Mentally she shook herself. Now wasn't the time to fall apart. She needed to think of a way out of this. She was alone, unarmed, and the design of her dress would hamper any attempts at defending herself. With all the noise downstairs no one would even hear her if she screamed. "What do you want?" she asked, hoping he wouldn't see her question for what it was—an attempt to stall until she figured out what to do.

"I was only supposed to scare you then. Send you running back to him. I wouldn't have hurt you too bad, but you broke my damn ribs." The knife pressed deeper against her throat. "Don't be trying none of that shit this time."

For an instant Frankie's brain whirred, trying to assimilate what he'd said. Robert had been the one to sic this man on her, though she couldn't fathom why. Third, this man didn't intend to leave her alive if he were so forthcoming about what he'd done. But if she were his prisoner, he was also trapped inside the house. "You'll never make it out of this house alive."

His only response was a low, wicked laugh that sent a chill through her. He yanked her toward him, lifting her off her feet. She couldn't allow him to drag her inside. At least out here, someone might notice the commotion of her fighting for her life, even if they couldn't hear the noise. Besides, she'd shimmied down the trellis outside her window enough times in enough variations of attire to be able to accomplish it now. All she needed was a few uninterrupted seconds.

She couldn't wait to act any longer. Luckily, he'd relaxed the pressure of the knife against her neck in order to carry her. She jerked her head backward, not hitting his forehead as she'd intended, but the bridge of his nose. That was good enough, considering she heard the dull crack of the bone breaking. He grunted in pain, his grip loosening enough for her to maneuver. An elbow to his ribs brought another grunt of pain. But he backhanded her, a blow that sent her sprawling to the ground.

Her ears rang, and from seemingly somewhere off she heard Nelson calling her. But he was downstairs, no use to her. If she were going to save herself she'd have to get off the damn floor. Using the latticework of the waist-high railing, she pulled herself to her feet, just as a loud crash sounded in the distance. The man rushed toward her then. For a second she stood frozen until he was almost upon her. At the last minute she stepped out of the way and pushed, sending the man flying over the side. She heard the man scream, then a thud, then the sound of metal scraping metal.

She leaned over the side, her ruined coiffure hanging down on one side. Beneath her, the man had impaled himself on the fence. One of the spikes could be seen poking through his shoulder.

A wave of nausea swept through her. She knew he wasn't dead because he was still moving. She hadn't noticed before, but he was dressed in the livery of the waiters hired for that evening: white jackets adorned with faux gold epaulets and black pants. Even in the dim moonlight she could see the blood staining his clothes, both from the blow to his nose and the wound in his shoulder. A small crowd of her mother's guests, those who had been outside, formed around the man, but for some odd reason most of them were looking up at her.

A pair of strong arms closed around her. She didn't have to guess to whom they belonged. "Nelson," she whispered.

"Come away from there," he said. His voice was surprisingly gentle, solicitous.

He didn't need to cajole her. She leaned back against

him, allowing his arms to close more tightly around her. Although her temple ached and her head swam, a smile formed on her lips. "What took you so long?"

Laughter rumbled in his chest. "I don't suppose I have to ask you if you're okay."

"Nothing a good lie-down wouldn't cure."

"Come on."

It wasn't until he turned her around and led her inside that she noticed her mother standing grim-faced in the center of the room. Not wanting her to worry, she brought another smile to her face. To her mother she said, "Nothing like a little entertainment to liven up a party."

"Oh, Francesca," her mother huffed, coming up beside her. "There's a man downstairs bleeding onto the rose bushes and you're making jokes." Margaret brushed back Frankie's hair. "Oh, my," Margaret said.

Frankie touched the temple that throbbed and her hand came back sticky. She must have banged it when she fell, but she couldn't remember the blow. No wonder she felt so light-headed.

Before she could protest, her protectors pushed her into a seat. "I'm fine," she protested. She touched her fingers to her scalp. Already the blood flow had stopped. "Or I would be if I could manage to stop whacking things with my head."

"Hush, dear, you're starting to babble," her mother said. Frankie didn't know where an ice bag had materialized from, but her mother pressed one to her temple. "Who was that man?"

"Someone Robert knows. I'm sure he's the one that attacked me in Atlanta."

She heard her mother's "oh" of surprise. Considering she hadn't mentioned being attacked before, it was a mild reaction. But Frankie wasn't concerned about her mother at the moment. She'd said that for Nelson's benefit, to let him know it wasn't some random thief or party crasher. She knew by the expression on his face that now that he knew she was relatively safe and unharmed, he intended to find out why this man had tried to harm her, not once but twice.

She also knew she'd have to do her own 'splaining. When Margaret looked over her shoulder at Nelson, all he said was "Take care of her."

"Where are you going?"

"You know damn well where I'm going."

She did and there was no use pretending she didn't. "Don't do anything I wouldn't do."

He winked at her. "You can count on that."

Oh, damn. That's what she was afraid of.

Nelson loped down the stairs, aware that the guests still assembled turned curious faces to him as he moved. They'd have to keep wondering for now. He headed toward the back of the house, out the glass doors that led to the side of the house. It wasn't hard to find the little garden below Frankie's window, even though the crowd that had been present a moment ago had dispersed. A series of lights had been turned on, casting the house and grounds in stark illumination.

Frankie's attacker had managed to free himself from the fence, but he wasn't going anywhere. A circle of men surrounded him, most notably the ancient Anderson, who had a gun trained on the man, and Frankie's father, who brandished a golf club. The farcical nature of this scene might have reached him if fury weren't the only emotion guiding him.

Frankie had told him Robert had something to do with this mess, but he wanted to know all of it now—before the police got here and messed up his plans.

Nelson strode to where the man knelt in the grass and hauled him to his feet by the lapels of his jacket. Pressing him back against the fence, he demanded, "Who the hell are you and who sent you here?"

The man glared at him but said nothing. Nelson could see the fear in his eyes. He'd known the man was a coward the moment he'd burst into Frankie's room. He knew Frankie thought this man was trying to attack her when he rushed toward her, but Nelson knew better. He'd been trying to escape. Obviously, this man didn't have any problem terrorizing a woman half his size, but he had no stomach for an equal. Too bad. He'd have to deal with one now.

Nelson drew back one hand and punched the man in the shoulder, right above his wound. Immediately fresh blood appeared on the jacket. The man howled and his head lolled back to one side, revealing a tattoo of a dagger on his neck. Seeing it, and the knowing that its presence confirmed the fact that this man was responsible for both attacks, fueled new anger in him. He drew back his hand again, but the threat was enough to get the man talking. He blurted out a name that meant nothing to Nelson.

"What's your connection to Robert Parker?"

"He owes somebody. Big time."

"For what?"

"Man doesn't know how to get up from a table without leaving all his money behind."

It gave him no pleasure to realize he'd been right about Parker. "So why'd you come after Frankie?"

"He needed her money. I didn't mind helping him."

He'd bet. And Parker had figured that if she were in danger she would have turned to him. It only proved how little Parker knew her. Frankie had turned the tables on both of them. But tonight, there was no chance of Frankie returning to Parker. Tonight served another purpose.

"Why now?"

"A warning."

Either Parker paid what he owed or he'd receive the same fate. He knew everything he needed to know now. Frankie was safe. He should let this man go and get back to her. But somehow he couldn't make himself do that. Rage still burned in him, though he'd kept it in control until now. The urge to give this man back some of what he'd given Frankie burned in him, too.

Then there was a hand on his shoulder. "That's enough."

The gentle note in Peter Hairston's voice snapped Nelson out of his trance. He'd been so focused on this man he'd forgotten about his audience. He let the man go, watching as he slumped to the ground. Then he turned to Frankie's father. "Thanks."

"Maybe you should see to my daughter now."

Nelson nodded and went back to the house. When he got to her room, he found Frankie pacing the floor, while her mother sat on the bed worrying the beading on her dress. Neither one of them fooled him. They'd probably run back from the balcony the moment they realized he was coming.

But for now, his concern was all for Frankie. She'd changed into a voluminous navy-blue robe reminiscent of the one she'd worn in Atlanta. Her hair was pulled back into one long ponytail. There was a small bandage at her temple. Aside from that, and the concerned frown on her face, she didn't look much the worse for wear, though he knew finding her attacker in her room must have, at the very least, shaken her.

Frankie's mother slipped from the bed. "I'll leave you two alone."

He would have thanked her, except she left too quickly, closing what was left of the door behind her. For a moment, neither he nor Frankie moved. The next thing he knew, she was in his arms, her mouth opening beneath his. His tongue plunged into her mouth and she kissed him back with equal fervor. When he finally pulled away, she buried her face against his chest.

He stroked his hand over her hair and along her cheek. "I'm sorry, baby," he whispered against her ear.

"For what?"

"For not being here when you needed me."

She lifted her head and cast him a patient look. "What are you talking about? You've been here every time I've needed you. How did you even know to come to my room?"

"Some of your mother's guests decided to go for a swim. They stumbled across one of the waiters in the cabana. He'd been knocked out, but was still alive. Luckily, I was with your mother when the guests came to report it. For what it's worth, the man downstairs has a tattoo of a dagger on his neck."

"So I didn't imagine that?"

"No. Parker probably told you that to keep you from figuring out that the man who attacked you was not the same one who killed the other girls."

"And it worked. I thought I was going crazy, dreaming the same damn thing every night that I thought wasn't real."

Speaking of reality, he had one last bit of it to lay on her. He knew he shouldn't have asked for her love without telling her, but somehow, down by the pool, it hadn't seemed the right moment. He took her hand and led her to the pair of chairs in her room. He sat in one and pulled her onto his lap. She came willingly, but he could see the questions in her eyes. He'd answer them all in a moment.

"The other day, I never did finish telling you why I left the force."

"You don't have to do that."

"Yes, I do. The man I attacked was my father."

She shook her head and her brow furrowed. "I thought you told me that your father disappeared when you were young and you never saw him again."

At the moment, he couldn't remember when he'd told her that. It didn't matter. "That was the man my mother married. Most marriages don't survive the rape of the woman, even if there isn't a child involved. Theirs was no exception."

She stared at him for a long moment. Various emotions played across her face: confusion, denial and finally understanding. "Oh, God, Nelson. How did you find out?"

"I overheard my aunts talking once when they didn't know I was in the next room."

"How did you know that man was your father?"

"I didn't. He told me. He was sixty-three years old and still preying on young women. Up until then, I think I'd downplayed my mother's experience in my mind. I didn't want to think of my mother in that way. Not all rapes are brutal, but I knew how bad it could get. When we picked him up he was sixty-three years old and still preying on young women. He insisted on telling me every detail. I lost it and he got exactly what he wanted. We had to let him go."

"And you lost your job."

He nodded. "I went a little crazy after that. That's when Sandy left me. Up until then I hadn't even told her how I was conceived." And in the back of his mind he'd wondered if that weren't the real reason why she'd left.

He gave her thigh a squeeze, waiting for some kind of response to what he'd told her. She did the last thing he expected. She touched her fingertips to his cheek and offered him an encouraging smile. "Why are you telling me now?"

"I don't want there to be any secrets between us, Frankie. I want you to know what you're getting. What he was is part of me, too. How do you think he knew who I was? I look just like him—the same features, the same coloring, probably the propensity for violence as well. The only difference is that I've always had an outlet for it—first football, then the force and now P.I. work." He took a deep breath and voiced the demon that had plagued him most of his life. "How do I know that with a little twist of fate I might not have ended up just like him?"

Frankie brought one of his hands to her lips and kissed the back of it. "Because I know you. Downstairs just now, you had the chance to beat the crap out of someone who hurt me and you didn't take it. I wanted you to. I wanted you to hurt him just a little bit, but you didn't."

"I had an audience."

"Is that what you were thinking about then?"

"No," he had to admit. He'd forgotten all about them. But in his mind, that didn't really change anything.

"Do you remember the first night we were together?"

"I have a vague recollection of that," he teased.

She smacked him on the arm. "I was so scared that night."

"Of me?"

"Of freezing up or flaking out," she said in a voice that suggested he should know better. "I wanted to be with you. I just didn't think I could do it. You made it safe for me. If I hadn't thought it would offend your manly sensibilities, I would have told you before. You're the gentlest man I've ever known. I so needed that, and not only in a sexual way, either. I watch you with your girls, even with your ex-wife. That's what freaked me out—to see you touch her the way you touch me. What I'm getting, as you put it, is a wonderful man who I adore. I'm going to quit talking now, because I'm starting to sound like a sap." She relaxed against him, laying her head on his shoulder.

He didn't know how to respond to either her words or actions. It hadn't occurred to him that he was looking for reassurance from her. He was only hoping his past didn't revolt her, given what she'd gone through. He hadn't had the courage to tell Sandy, and he realized that he had more faith in what he and Frankie had than he'd ever had in his marriage. He closed his arms more tightly around her and kissed her temple.

"So when are you going to do this hand-asking thing you have to do with my father?"

"Soon. Maybe we should go downstairs and talk with the police first. I'm sure they have their own asking thing for us."

She grinned up at him. "I guess we could do that. Then I'm going to hold you to getting out of here. We'll take the limousine so that I can ravish your body in the car."

Nelson threw back his head and laughed. That sounded like a plan to him.

Epilogue

One month later

Nelson woke to the sound of tropical birds cawing outside their window. Bright sunshine poured in the window, letting him know they'd slept away the first few daylight hours of their honeymoon. Frankie, still pressed up against him, slumbered on. That was fine with him. The last few weeks had been turbulent ones for her, between planning the hasty wedding with her mother and the discovery of all that had gone on in the town she once called home. He hadn't seen any reason for the rush on the wedding, but he suspected Frankie wanted something to take her mind off the other goings-on.

The minute Robert Parker had been confronted by the police, he'd broken down and admitted to sending someone to scare Frankie, as well as to tampering with her birth control pills to get her pregnant in the first place. When Frankie heard this, she laughed it off, but Nelson suspected she hid her hurt from him. He knew her well enough to know she'd get around to sharing eventually, so he let her be.

Tara's owner, the man who'd sent his goon after Frankie the second time, turned out to be Rita Forbes's husband. The entire club was shut down, including the back room where Parker had unwittingly lost all his money to his own brother-in-law. When they came to get Forbes, he closeted himself in his study with his revolver and took his own life. Rita Forbes did not attend the funeral.

Only time would tell if the charges against Harry Brandt would stick, but Julia was granted immunity for her testimony against him. This time Frankie intended to testify.

Now, in the present, she stirred beside him. She brushed her hair from her face and looked up at him. "How long have you been awake?"

He scrubbed his hand up and down her side. "Not long."

"I had a nightmare," she said.

"Oh?" he said, dreading the worst. Although the episodes had gotten less frequent and terrifying, she still sometimes woke up needing his reassurance.

"We were old and fat and living in Florida. Our grandchildren only visited to swim in our pool."

"Grandchildren? We haven't even discussed having children yet."

She stretched in an appealing way. "Well, I want a whole bunch of them. All girls. We can make a soccer team and go around challenging other families."

"Exactly how many other families are you expecting to find with enough children for their own soccer team?"

She frowned up at him. "Killjoy. You couldn't let me have my dream for five minutes."

"You can have whatever you want, baby. You know that."

"I know." She sighed in a way that suggested something was on her mind.

"What is it, sweetheart?"

"There's something I should have told you before we got married."

"What's that?"

"I had this crazy great-aunt who left me some money in her will, if I met with certain, well, stipulations."

"Okay." He had no idea where this was leading. He knew she had already had a healthy trust fund, the allowance from which she was presently living off since she didn't have a job. Even so, he'd signed a premarital agreement to keep her money hers. If she hadn't suggested it, he would have, but by asking him to agree she'd proved he hadn't married a frivolous woman. "What was the stipulation?"

"I had to be married by my thirtieth birthday, which is in November."

"How much is the inheritance?"

"Not much. Five million dollars."

Nelson's breath stalled and he simply stared at her. "What did you say?"

"I said, we are now the proud owners of five million dollars."

"Is that why you wanted to get married so quickly?"

"No." She bit her lip. "I didn't want to give you the chance to change your mind."

It hadn't occurred to him that she needed reassurance from him, too. "I wasn't going to do that. If you know anything about me it's that I stick." He pulled her closer and planted a kiss on her shoulder. Then a thought occurred to him. "Wait a minute. What do you mean we? What about the agreement?"

"Oh, I'm keeping everything else, but that belongs to both of us. I couldn't have gotten it without you. I didn't even want it in the first place."

The idea of turning down that much money boggled Nelson's mind. He'd never been poor, but he certainly didn't have millions to toss aside casually, either.

Frankie pulled back to look him squarely in the face. "I'm going to tell you something now that if you repeat to another living soul, I will kill you. You know how rumors fly in our family."

He wasn't sure whether to take this seriously or not. "Tell me."

"The worst part of everything that happened to me personally was losing that baby, Nelson. I was only teasing before, but I want another daughter to make up for the one I lost."

"When? Now?"

She offered him a watery smile. "No. Not now. I want a chance to enjoy my husband for a while and get to know my stepdaughters. But soon."

He hugged her to him. For all the hard edges on the outside she was a soft woman where it counted. "You let me know when, sweetheart. I'll be ready."

Leila Owens didn't know
how to love herself let alone
an abandoned baby
but Garret Grayson knew
how to love them both.

She's My Baby

Adrianne Byrd

(Kimani Romance #10)

AVAILABLE SEPTEMBER 2006

FROM KIMANI™ ROMANCE

Love's Ultimate Destination

Silhouette® Desire®

**Introducing an exciting appearance
by legendary
New York Times bestselling author**

DIANA PALMER

HEARTBREAKER

He's the ultimate bachelor…
but he may have just met
the one woman to change his ways!

Join the drama in the story of a confirmed
bachelor, an amnesiac beauty and their
unexpected passionate romance.

"Diana Palmer is a mesmerizing storyteller
who captures the essence of what
a romance should be."—*Affaire de Coeur*

Heartbreaker *is available from Silhouette Desire
in September 2006.*

Introducing...

nocturne

**a spine-tingling new line
from Silhouette Books.**

**These paranormal romances will
seduce you with dark, passionate tales
that stretch the boundaries of conflict,
desire, and life and death, weaving
a tapestry of sensual thrills and chills!**

Don't miss the first book...

UNFORGIVEN

by *USA TODAY* bestselling author

LINDSAY
McKENNA

*Launching October 2006,
wherever books are sold.*

Page-turning drama...

Exotic, glamorous locations...

Intense emotion and passionate seduction...

Sheikhs, princes and billionaire tycoons...

This summer, may we suggest:

THE SHEIKH'S
DISOBEDIENT BRIDE
by Jane Porter
On sale June.

AT THE GREEK TYCOON'S
BIDDING
by Cathy Williams
On sale July.

THE ITALIAN MILLIONAIRE'S
VIRGIN WIFE
On sale August.

With new titles to choose from every month,
discover a world of romance in our books written
by internationally bestselling authors.

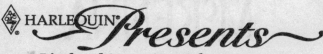

HARLEQUIN® *Presents*

It's the ultimate in quality romance!

Available wherever Harlequin books are sold.

www.eHarlequin.com   HPGEN06